Born in London to ⸍, Anita
spent her childhoc ⸍ ⸍s. She
met her husband when she was eighteen and they laid down
roots in sunny Dorset to raise their four children. With the
children now grown and flying the nest, and the family
expanding, Anita divides her time between tracing her
ancestral roots across Ireland, England and Scandinavia, and
writing in her nature filled garden with her cats.

For more information on Anita, on her writing and books,
read her blog on anitagriffiths.blogspot.com, follow her on
Instagram anita_griffiths_ and Twitter@anitaegriffiths and
join her on Facebook @anita.e.griffiths (Anita Griffiths Writer)

Also by Anita Griffiths

Beyond the Ironing Board – an autobiography about motherhood and life in the real world.

Cobbled Streets & Teenage Dreams

Zara

Close Your Eyes

Anita Griffiths

Copyright © 2019 Anita Griffiths
First edition

All rights reserved. This book or any portion thereof may
not be reproduced or used in any manner whatsoever
without the express permission of the author except for the
use of brief quotations.

This is a work of fiction. Names, characters and incidents
are the product of the author's imagination and any
resemblance to actual persons, living or dead, is entirely
coincidental.

Any reference to places or events is purely from a personal
opinion.

ISBN 9781095148426

Cover design by
Inkpots & Paper

For fellow Brontë fans everywhere.

Thank you C, E & A for your unforgettable stories

*

Dedicated to the teenager who climbed up drainpipes

to be with his love

xxx

Chapter One

"Good morning, class!" The burly figure standing in the doorway commanded attention, his brash, Mancunian tone cutting through the cacophony that filled the room. The response was immediate; the room fell silent, bar the scraping of a dozen chair legs as the students hurriedly got to their feet and stood to attention behind their desks.

"Good morning, Mr Nelson," they chorused; some more enthusiastically than others. He remained in the doorway, surveying them in silence. A towering, well-built man in his early thirties, he was smartly dressed in a navy suit, pale blue shirt and matching striped tie. And yet, he looked uncomfortably restricted, as if his muscled frame was aching to burst free of its cloth constraints.

"I could hear you from the other end of the corridor," he said steadily, pointing behind him to reinforce his statement. He didn't need to waste any more words to convey his disappointment in them; the look on his face spoke volumes. Mumbled apologies rippled across the room. He noisily drew in breath through his nose to indicate he was satisfied with their remorse. Closing the door behind him, he moved over to his desk in front of the large blackboard, and deposited the pile of books and folders he had been carrying. He perched on the edge of the desk to address the class once they were seated again.

"Welcome back, year thirteen. I hope you all had a good Christmas." He held up a hand to stem the outpouring of comments.

"I didn't ask you to *tell* me about it. I was simply hoping you'd had a good one," he stated. He waited for absolute silence before continuing, watching the class thoughtfully.

"Right, I've come to a decision. I have decided that this is the year you are going to achieve your goals: make yourselves proud. Make *me* proud. Make people sit up and notice you. This is it – 1994 – this is *your* year to succeed. This is the year we put Keighley on the map. Hang it, this is the year we put Yorkshire on the map!"

A cheer went up and a sea of grinning faces waited expectantly for his next words. He had them in the palm of his hands. As he always did. Fair but firm, Mr Nelson was without doubt, the most popular member of staff in the school. He had a way of engaging the hesitant, and encouraging the reluctant. He was renowned for his pep talks.

"So, in order to achieve that, we need a serious shake-up here because, quite frankly, your test results from last month were shocking. Appalling. Where were your heads? Certainly not here." He forcefully tapped a finger on his desk to emphasise the point and shook his head in despair, widening his eyes. A few laughed awkwardly, the rest stared back at him, not sure what to say.

"Did you have a good wedding, Sir?" Ryan piped up, skilfully changing the conversation. Mr Nelson smiled and nodded.

"Yes, I did, thank you."

"Where did you get married?" Jennifer asked, with genuine curiosity.

"Manchester," he replied. He could feel the buzz of questions hanging in the air and decided to relent for a moment.

"Is she from Manchester too then, Sir?" Jennifer persisted.

"Yes, she is. We moved here together four years ago." He clapped his hands together indicating enough questions but Ryan hadn't quite finished with his distraction tactics.

"What does she do, Sir?"

"She's … no, enough chat now. We've got things to do here," he stated, giving a determined nod.

"Ooh Sir, is she a secret agent? … or a pole dancer?"

Mr Nelson laughed in good humour but his grey eyes flashed a warning at the young reprobate. He was pushing too far.

"Well, Ryan, did I ask for a comedian? Because all I'm getting is an idiot," he challenged. Ryan grinned nonplussed and cocked his head as laughter and jeering ensued at his expense.

"Right, enough now, class," Mr Nelson held up his hand for silence. "We had a lovely wedding, thank you. My wife is a primary school teacher, here in Keighley. And we are both very happy. Okay?" He looked pointedly at each of his students and when his eyes fell on Mary O'Shea, he gave her a slight wink and smiled. Mary was one of his hesitant students; actually, she was his most painfully shy student. And she knew his wife, Nicola. They had met the previous summer at the Brontë parsonage museum, in the nearby village of Haworth, where Mary had a part-time job. During term-time she worked each Saturday but during the holiday periods, when the museum was at its busiest, she worked most days. It was no surprise to him that she should be working there; every teacher in the school knew that Mary had a love of the Brontë sisters, and literature in general. She was always top of the class in English. But what did surprise him, was how readily she had struck up a conversation with his wife. Ordinarily, she would just about bring herself to answer the register, she was that lacking in confidence, and yet, she talked to Nicola with such earnest, desperate for a kindred spirit to converse with about her favourite books. Nicola had returned many times to Haworth, to talk with

3

Mary and share their passion, and to slowly draw her out of her shell.

"Look after her, Jim", she had said. "Take her under your wing, help her to find her feet. I get the feeling she's completely overpowered by her father. He doesn't give her room to breathe, let alone, grow."

Jim Nelson could see that. He had taken an instant shine to Mary when she arrived from Northern Ireland as a new student at the start of year Twelve, but found her father to be quite overbearing and forthright. It was clear he was used to being in control and expected others to do as he said. Perfect qualities for his position as a chief inspector but not so appealing in his role as a father. Jim Nelson was used to turning on the charm and diplomacy during parents' evenings but even he had struggled to hold a conversation with Donal O'Shea.

Snapping back to reality, he addressed the class.

"Right, this is how it's going to work," he said, leaning over to retrieve a list of names from his pile of notes.

"I am going to call out some names. When you hear your name, stand up. Then I'll tell you where to move to…" He stopped abruptly when loud groans and complaints were emitted, and stared across the room defiantly.

"What is your problem, year Thirteen? This is for your own benefit, not mine. I'm going to put you in pairs that I think will work well together. The time for cosy chats and lazy minds is over. Your mocks are looming and before you know it, your final exams. So, stop acting like babies, and start acting like young adults. Come on, half of you are old enough to vote now – surely you can cope with being moved from your best mates for an hour a day?"

Satisfied that his message had got across, he read the first name out. Hushed tuts of frustration filled the room as he

4

worked his way down the list and reluctant students moved places. Mary sat nervously waiting for her name, dreading who she would be paired with.

"Mary O'Shea," Mr Nelson's nasal tone softened ever so slightly and he waited for her to get to her feet. She stared down at her hands, hiding behind the long, brown fringe that fell across her face, acutely aware of the red tinge slowly creeping up her neck and across her cheeks.

"Not Ryan, not Ryan," she muttered under her breath.

"Go and sit with Richard White."

Mary's head snapped up, wide eyes staring at her teacher for an instant in utter disbelief. She glanced across at her friend on the adjacent table who grimaced in response. Her face flooded with colour, she gathered her books together and headed for the table at the back of the classroom. Richard was leaning right back in his seat, pushed away from the table, with legs stretched out in his customary fashion. He stared out of the window, completely blanking Mary as she slid into the seat next to him. Ryan didn't let the moment go unnoticed.

"Oooh, looks like the Virgin Mary got lucky at last. That's how you like them, eh, Richard?" he taunted. Quick as a flash, a thick textbook went flying through the air and caught Ryan smartly on the back of his head. Instinctively, he turned and threw it back at Richard, jumping out of his seat to propel it with more force. Mary put her arms across her face and ducked as it flew towards her. Richard blocked it, snatching it up in mid-air and was about to launch it back at Ryan again but hesitated, glaring steadily at him.

"Richard, get out! Now!" Mr Nelson bellowed, taking two steps towards him and pointing angrily towards the door. As Richard got to his feet, Mary braced herself for his chair to go flying across the room next but to her surprise, he walked slowly towards the door, his eyes fixed firmly in front of him.

"Wanker!" Ryan snarled as Richard passed his table. Frustrated at not getting a response, he spat at Richard's back.

"And Ryan, come and stand by my desk. You're seventeen, not seven!" Mr Nelson stood for a moment, angry eyes boring into Ryan's, who in turn, tried to look defiant but shifted his feet nervously where he stood in front of the desk. Mr Nelson indicated with his finger that Ryan should stand behind the desk, with his back to the class.

"You stay there," he instructed in a quiet, steely tone. Perching back on the edge of his desk, he looked down at his list again.

"Jessica Stanley, sit with Matthew Jones." He continued reading out names as if nothing had happened, until the list was complete.

"Right, I want you to turn to your partner – those of you that still have one – and discuss your strengths and weaknesses in maths. Be honest with each other." With that, he left the room. Mary watched him through the classroom window that overlooked the corridor. He stood in front of Richard, hands in pockets, talking quietly to him. Richard, easily one of the tallest in the class, leant up against the wall, one foot resting on it as if ready to launch himself and run at any given moment. He stared off down the corridor, refusing to hold eye contact, but seemed to be listening to what Mr Nelson had to say.

"Bad luck, Mary. Richard's a nightmare, he's vile. I know you hate him, don't you?" Tracy whispered, crouching by Mary's table, making sure she couldn't be seen through the window by their teacher. Mary nodded, her eyes drawn back to Richard. She'd never had a chance to look at him before; not properly anyway. She was always seated at the front of the class and he was invariably at the back. His black hair was as close to being shaved as school would allow, high on the sides and back, leaving a two inch crown and fringe. Although tall, he wasn't gangly with it; quite the opposite, with broad shoulders and muscular arms. He pushed his shirt sleeves up, growing agitated at what was being said, and Mary caught a glimpse of his heavily inked skin. Mesmerised, she wondered what the tattoos were like under his shirt. How far did they go? Was his chest tattooed too? Suddenly aware that she was staring, she blushed and dragged her eyes away, turning back to Tracy.

"Yes, I hate him," she whispered in reply. Glancing round, she caught his eye. He stared at her, his steely blue eyes cutting through her. She blinked and looked away, turning crimson.

"I really hate him."

Richard returned to his seat minutes later and the lesson continued in a more subdued fashion. Mary kept her eyes on Mr Nelson, not daring to move her head or glance in Richard's direction. Even so, she knew that he wasn't paying her the slightest interest; he spent the remainder of the lesson staring straight ahead, unnervingly still. Mary felt sure that Mr Nelson had swiftly changed the pitch of his lesson - nothing involved partnered work – and she let out a sigh of relief when the bell went. Richard was out of his seat and through the door before the class was dismissed; usually something Mr Nelson would pull a student up on but he decided to let it go. Watching the class file out, he beckoned for Mary to stay behind.

"Do you understand why I have paired you up with Richard?" he started. Mary shook her head.

"Because he's very, very bright. I know that's a surprise but there it is. Richard White will undoubtedly get an A in his maths exam, without even trying. The same with science." He smiled encouragingly. "Look, Mary, I know you struggle with maths and I know Richard isn't exactly friendly but he can help you." He fell silent, watching as she took in what he was saying.

"Here's the thing: my wife is adamant that you'll make a fantastic teacher and I don't doubt her judgment for a minute but …" he paused, gauging her reaction, "if you want to teach at secondary school level, then you're going to come across a dozen or more Richards and Ryans of this world, so you may as well get used to them now. And at the same time, make the most of Richard's knowledge. He *can* help you. And he will; I spoke to him." Sensing he was winning her over, he raised questioning eyebrows for confirmation. She nodded and gave him a weak smile.

"You've got your university application done, haven't you? And you put York as your first choice?"

Mary nodded.

"Good, so we just need to get you up to speed with maths, and possibly science. Are you happy to have some help with science too?" He could see she was feeling overwhelmed as she nervously chewed her lip, nodding in response to his questions. He dropped his voice to barely a whisper, trying to reassure her.

"If you ever need to talk, I'm always ready to listen. Not just about maths, I mean. Anything. Anything at all." He paused, deliberating how to word his next sentence.

"My dad's retired now but he was a headmaster in his day. A brilliant one. Very strict though: expected his family to jump through hoops all the time. He treated us the way he treated his students. You'd think, working with children all his life, he would've understood them. What makes them tick. But sadly, no. Too busy being in charge." He waited for her reaction, hoping he hadn't overstepped the mark. He could see something in her that he recognised.

"I think our dads would get on like a house on fire then," she ventured, a daring look in her eye telling him she knew exactly what he was getting at. It felt good; even just hinting that her father was controlling was a brave move for her. It was strangely liberating. In that moment, Jim felt sure he'd just seen a glimpse of the Mary that his wife had befriended.

"Ignore Ryan, he's an idiot," he said, gathering up his pile of paperwork and walking with her to the door. "He's Josh's stooge and does whatever he's told to wind Richard up. Josh and Richard have had a longstanding rivalry for years. You just got caught up in the middle of it today. Don't let it upset you." He nodded and gave her a wink by way of ending their conversation. As he watched her walk down the corridor, he wondered at the wisdom of his decision. Richard was undoubtedly the brightest lad in the class but also the most volatile. Pairing him up with such a delicate soul as Mary felt wrong and yet, he did think it could work. They may even balance each other out.

"Bye!" Kelly waved to Mary as they parted by the park in Haworth where the bus had dropped them off. As she turned to start the slow walk up the steep, cobbled Main Street, Mary hesitated. Richard was walking just ahead of her; he paused to light up and, flicking his match into the street, turned to look at her. She forced a smile as she drew level with him. He nodded in response and to her surprise, started walking next to her. Hardly daring to breathe, she tried desperately to think of something to say. He beat her to it.

"So what's your maths like then?"

She gave an embarrassed laugh.

"Appalling. So is my science to be honest. I just don't get it."

He didn't respond.

"Sorry about today. Y'know, with Ryan," she said quickly.

He frowned and gave a shrug.

"Not your fault. He's a dick."

"You shouldn't let him rile you then," she replied, looking away quickly when he shot her a cold look.

"I don't."

They walked on in silence. Mary noted how easily he strode up the hill; she was struggling to keep up.

"Why do it then?" he asked. She looked confused.

"Do what?"

"Maths and science. If you're no good at it, why bother?" He almost sounded cross.

"I need it for uni," she explained. He stopped walking, looking at her in wonder.

"Uni? You want to go to uni? Why?"

She ached to smile at his surprise. There was a look in his eye that pleased her. She had got his attention.

"Because I need to. I want to be a teacher." She made it sound so simple; she wished she could believe it would be. Richard thought about it for a moment, slowly moving on.

"You've seen Nelson's job. You really want to do that for a living?"

Not sure how to respond, she opted not to and they fell silent again.

"It's not maths you want to teach, is it?"

Mary couldn't tell if he was joking or not, his stony face was so hard to read. She didn't think he laughed much, if at all.

"No!" She pulled a face. "That would be madness. No, English Literature; that's what I want to teach. And my dad wanted me to do 'proper' subjects as well. So …" She shrugged her shoulders.

"Your dad chose your A-levels for you? Do you always do as you're told?" he challenged. She looked away, hurt by his tone. He had hit a nerve. He dropped his cigarette onto the cobbles and ground it with his foot. Squinting at her, he nodded slowly, taking her silence as meaning 'yes'. They had stopped outside the café at the top of the hill. Mary glanced nervously at the doorway, checking to see if she had been spotted. About to say something, she turned back to Richard only to see he was already walking away. Her heart sank; she hated herself for being so awkward and ordinary. She wished she could sparkle, be noticed. With a final look as he disappeared up the street, she headed for the door just as he turned back to her. He nodded and half-raised his hand. She reciprocated, a shy smile spreading across her face.

Mary's alarm woke her at quarter to seven the next morning; it always coincided with the chimes from the church clock opposite. Five minutes later, her mother knocked on the door with a mug of tea for her which she drank by the window before jumping into the shower. It was the same routine every morning: up, drink tea, shower, breakfast with her parents, wave her father off to work and then leave for the school bus as her mother opened up the café. Regimented from a young age, she knew that her father expected the morning to run smoothly, like clockwork. She usually did everything on autopilot but this morning was different. She woke with butterflies in her stomach and a curious mix of feeling elated with a sense of trepidation. Sliding out of bed she headed straight for the window overlooking the street and pulled back the heavy, dusky pink curtains. She smiled at the scene unfolding beneath her and

11

let out a contented sigh. It was her favourite time of day: first thing in the morning as the world around her was coming to life. It was still dark but the dawn chorus had already swung into action with the blackbirds hitting the high notes as they perched in the treetops of the adjacent churchyard. The frost covered cobbles gleamed in the amber glow of streetlights and lighting from the pub and church opposite. Mary loved living in Haworth; more particularly, she loved living on Main Street. It was a far cry from her isolated, rural upbringing in Ireland. Here, she was in the thick of it, living above her mother's café and opposite the Black Bull pub, renowned for being one of the most haunted pubs in England. Beyond it, wide church steps led from the street to St Michael & All Angels Church and the Brontë Parsonage Museum. She cast her mind back to her first day in Haworth and the excitement she had felt at seeing all the little boutiques and gift shops up and down the street. It was teeming with tourists, more so than usual as they had arrived in the height of the summer season. She felt like she was on a permanent holiday for the first few months.

The old, mill village in West Yorkshire was built on the side of a steep hill and edged by desolate moors. In its heyday, Haworth was a busy trade village with purpose-built shops hugging the Main Street; notably tailors, drapers, clog and bootmakers, stone masons, joiners and blacksmiths. Weaving spilled out from the surrounding twenty five mills into homes where handloom weavers would work from their kitchens in the village. When Mary and her parents arrived in Haworth in 1992, the traditional trade shops had long since been replaced by antique book shops, local art and crafts, Brontë inspired gift shops, clothes boutiques and a plethora of quaint tea shops. Standing proudly at the top of the popular Main Street stood the café that was to become their new home and business. Like all the other buildings, the café was built of local sandstone and gritstone, darkened to almost black with age. The ground floor housed the café and a further two floors provided living quarters, as with most of the shops along the street. Everything about the building, from the creaky floors to the dirty, soot laden exterior, thrilled Mary. She readily embraced the spirit of the village, quickly falling in love with its literary history and brooding landscape, and became a regular in the neighbouring shops.

Grabbing her hairbrush, she methodically pulled it through her wet hair, watching her reflection as she did so. She was nothing special, she knew that. Lifeless mousy hair that hung half way down her back: eyes a little too big, a little too blue. Not a sparkling sapphire blue, more a washed out sky blue; their only saving grace being the thick black lashes that framed them. Her soft, pink skin was splattered with freckles, and they didn't just limit themselves to her face. They covered her entire body. She hated them. So much. Family would tease her about them in varying degrees, depending on the relation. Kind aunts would say, 'they are kisses from the sun', or 'God's blessing'. Patriotic uncles would claim, 'it's your Irish blood', and cruel cousins would tease, 'somebody attacked you with a brown felt tip, and they did a proper job of it!' She loved the idea of kisses from the sun, was proud of her Irish blood though not so sure about a blessing from God, and in truth, she mostly felt as if she had indeed been attacked by a felt tip pen.

Mary's father was in his usual spot at the head of the table, studying the newspaper with a fixed frown. He looked up as Mary entered the room and afforded her a brief incline of his head, glancing at his watch.

13

"Running late today, Mary? Did you not sleep well?" His strong Belfast tone was curt, and she knew he didn't expect a response. She mumbled an apology and sat down, smiling her thanks when a plate of buttered toast was put in front of her. Her mother smiled back and patted her shoulder, glancing at her husband. Mary spread raspberry jam on her toast, taking care not to spill any on the white, linen table cloth. Tiny specks of pink were still visible from previous spillages and every now and then, her father would look at them and tut, rubbing his finger across the stains to highlight his displeasure. He was much older than his forty-eight years, both in appearance and attitude. His once dark brown hair was now more dark grey, and his deeply furrowed brow emphasized his permanent state of disapproval. Folding the newspaper in half and carefully placing it in front of him, he commanded Mary's attention with a sharp intake of breath.

"I had a long telephone conversation with Mr Nelson last night. He tells me you are struggling with maths."

Mary shot a look of despair at her mother, putting her half-eaten toast back on the plate. Her mother spoke up for her.

"We discussed this before Christmas, Donal. I told you Mary was finding it difficult."

"Did you, Bridget; I don't recall that conversation at all." He turned steely eyes on his wife. "Because if I had recalled that conversation, then I would not have felt such a fool talking to Mary's teacher, would I?" His tone was unnervingly measured, barely concealing his rising anger.

"I do not expect to be told, over the phone, that my daughter is so behind with her maths that she needs help from another pupil."

"Well, surely that is a good thing? They can work together," she tried to placate him. "Mary, who's helping you?"

"Richard White." Mary's voice was barely a whisper. Her mother's eyes widened slightly and uncertainty flickered across her face. She deliberately avoided looking at her husband but was acutely aware of his eyes boring into her.

"Oh. I see. Is he … helpful?"

Mary nodded.

"Are you alright about it?" her mother encouraged.

"Yes. He's alright, Mam, really," she gave a nervous smile. Too late, she realised her folly.

"Oh, is that a fact?" her father's words dripped acid. "And what makes you think you are a good judge of character, Mary?" He pushed his chair back slowly from the table and stood up. Despite his short, stocky frame, he seemed to tower over both women, scowling at them. He pointed a finger at Mary.

"You make sure you work twice as hard now, so we can have an end to this nonsense. No more time-wasting. I am not happy about this." He paused. "Mary, do you hear me?" he barked. She nodded quickly, balling her hands on her lap and digging her nails into her palms. With a final glare at his wife, he marched out of the kitchen. Bridget dutifully followed after him, making sure he had everything he needed for work. Mary let out a shaky breath, slowly uncurling her hands.

"He will not make me cry. He will not make me cry," she chanted under her breath, gently rocking in her seat.

Mary was already on the school bus when Richard got on further up the road. Kelly was sitting next to her, talking loudly about her cousin's new puppy to the girls in the seat behind them. Mary looked up at Richard, ready to smile, but he completely blanked her as he made his way to the back of the bus. It was as if their conversation the previous day hadn't taken place. She wasn't sure why it bothered her but it did. She feigned interest in Kelly's tale and took the opportunity to steal a look at the back seat when she turned to talk to the friends behind her. She kept turning round but he was staring out of the window. Kelly said something that made the small group laugh out loud; finally he looked in her direction and she smiled. He raised an eyebrow in a half-hearted acknowledgment, then shooting a contemptuous look in Kelly's direction, returned his attention to the passing scenery.

The first lesson of the day was double science. As the class filed in, their teacher raised his hand for their attention.

"Before you take your seats: I have decided to take a leaf out of Mr Nelson's book and move some of you around. So, listen out for your names and I shall tell you where to sit."

As he worked his way down the list, it was clear he had not just taken a leaf, but copied Mr Nelson's list almost to the letter.

"Mary O'Shea and Richard White, sit over there." He pointed to a table in the middle of the room. Ryan wasn't in their science class but Josh was. Mary could sense he was aching to say something, judging by the cocky grin on his face as he watched them take their seats. He was seated towards the back of the class.

"Alright, love?" he called to Mary and gave her an exaggerated wink, clicking his tongue as he did so. Flustered, she pretended she hadn't heard, busying herself with rifling through her pencil case for a pen. Richard glanced at her hand, noticing how it shook. He silently passed her a pen from his pocket. She wanted to say thank you but he didn't look at her. She could tell by his straightened back that he was on high alert, waiting. Sure enough, a fist-sized, screwed up ball of paper hit him on the back of his head, barely

16

making an impact before landing noiselessly on the floor by his seat. Richard didn't flinch or react but taking a sideways look at him, Mary could see how his jawline twitched as he clenched his teeth. Her stomach twisted, anticipating a repeat of the previous day.

"Joshua Higgins, stand up!" Mr Platt sounded exasperated. "Two minutes: that has to be a record, even for you. Get out!"

Josh left the room with a wide swagger, grinning at his friends. He flicked the back of Richard's head as he passed and winked again at Mary. Neither of them responded and for a moment she felt strangely on a par with him. As if reading her thoughts, he gave her a sideways look.

"Okay?" he asked with no hint of emotion. She nodded.

"Yes. You?"

He looked surprised, then annoyed, frowning.

"Why wouldn't I be?"

Mary looked away, willing herself not to blush. She hated that she would turn beetroot at the drop of a hat; it had always been the bane of her life. Sighing, she watched Mr Platt hand out past exam papers and smiled her thanks when he reached their table. He hesitated, about to say something but decided against it. He addressed the room.

"Right, class; I have a stack of these for us to work through. Take a look and highlight anything you're unsure of, then swap with your partner and see what they've highlighted. Discuss, help each other as best you can, and then we'll go through it as a class. Ten minutes; off you go."

Mary opened her paper and her heart sank. Deftly pulling the lid off her highlighter, she systematically worked through, trying not to let panic engulf her. Turning to Richard, she tentatively pushed her paper towards him. He slid his across towards her, the highlighter untouched by his side. She watched him flick through her paper, noting the abundance of pink splodges.

"Did you just colour in the whole thing?" he asked dryly. She gave a nervous laugh, mortified by the look on his face.

"I did warn you," she tried to joke. The crack in her voice didn't go unnoticed. He stared at the paper for a moment, deliberating. He pushed it back to her.

"Go through it again and mark - with a normal pen – the questions you don't understand *at all*. You must get some of this, surely?"

Mary hung her head. Her stomach twisted into knots again and she felt shaky inside. Richard was watching her face, reading her mind unnervingly clearly. He lowered his voice,

"None of it?"

She shook her head. He sighed deeply, opening the paper again.

"Looks like we've got our work cut out then, doesn't it. Please tell me maths is your stronger subject." He let out a defeated expletive when she shook her head.

"I'm sorry," she murmured.

"You owe me." His voice was challenging but she could see a flicker of humour in his eye.

"I can pay you in cake," she ventured. He snorted.

"Cigarettes then?"

"I was joking, you don't need to pay me. Just … just stand up to your dad next time," he almost sounded sympathetic. Her face dropped and she could feel her cheeks burning. She swallowed the lump in her throat. She had a crazy notion of getting up and walking out but of course she would never have the courage to do so.

"Mary?" Richard's use of her name made her start. It seemed so alien coming from his mouth but she liked the way it sounded. His broad Yorkshire accent softened her name in a way her father's voice never could. He was looking at her expectantly.

"I …" she faltered.

"It's okay," he nodded. She smiled; he didn't smile back but his icy blue eyes darkened, softening just for a moment. He picked up the paper and prepared to work through the first question with her.

"It better be a huge cake," he muttered. This time she could tell he was joking and she laughed, nodding.

"It will be!"

Happy that they'd broken the ice, she moved her chair a little closer to his and listened intently as he explained aluminium extraction using electrolysis, making it seem so simple.

Chapter Two

Their first week back at school was a three-day one which ordinarily Mary would have been pleased about but she felt disappointed when Saturday came around. Despite their shaky start she had actually enjoyed her lessons with Richard. Yes, he was edgy and hard to read, but he made her feel buzzy. Daring even. It was a feeling she liked. When he was explaining something to her, watching her to see if she had understood, he made her feel like they were the only two people in the room. She knew it was silly; the minute they left the classroom she became invisible to him again.

The Brontë Parsonage museum was closed for cleaning and she wasn't needed on the rota for two weeks, so she had a free Saturday and had planned a walk with Kelly up to Top Withens. It was her favourite walk; not just because the derelict farmhouse, known as Top Withens, was famed to be the setting for *Wuthering Heights*, but also for the sheer beauty of the landscape across the moor leading to it. She loved the fact that the Brontë sisters had walked that same path many times over, creating characters and sharing secrets. Mary often traipsed alone across the bracken, lost in thought, letting her mind wander. She could almost hear the thunder of Heathcliff's horse as he rode at speed up to the farmhouse.

"Who's your favourite: Heathcliff or Rochester?" Kelly had asked when the pair of them first became friends.

"Hard to say, really. I love them both. They're both broken souls and so misunderstood. How about you?" Mary eagerly anticipated Kelly's reply. Nobody else her age got why she was so fascinated with those novels. Kelly shrugged.

"Neither. They're both losers. Let's face it, Mary, I wouldn't bother with either one of them!"

Mary hadn't broached the subject since. She preferred to keep her fantasies in her head, and not try to share them with her cynical friend. They did however, both enjoy their walks together across the moor.

Kelly Wood and Mary had struck up a friendship at the beginning of the new school year the previous September, when the changed seating plan in English had paired them up. They hit it off from the onset, despite being like chalk and cheese. Kelly was outgoing and streetwise; an opinionated extravert with a sharp tongue who didn't suffer fools gladly. For some reason, she had claimed Mary as her best friend and Mary didn't question it; she was relieved to be on the right side of Kelly.

As Mary walked round the side of the church and through the graveyard, a liver and white springer spaniel came bounding towards her, barking. She crouched down to greet it, stumbling as it jumped up at her, wagging its stumpy tail in excitement.

"Well hello, Genevieve!" Mary lavished the dog with attention, grinning up at Kelly as she approached them.

"Away, Gen," Kelly commanded, then patted the dog's head when she promptly obeyed, returning to sit at Kelly's feet. Mary straightened up, brushing muddy paw prints from her jeans.

"Yeah, sorry about that. She's already been through three puddles on her way here", Kelly explained, not really worried. She knew Mary didn't mind.

Never short of things to talk about, Kelly dominated the conversation as they carried along the path leading to Top Withens, stopping to pet the horses that hung their heads over the low, stone wall that separated the narrow path from

21

the fields surrounding the back of the Parsonage. As the path inclined, they paused to catch their breath and wait for Genevieve to re-emerge from the undergrowth. Mary gazed off into the distance at the rolling, lush green hills, partitioned by snaking stone walls and dotted with stone dwellings. She let out a contented sigh. Kelly followed her gaze.

"I love this place. However much I moan about it, I'd miss it if I ever left," Kelly said. "I wouldn't miss my brothers though!"

"I bet you would," Mary laughed. She had listened to Kelly complain about her siblings on numerous occasions but she still felt envious. She would love to be part of a big family, to belong to a unit. The bickering was just part and parcel of that, she was sure, and she knew that part of Kelly's supreme confidence came from feeling secure within her unit.

They carried on the walk, quickly reaching the edge of the moor on Dimples Lane. The landscape changed quite dramatically, levelling out to a vast expanse of rocky outcrops, hillocks and heather, blackened in places from the unforgiving frost. A well-worn, stony path led them across the moor, the open terrain offering no protection against the sharp wind that hit their faces and whipped about their ears. Undeterred, Kelly chatted on, hardly pausing for breath, and Mary walked beside her with her head cocked trying to catch what she was saying. The wind dropped as they approached the descent to the Brontë Bridge and waterfall; the slippery, rough, stone steps proving hazardous underfoot. The terrain had changed once again; a ravine cut through the moorland, with the path falling away sharply to the right of them where the chattering Sladen Beck rushed by. Its route cascaded down through the heather and stone ahead, before levelling out and bubbling along under the clapper bridge. To the left was the familiar sight of the Brontë Falls, the swollen water hissing and splashing as it tumbled, smacking against the dark stone. It was always more spectacular after heavy rain; during milder weather the stream was less urgent, more peaceful. Mary preferred it when it was angry; an unstoppable force of nature. She loved the powerful sound of water against rock, and felt inspired by its energy. They paused by the bridge, enjoying the brief respite from the relentless wind that swept across the moorland, by-passing the ravine. The original stone bridge had been destroyed during a flash flood five years previously but had been quickly rebuilt in a similar, yet more robust style. A commemorative plaque from the Brontë Society, embedded in a large boulder on the far side of the bridge, marked the occasion and served as a reminder of the destructive power of nature.

Crossing the bridge and scrambling up the far side of the ravine – avoiding the slippery, man-made stone steps - and using protruding rocks as hand-holds, they quickly reached level ground once more where they were instantly buffeted by the wind again. As they tramped through heather and clay-like mud, the sun started to warm up, taking the edge off the wind, and the moor started to rise again, slowly taking them to a higher plateau. At its peak lay the ruins of Top Withens farm; once a remote farmhouse, which had been left uninhabited since the mid-nineteen twenties. Now the shell of the old stone house was all that remained, with another plaque from the Brontë Society, marking the building's historical importance for the scores of literary fans that visited the spot. It had, over the years, become a place of pilgrimage and yet, had thankfully been left completely untouched by commercialism. The grey bricked ruins and the neighbouring pair of trees were photographed relentlessly and featured on many postcards, paintings and in several books. But when Mary and Kelly reached their destination, they were the only two there; the only sounds to be heard were from nearby sheep and windswept birds. It was hard to see what all the fuss was about, unless you were a lover of *Wuthering Heights.* To the untrained eye, it was just another farmhouse left to the ravages of time, the occupants long gone; either driven away by hunger and better prospects, or death – their way of life dying with them. It was remarkably ordinary for such a revered spot.

Kelly pulled an old ice-cream tub from her bag and filled it with water from a plastic bottle. Genevieve noisily lapped it up before running rings round the bricked walls, sniffing in every corner, as she did with every visit.

"Drink?"

Mary nodded, catching the can that Kelly threw towards her. She reciprocated by pulling two cup-cakes from her bag, handing one to Kelly. It was their usual thing; Kelly brought a drink and Mary brought the cakes. They sat on the one of the walls, their legs dangling over the edge, gazing off into the distance as they munched in contented silence. An undulating patchwork of brown, burnt orange, and varying shades of green, stretched for as far as the eye could see. Sunlight flickered across the moor, briefly bringing the colours to life before being masked again by cotton-ball clouds that drifted across the winter sky. Genevieve barked to remind them of her presence. She had finished exploring and was restless, keen to get going. Packing away their things, they started the three-mile walk back to Haworth.

As they carefully made their way down the sharp drop back to the Brontë Bridge, Mary glanced up from her feet as Genevieve charged past her, surefooted on the slippery stone path. There, on the other side of the bridge, was a figure she recognised instantly. Richard was sprawled on the stony ground, staring up at the sky. Or was he asleep? She couldn't tell from where she was. Genevieve barked as she approached him; Richard propped himself up on his elbows, staring at the dog but made no attempt to greet her. From behind her, Mary heard Kelly swear under her breath and let out a piercing whistle. Without hesitation, Genevieve charged back up the incline to Kelly's heel. Richard watched her progress and recognising the girls, looked away. Mary's heart sank. She was acutely aware of looking a mess. Her hair was windswept, nose bright red from the sharp cold, and her jeans were caked in mud around her ankles.

"Stupid dog, why does she have to greet everybody?" Kelly cursed quietly. "She has no morals," she snorted, deliberately turning her head away from Richard as they crossed the bridge. He watched them pass, and catching his eye, Mary smiled and mumbled, "Hello." He nodded, then looked away, dismissing her completely. She blushed.

"Why are you talking to that tosser?" Kelly muttered angrily, shooting Mary a look of disapproval. "And why have you gone bright red?"

"Because it's really embarrassing sitting next to him in class and have him teach me stuff. I feel so stupid, and he's so clever," she explained quickly. Kelly grunted in sympathy.

"Yeah, don't let it fool you," she warned, marching on. Mary shook her head meekly. She turned to look back at Richard; he was staring at her. She tentatively put her hand up to wave but he looked away again.

"What's he doing up here anyway?" she wondered, catching up with Kelly.

"Getting off his head; that's what he usually does up here."

"Really?" Mary glanced back and saw he was lying on the ground again.

"How do you know he's…" she looked at Kelly expectantly.

"Didn't you smell it? I got high just walking past him!"

Mary stared at her in surprise, realisation dawning.

"Is *that* what that smell is? It's weed? I never knew." She thought back to the number of times she had come across the sickly sweet smell lingering in the air along one of her walks, or in the park.

"Oh, Mary, you really have a lot to learn," Kelly teased, tucking her arm through Mary's. "What would you do without me, eh?"

Mary laughed, embarrassed. She wished she could be more like Kelly and less like an awkward, frumpy child. She wished she had Kelly's confidence and forthright manner. Kelly had the boys hanging off her every word and the girls desperate to be her friend, and yet she could shoot them down with one scornful remark or glare, knowing that they would lap it up and come back for more. Mary still couldn't fathom how she did it; how she was so popular and yet so cutting.

"Shall we drop Gen off home and then go back to yours to watch *Pretty Woman* then?" Kelly prompted as they approached the edge of the village.

"Absolutely," Mary agreed. She knew her father was out for the day, so they would be undisturbed. He hadn't objected to her friendship with Kelly as such, although initially his disdain was more than clear but Kelly had managed to charm him, winning him over in her inevitable way.

Kelly flopped down on the sofa in Mary's room and threw her a packet of crisps from the bag in front of her. She let out a deep sigh as she relaxed.

"I love your room," she enthused with unmasked envy. Mary's room, adjoining spare room, and bathroom across the small landing, took up the entirety of the third floor. Her room was a little old-fashioned; faded pink and navy chintz paper covered the walls, with a once-thick, worn, shaggy carpet underfoot, in a matching pink. Remnants of the previous occupiers, it had been Bridget's intention to decorate the room with fresh paint and carpet, but like most things, it was put on the back-burner until 'life has settled down a bit'. Mary didn't mind the tired décor, she was just grateful to have her own space, away from her parents. The spare bedroom that led on from her room was small, housing a bed sofa, wardrobe and desk. She used it as a dressing room and study, as guests were thin on the ground. Again, the faded walls cried out for a make-over from the drab, mushroom coloured woodchip. It could have been jazzed up if she had the inclination but as far as Mary was concerned, it served its purpose. Her room was above the lounge and just as large, with two windows overlooking the Main Street. The spare room overlooked the back, with views reaching across to Brow, on the far side of Haworth village. Rows of grey and brown houses, interspersed with tall, broad trees, were framed by the rolling hills that stretched off into the distance. Directly below the window was the wide, flat roof of the kitchen extension. Below that, the kitchen of the café.

As Mary had no need for more wardrobes, her bedroom was uncluttered and spacious. A small, iron-framed, double bed was at one end of the room, positioned to have a perfect view of the pub and church steps from the window. The patchwork bedspread that covered her pink bedding clashed with the wallpaper and yet the contrast seemed to fit. A low, wide chest of drawers doubled up as a bedside table for a lamp, books, CD player and a cloth covered jewellry box. A large, comfy, slightly lumpy, sofa was positioned at the foot of the bed, facing the opposite wall where her television was perched on top of a wide, pine unit. The sofa was covered with a cream, fleecy throw. In between the television and the window, a low, velvet upholstered chair beckoned and was

Mary's favourite spot to watch the world outside. Some of the furniture was already there when they moved in, and some had been picked up from second-hand shops. The velvet chair with mahogany, ring turned legs was Mary's find. She had fallen in love with the deep, midnight blue colour of the button back bedroom chair and against her father's better judgment, he had begrudgingly agreed to the rather steep price. She found an old, silk shawl with a rose print and elaborate fringe in the same shop, which she draped across the chair. When she sat in it to either read or daydream, she was transported to another time, another world. She called it her 'wishing chair', after her favourite childhood book; a book that still had pride of place on the shelf. Two wide, wooden bookcases dominated the room; one on the other side of the television and one next to her bedside chest of drawers, near the door . Both tall and both laden with her treasured books. There were a couple of second-hand book shops on Main Street and she was a regular, picking up bargains or saving up for the more costly, collectors editions. Books were her salvation, her escape. She could be whoever she wanted to be when she was reading, immersing herself in the lives and personalities of her favourite characters. Returning to reality was always a wrench. However much she loved being at the heart of the community, she still felt invisible. Trapped, like a caged bird; able to see, smell and hear the world but not able to lose herself to it.

"You're so lucky," Kelly insisted, watching Mary insert the film into the video player. "I have to share with my two sisters. My brothers are always fighting and their friends are always round. There's no peace anywhere. This is like heaven here!"

Although pleased with her response, Mary wasn't convinced about it being 'heaven'. Kelly was the fourth of five children; Gillian was the eldest, aged twenty-two, the twins, Kimberley and Kevin, were twenty, and James, fifteen. Both parents worked flat out to support the family and only now that the three eldest were also out at work, life was starting to get easier for them. There was occasional talk of Gillian and Kevin moving out but neither of them seemed in a hurry to do so. Kimberley declared often that she had no intention of leaving home as it was too expensive. What she really meant was that life was easier at home and she enjoyed the spare money. Mary had been warmly welcomed by them all into their chaotic home and she loved going there whenever she was allowed out.

She thought about her reply, always nervous to really speak her mind to Kelly.

"I think I'd rather have your life to be honest. Yes, I can watch the tv in peace whenever I want. Eat cake all day! But I'm lonely up here in my ivory tower. I've no-one to watch films with or listen to music with. The pub over the way is always so lively and I'm ... stuck *here*. The world outside is rushing on by. Busy, busy! And I'm bored. There's no excitement in my life. I'm watching others but for me ... there's nothing."

Kelly stared at her, stunned into silence by her frank outburst. She slowly swallowed her mouthful of crisps, a triumphant smile spreading across her face.

"Right, that's it. We need to get you out more! I'm still mad at you for not coming to Angela's party at Christmas." She pulled a mock scowl but her eyes told a different story; she was busy plotting.

"I know, but I told you why," Mary defended. She had desperately wanted to go to the party; it was the first one she had been invited to and she knew she had Kelly's friendship to thank for that. Before Kelly, nobody beyond a couple of school friends had ever bothered with her. Kelly was not going to be deterred, she was on a mission now.

"Yes well, your dad is just going to have to get used to it. You're nearly eighteen now, not his little baby anymore."

Mary looked uncertain, hovering by the television with the controls in her hand.

"It's not that simple," she mumbled.

"Of course it is. Your dad's alright, he's just a bit over-protective, that's all. Behind that scarily fierce face, I bet he's a teddy bear!" she laughed. Mary gave her a weak smile, knowing it was futile to argue.

"Next weekend, you're coming with me to that party I told you about," she beamed.

"Your brother's friend?" Mary felt panic clutching at her chest. She had met Kevin's friend; he was three years older and in a completely different league. He made her feel like she was twelve, not seventeen.

"Adam, yes. Here's what we'll do. You come over to mine in the morning and we'll go shopping in Keighley. Then I'll give you a make-over; you'll look fantastic, trust me," she rubbed her hands together, pleased with her plan. Mary could tell there was more to come. Kelly's eyes sparkled with mischief.

"What you need is a date. I'm going to fix you up!"

"No! No, please don't," Mary tried to sound as firm as she could. Kelly regarded her for a moment.

"Okay, but that's what you need, Mary. You need to start living a bit."

Mary could tell that despite her admitting defeat, Kelly wasn't going to give up so readily. She had every intention of 'fixing her up' with somebody. Mary decided to change the subject.

30

"Why do you hate Richard so much?" She tried to sound nonchalant but her voice was a notch too high and the words stumbled out abruptly. Kelly recoiled her head dramatically.

"Wait, how did we get from finding you a boyfriend to talking about that tosser?" She gave a derisive snort. Mary floundered.

"It wasn't … I didn't … think it because of that, I just remembered what we were saying earlier, that's all," she recovered swiftly. She couldn't admit to Kelly that he was on her mind most of the time. She was fascinated by him.

Kelly slumped back in the sofa, wriggling to make herself comfortable, thinking about the past.

"We used to be really good mates when we were kids, y'know, right through primary school. He was cute. I used to say I was going to marry him!" She paused, lost in thought as old feelings resurfaced.

"I felt sorry for him when his dad left, it was awful," she admitted, her voice trailing off as she recalled what had happened.

"His dad left?"

"Yeah, he ran off with Josh's mum. They'd been at it for ages, she was a right flirt, and then she just left the kids with her hubby and buggered off with Richard's dad."

Mary sat herself down next to Kelly, stunned by what she was hearing. Visions of Richard as a distraught young boy tugged at her heartstrings.

"That's why his mum drinks, I reckon. She was left with Richard and had to move back in with her parents. He's a nasty piece of work, her dad. Evil."

"Evil? How?"

Kelly sighed. She fiddled with the edge of a blue, plush scatter cushion.

31

"Well, my mum was friends with her at school and she said that Richards granddad was knocking her about. Hayley, Richard's mum, always had a black eye or bruised face. Anyway, there was talk that he was doing more stuff to her … y'know, behind closed doors." She screwed her face up with disgust, not liking what she was relaying. Mary was horrified, unable to comment. It was a much more disturbing tale than she had expected. Kelly shot her a look, nodding.

"I know, like I said, evil. But she had no choice. She had Richard, no job, lost the house, so she had to go back home. And I know for a fact that he knocks Richard about but she's too drunk to stick up for him."

They both lapsed into silence, taking in the weight of her words. Mary's mind was racing; she wanted to ask why Kelly had turned against him when surely he needed all the friendship he could get. As if reading her mind, Kelly continued,

"And then when Richard's dad died suddenly, he changed. Like, a massive change. He became really angry and moody. Josh's mum came back home. Her husband took her back and they carried on as if nothing had ever happened. Then Richard and Josh had this big argument and he beat Josh to a pulp. Seriously, psycho stuff. He just flipped, he wouldn't stop. I thought Josh was dead!" Her eyes widened as she relived it, shaking her head. The sight of Josh's bloody face against the hard tarmac was an image she could never shake off.

"I mean, looking back I can see how he must've been angry. He lost everything when his dad left with *her*, and then she came back to the village as if butter wouldn't melt. So I kind of understand it. But then a couple of years ago, he beat Josh up again for no reason. I mean, seriously badly. I didn't see it happen that time but it was worse than the first fight. He put

Josh in hospital. I haven't spoken to him since and I don't ever intend to. He's bad news, Mary. Real bad news."

They lapsed into silence once more. Mary stared unseeing at the carpet, trying to process everything she had just learnt. She was appalled to think that Richard could have been so violent but at the same time, she couldn't help but feel disappointed in Kelly. She should've supported him, not turned her back on him, when he was so obviously crying out for help. They had been friends since they were little; why didn't she see what he was going through? He must have been so broken and felt so betrayed.

"To think I nearly slept with him!" Kelly's stark admission snapped Mary back to reality. She blushed.

"You did?"

"Yeah. He would've been my first. Can you imagine that?"

Mary didn't want to but curiosity got the better of her.

"What happened? When was this?"

"A while ago, when I was fifteen. He said he wasn't interested but I knew he was. I think he couldn't handle me, I was too much for him!" She gave a raunchy wink.

"So what happened then?"

"I slept with Josh instead."

That wasn't what Mary was expecting to hear either and she barely contained her disbelief.

"*Josh*?"

"Yeah, can you blame me? He's always been gorgeous, everybody fancies him. I still do a bit but he's just like a big kid now. I prefer them older," she laughed, slipping back into the outrageous Kelly that Mary was used to. But Mary wasn't quite done with her questions.

"So, is that why Richard and Josh had the second fight? Because you slept with Josh?"

Kelly shook her head.

"I doubt it; it happened months after. Although Josh did brag about it in front of Richard but he didn't seem bothered. No, I think he's just evil, like his granddad." She was getting tetchy with all the questions and dragging up the past. She hated Richard and it irked her that Mary wasn't backing her sentiment wholeheartedly.

"Trust me, Mary. Don't get mixed up with him, you don't know what he's really like." She could see Mary was feeling anxious about everything she had heard and Kelly regretted being so honest. She sometimes forgot how naïve and innocent Mary was about life. It wasn't her fault she had been thrown together with Richard at school. She straightened up, determined to lighten the mood and forget about him.

"So, are we going to watch this film, or what? I've already finished my crisps!"

Chapter Three

The next week at school continued in a similar vein to the previous one; during lessons, Richard would give his undivided attention to Mary but as soon as they were away from the classroom, he barely seemed to notice her. To save herself from embarrassment, she had stopped looking up from her seat to say 'hello' when he got on the bus. She knew he wouldn't acknowledge her anyway. His patience with her during lesson though, had taken her by surprise. He seemed the most unlikely person to be such a good teacher, taking pains to make sure she understood exactly what he was telling her.

"How do you make it seem so easy?" she had asked.

"It *is* easy. You just have a way of making it seem hard. You're thinking way too much, over-complicating it."

Since her conversation with Kelly, she was seeing Richard in a new light. She really felt for him and how he must have been so damaged by his family; abandoned by his dad and abused by his granddad. She was seeing Josh in a new light too. Initially, she had been a little in awe of him, fancied him even; as Kelly had quite rightly pointed out, he was by far the most popular boy in their year. Tall, good-looking without making much of an effort, with cute dimples and a cheeky smile. The proverbial blonde-haired, blue-eyed boy. He even had the teachers under his spell, turning on the charm to his advantage. As far as they were concerned, he was exasperating, nothing more. Through different eyes, Mary could see how blatant he was with his flirting, and how he intimidated those not in his friendship group. He was a bully; an arrogant, self-assured bully who took pleasure in belittling others. She hated the way he taunted Richard at every opportunity, and with each passing day she was feeling more protective towards him.

By Thursday, Mary had had enough of Josh's constant snide remarks directed at their backs, and the tiresome barrage of tightly screwed up balls of paper, aimed at Richard's head. One skimmed the side of her face as she was leaning towards Richard to hear him, and landed with a thud on their table. She snatched it up angrily and was about to turn to throw it back. Richard put his hand over hers to stop her.

"Don't do that," he said flatly.

"But I'm sick of it; aren't you?" she said, feeling unusually annoyed. Richard shrugged. She could see he was surprised by her reaction. Suddenly aware of his hand on hers, she started to blush. He moved it and looked away. Luckily their positioning meant that the awkward moment was masked from Josh, otherwise there would have been no end to his goading, she felt sure.

As their Friday maths lesson came to an end, she reached into her bag and discreetly handed him a small, mint coloured cupcake box under the table. He took it, turning questioning eyes to her. She smiled shyly.

"It's a muffin. Just to say 'thank you'. Last night was the first time I actually understood my maths homework!"

There was the merest hint of a smile in the corners of his mouth but it didn't amount to anything.

"Thanks," he said quietly, staring at the box, then reached for his backpack and stuffed it inside.

"I wasn't sure if you were a cranberry, blueberry or chocolate chip person, so I took a gamble and went with choc chip," she said brightly, trying desperately not to show how nervous she was. Her insides were shaking but she was relieved that for once, her face was not turning its usual shade of beetroot. The bell went and as they stood up simultaneously, Richard leant towards her.

"You guessed right," he said, nodding. She smiled, pleased. Without a second glance, he was through the door and swallowed up by the throng in the corridor. Mary stared after him, suddenly feeling small.

Kelly was waiting for her by the school gates and they walked arm in arm to the bus. She talked loudly all the way home about their plans for the following day, telling anybody that would listen about the age of the boys at the party and how she was going to fix Mary up with one of them. It was light-hearted banter and Mary laughed at her teasing, pleased to be centre of attention for a change. She caught Richard staring at her out of the corner of her eye, but resisted looking directly at him. He was clearly listening to what was being said and she could see his clenched jaw twitching; a sign she now knew of him being agitated. Kelly must really rankle him, she thought, and felt a fleeting pang of guilt at being part of her loud display.

Mary turned her alarm off as soon as it rang the next morning and snuggled down into her duvet, stretching and then curling her toes before drawing her knees up to keep as much heat in as possible. Her mother appeared with the customary mug of tea and perched on the edge of the bed, an indulgent smile on her round face.

"You stay here for a little while longer. Your father is on his way out to golf shortly."

"Does he know about tonight?" Mary asked nervously. Bridget shook her head.

"He knows you are spending the day with Kelly, yes. And as far as he is concerned, you will be home late as you've been invited to stay there for a film night. He wasn't happy, Mary, but I convinced him that it would be fine and I will wait up for you. So for goodness sake, please be home by midnight because, believe you me, if you're not, he won't let this happen again. You can be sure of that!"

Mary sat up and hugged Bridget.

"Thanks, Mam. I'll be home before midnight, I promise," she grinned. Bridget nodded, straightening up.

"This party is going to be alright isn't it? There'll be no drink and drugs will there?" Her question lacked conviction; she didn't' think for a minute that Mary would undertake going to that kind of a party but she felt the need to ask nevertheless.

"Of course not! I told you, it's at a friend's house, so there will be parents there," she said, trying to sound convincing.

"And this is James's friend? Kelly's younger brother?"

"Mmm-hmm," Mary nodded, holding the mug of tea to her face to hide the tell-tale colour creeping up her neck. Bridget didn't seem to notice; her mind was on more practical things.

"I don't have any money to give you, Mary. Why are you going shopping in Keighley? Surely you have plenty of tops to wear?"

"It's alright, Mam, I've got money from my wages. And I just wanted something new. It's my first party, y'know," she reasoned. Bridget patted her leg and nodded.

"I know that. You have fun, but I honestly don't think a bunch of fifteen-year-old boys will even notice you."

Mary knew she didn't mean to cause upset with her thoughtless comment but it hurt nonetheless. As soon as Bridget had left the room she started to get herself ready. She had such butterflies in her stomach. She knew she was running a huge risk by bending the truth as far as the party was concerned but the knowledge that her mother was also bending the truth on her behalf, made her very nervous. She knew what the consequences could entail.

An hour later, she was walking down the steep hill of Main Street, her large shoulder bag banging against her hip. She waved to several of the shop keepers as she passed by their windows.

'At least they notice me,' she thought to herself, dwelling once again on her mother's words. By the time she and Kelly were on the bus to Keighley, she had forgotten all about it and her stomach had butterflies of a different kind. She could barely contain her excitement, giggling with Kelly as they discussed make-up, clothes and which shoes to wear.

"Don't kill me," Kelly said, her eyes twinkling and a huge grin on her face, "but I've booked you in at the hairdresser's!"

Mary's face dropped.

"No! Why? What … what am I having done?" Her dismay was quickly replaced by more giddiness as they debated the possibilities. She shot an envious look at Kelly's bleach-blonde hair.

"I can't possibly have it coloured. My dad would literally hit the roof!"

But as she sat in the padded, vinyl, swivel chair staring at herself in the salon mirror, embarrassed by how dreary her hair looked, she had a moment of recklessness and agreed to all that the stylist suggested. Two hours later, she stared once again at her reflection, not quite able to believe the transformation. Kelly could hardly contain her delight.

"You look amazing, absolutely amazing!" she squealed, her expression matching Mary's.

The length had been cut to just below her shoulders with face-framing layers and longer layers throughout, lifting the weight dramatically. Her dull, brown colour was brought to life with glowing, caramel highlights, softening her face and emphasising the blue of her eyes. Her heavy curtain of fringe had been cropped to hover by her mouth, and softly brushed

39

to the side. Mary ran a finger along the outline of her face, transfixed.

"Is that really me?" she murmured, a slow grin spreading across her face. She looked at Kelly through the mirror, dropping her mouth open in exaggerated shock. Kelly copied her.

"I can't get over it! You look so different, Mary. Gorgeous!" She clapped her hands together decisively. "Right, all we need now is make-up and clothes. Come on!"

They got back to Kelly's later that afternoon; tired, giggly, and full from the chips they'd eaten on the way home. Dropping their bags on the bedroom floor, they both threw themselves across Kelly's bed, letting out exhausted grunts. Kelly reached for Mary's hand and squeezed it.

"It's been great today. I've been dying to do this with you for months." She rolled over onto her side to look at Mary's hair again.

"I can't believe how much it changes you."

Mary sat up, frowning.

"Don't say that; what's my dad going to do when he sees it?" She was beginning to regret being so reckless.

"Oh, sod your dad! This is your night, Mary, and I'm going to make sure you enjoy it!" She disappeared out of the room only to return a few moments later with two glasses in her hand. Opening one of the wardrobes, she pulled a large, white bottle out and waved it at Mary.

"Ever tried Malibu?" She knew the answer even before Mary shook her head.

"Oh, you'll love it. It tastes like coconut ice-cream," she said, pouring a generous measure into each glass. Mary took a gulp and nearly choked. Her throat burned, making her eyes water.

"That's not quite ice-cream," she said hoarsely. Kelly laughed, raising her glass.

"Get it down your neck, go on. Cheers, duck!"

By seven o'clock, Mary's transformation was nearly complete. Gillian and Kimberley had also been getting ready for the party, and adding their advice on Mary's make-up. The bottle of Malibu did the rounds as they crowded round the dressing table mirror, elbows jostling for room, trying to avoid knocking the pile of make-up pots to the floor. Frustrated, Kimberley marched out of the room and shouted at the bathroom door.

"Shift your arse, Kevin! I need the mirror!"

Kevin swore at her from the other side and thumped the door. Kimberley thumped it back. He swore again and yanked the door open.

"Jesus, Kim, you're right! You do need the mirror. You look like shite!"

Kimberley swore at him and punched his arm. He growled and then laughed, slapping her arm. She pushed him out of the way, laughing.

"Get lost, you moron. We both know I got the looks *and* the brains," she taunted. He shrugged.

"With looks like that you can keep them, thanks." He jumped backwards as she aimed a kick at his shin. She slammed the door in his face, complaining loudly about the smell of aftershave in the bathroom. Kevin laughed and sauntered into the girls' room.

"Alright, ladies?" He couldn't hide his surprise when he saw Mary but recovered quickly, smiling at his sisters and nodding with approval.

"Looking good, ladies. Looking good."

Gillian offered him a drink from the bottle. He held his hands up in mock horror.

"Malibu? Do I look like a girl?"

"You act like one, the amount of time you spend in the bathroom," Kimberley shouted from across the landing. Kevin turned to shout back, then catching Mary's eye, winked at her and smiled. She smiled back, her confidence soaring. She turned to the mirror, copying Kelly as she applied a thick layer of lip-gloss. Standing back to inspect Kelly's artwork, she liked what she saw. Black glitter eyeliner accentuated the shape of her eyes and a heavy dusting of iridescent denim blue eyeshadow made them sparkle. The blusher and foundation were applied more subtly.

"The trick is to make your eyes stand out," Kelly explained as she methodically brushed black mascara on to Mary's lashes.

After an afternoon of trying on outrageous outfits in the shops and giggling hysterically, Mary had finally settled on a pair of high shine, black satin leggings and a sleeveless, roll-neck top. A left-over from the post-Christmas sales, the slinky, red and black tartan top had gold lurex thread running through it and hugged her figure in a way she wasn't used to. Ordinarily, she would be feeling very self-conscious of her bare arms but the Malibu was quashing her inhibitions. A warm haze settled over her and her stomach felt bubbly with excitement.

"Not those, not those!" Kelly insisted, putting a hand out to stop Mary as she slipped her black ballet pumps on.

"I told you: you need heels. Here." She handed Mary a pair of black strappy sandals with long stiletto heels. Mary shook her head.

" I cannot wear those! For one, I won't be able to walk in them and two, if my dad saw me coming home in those, he would have a fit! At least I can cover up my clothes with my coat but those … no."

She surprised herself at how firm she sounded. Kelly shrugged, carelessly tossing the sandals onto her bed.

"What would your dad think to Kelly's outfit then?" Kimberley asked, tongue in cheek. Kelly stuck her hands on her hips and pushed her chest out, blowing Kimberley a kiss. Her black, skin-tight, sleeveless mini dress left little to the imagination. She had back-combed her hair up into a messy bun with a gold bandana tied round it. A thick, gold chain belt hung loosely about her curvy hips, serving no purpose other than to draw attention to them.

Mary gave her a derisive look.

"If my dad caught me wearing that, he would skin me alive!"

The sisters fell about laughing.

"How is that funny? He would literally skin me alive, I'm telling you." She started to laugh with them and accepted the near empty bottle from Kelly.

"Drink up and shut up! I'm telling *you*, your dad is a pussy cat. I bet he wouldn't mind *me* curled up on his lap, purring." Kelly made purring noises but stopped short when Kimberley threw a pillow at her.

"Hey! Watch the hair!" she whined, glaring at her sister. Gillian ushered them all out of the room and they noisily made their way downstairs, taking their time in their teetering heels. Kevin was waiting for them in the front room. Their mother stood up and gave them a hug, murmuring compliments to each of them. She hugged Mary.

"You look lovely, Mary. You go and enjoy yourself now."

James didn't turn from the television to acknowledge them. He was still annoyed that he was excluded from the party because of his age.

43

"But I'm *fifteen*!"

His mother looked at him steadily.

"Yes, that's right. You're only fifteen." She held a hand up to stop his retort. "End of story, James." She was more strict with him than with the others. Being the youngest, he was always trying to keep up with Kevin but was testing the boundaries to the limit. More sullen and outspoken than any of them, he concerned her and she was determined to check his behaviour.

Kevin leant over the back of the sofa and ruffled James' hair.

"Don't wait up, Jamie baby," he cooed.

"Get lost, faggot!" James pulled his head away, scowling at him. Ignoring it, Kevin kissed their mother and gallantly made way for the four girls to leave the room before him, smiling widely as they each thanked him. Turning at the door, he stuck his middle finger up at James.

"Later, loser," he winked smugly. He shut the door, blocking out the insults James was shouting in vain.

M People's *Moving on Up* was blaring out through the open door and the party was already in full swing by the time they arrived. Mary followed closely behind Kelly, holding her head down as she passed the crowd gathered by the door. Once inside, Kevin pointed up the stairs.

"Stick your coats in Adam's room. He won't mind." Then he disappeared into the kitchen, loudly greeting a group of look-a-likes, all preened for the occasion.

Once Gillian and Kimberley had gone back downstairs, Kelly sat on the edge of Adam's bed and pulled a bottle from her bag, offering it to Mary.

"I call it, 'Kelly's cocktail'," she told her. "It's a bit of everything."

They sat in the semi-dark for a while, passing the bottle between them. Mary quickly got used to the burning sensation at the back of her throat from the concoction of whiskey, Baileys and Amaretto, and had to admit, Kelly's cocktail tasted good.

The rest of the evening was spent in the company of four lads, all vying for their attention. They all knew Kelly but Mary was a new face to flirt with. Very unsteady on her feet, she swayed on the spot, giggling and trying to hear what was being said. Most of it was drowned out by the music but that didn't matter to her. She wasn't good at conversation anyway, she was just enjoying being centre of attention. The drink in her hand tasted like lemonade although she was fairly certain it was more than that. It was a comforting distraction for her as she watched Kelly flirting with Marcus. He was the one she had spent the whole day talking about and Mary could see it didn't take much effort on Kelly's part to get his attention. Somebody appeared in front of her, offering her another drink and she leant closer to hear what he was saying. Turning round, she saw Kelly had moved. She was sitting on Marcus's lap, kissing him. His hands were roaming all over her body. Not so much roaming, Mary thought, more like galloping. She looked round to see the others reaction only to discover they had all disappeared. She stood alone, watching Kelly, not sure what else to do. Somebody pushed past her and she stumbled backwards, landing with a bump on the floor by the wall. The room started to spin and her head felt disconnected from the rest of her body. The urge to lie down was too great to resist; she pressed herself against the cool wall and closed her eyes.

She came to when somebody stepped heavily on her ankle. Wincing with pain, she pushed herself up. Her stomach lurched, but more urgently, she needed to pee. Thankfully, the room had stopped spinning, nevertheless she clung on to the bannister with both hands to steady herself as she made her way up to the bathroom. Studying her reflection under the harsh light, she was impressed to see that her make-up was still immaculate and she didn't look anywhere near as pale as she felt. Back downstairs, she scouted round for Kelly who was nowhere to be seen. Neither was Marcus, or the other three lads that had been paying her so much attention earlier. With a sinking heart, it dawned on her that all of the flirting was aimed at Kelly, not her. She felt inconspicuous once again, blending into the shadows. Making her way back upstairs she went in search of her coat, and discovered that Kelly's wasn't there. She had clearly already left without letting her know.

Clutching her coat to her chest, she squeezed through the crowd that hadn't seemed to move from the open front door all night. Nobody noticed her; they carried on their banter over her head. A large group of lads had spilled out into the front garden, oblivious to the elements in their short sleeves. House of Pain's *Jump Around* started up and their raucous singing was punctuated with drunken laughter. A couple stepped aside to let Mary pass although nobody acknowledged her or gave her a second glance. As she looked up before crossing the road, she spotted Richard sitting on the garden wall on the opposite side, smoking. He looked away but she knew he had already seen her.

"Hello," she said, slowing down as she drew nearer. She smiled awkwardly. He looked up, and gave her a brief nod.

"Alright."

"You weren't at the party, were you? I didn't see you," she faltered, aware that he was watching her; more specifically, he was staring at her top which shimmered as the street light caught it. She fumbled with her coat, trying to put it on,

46

struggling to push her arms through and keep herself steady at the same time. Richard watched her, waiting until she had finished before replying.

"No, I wasn't. Why, did you look for me?"

She was startled, not sure how to respond. Colour flooded her cheeks. Silently cursing herself, she opted to joke it off.

"Well, you know, I had some pressing maths questions to ask you, that's all," she smiled. He smiled back, giving a little laugh. For a fleeting moment, it transformed his face, softening his normally set features. Caught off-guard, she audibly gasped which she quickly covered up with a cough, pulling her coat together against the cold. She took a step closer, hesitated, then sat next to him on the low wall.

"So, what are you doing here then?" she pressed. He drew in a deep breath, deliberating his reply, then shrugged lightly.

"Having a smoke," he shot her a look. "Waiting for you."

"Wai… waiting for *me*?" She could barely speak, her mind was racing. Did he just say that? Before she could stop herself she heard her blurted response.

"But why?"

Richard turned his full attention to her, studying her face.

"Have you been drinking?"

Flummoxed by his directness, she nodded. He looked away for a second, frowning.

"Thought so."

"What does that mean?" She was trying desperately to make sense of what was going on but the fresh air was having a strange effect on her. She swayed a little, her shoulder nudging against his. He put a hand out to steady her, then stood up.

"I thought you might need someone to walk you home," he said in a matter-of-fact tone. "Unless you want somebody else to?" he asked, nodding his head towards the rowdy bunch over the road. Mary inwardly laughed at the thought of any one of them offering to walk her home.

"No, no, you'll do," she looked up at him.

"I'll 'do', will I?" he teased. There was that smile again. Her stomach did a strange flip as she bit down a grin. Instinctively, she held out her hands for him to pull her up from the wall. Letting his half-smoked cigarette dangle from his lips, he effortlessly pulled her to her feet and steadied her, making sure she was stable before letting go of her hands.

"Alright?"

She nodded, stumbling over her own feet.

"Short-cut through the park?" he suggested. She nodded again.

"Is it a short-cut though?" she asked. He shook his head.

"Not really, no. But I think you need to sober up a bit before you get home, otherwise your dad'll have a word or two to say."

Not knowing how to respond to that, she walked beside him in silence. The significance of what he was doing slowly filtered through her muddled brain. She'd never had anybody looking out for her before, or understanding how fearful she was of her father.

"Thanks, Richard," she said softly. He looked away.

"That's okay."

"Are you allowed to drink?" she asked, fairly certain that he did so regularly.

"Probably. But I don't."

"What, ever?" she stopped in her tracks and stared at him. That wasn't the reply she was expecting. He gave her a look she couldn't fathom.

"No. I don't like what it does to people. Alcohol changes your whole personality. It's nasty stuff." He carried on walking.

"I'm sorry," she mumbled, feeling incredibly foolish and naive. He waited for her to catch up.

"I'm guessing it's your first time?"

She looked away. She hated that he could see right through her. She hated that she couldn't pull off being cool or sophisticated. She just felt like an idiot.

"And I bet Kelly bought the drink?"

Mary nodded.

"And then I bet she copped off with somebody and left you there alone." It wasn't a question; he knew the score. Seeing her face crumple a little, he swore under his breath. She sniffed and rummaged around in her pocket for a tissue. Richard took her arm and guided her over to a bench under the towering, dense rhododendron that edged the park. He watched as she tried to subtly blow her nose and hastily dab away tears. She was surprised by her own reaction, she didn't usually cry. Richard seemed angry.

"I've known Kelly all my life and she's always been an unreliable cow," he stated forcefully.

"But she's my best friend!" Mary tried to defend her but had to admit, she was feeling hurt by her actions.

"Yeah, well, 'best friends' have a way of turning. They let you down in the end. I don't trust anybody. It's easier that way."

Mary stared at him. The dim street light cast shadows across his face; his eyes flashed angrily as he spoke. Reaching for his cigarettes, he offered her one knowing she would refuse, before lighting up again. She waited for him to continue talking but he didn't. They sat in silence for a while. The air was crisp and still. In the distance a dog barked and somebody shouted; overhead an owl screeched as it coasted the tree tops. The faint crackle of Richard's cigarette and his steady breathing as he inhaled, then exhaled, was surprisingly comforting. She started to relax. Flicking his cigarette butt across the path, he finally broke the silence.

"So, what was that pressing maths question you had for me?" he jibed. She laughed at his teasing.

"Oh, that can wait til Monday," she dismissed. He smiled for a moment, thinking of a reply.

"I have never met anybody so shockingly bad at maths. Or science." He shook his head in despair at her as she landed a playful punch on his arm.

"You're hitting me now? After all I do for you?" He held his hands up in mock defence. Mary laughed and punched his arm again. He snatched her hand up and held it tightly, his whole body going still, watching her closely. She swallowed nervously, praying that he couldn't feel her shaking with anticipation.

"I have never met anybody so shockingly bad at punching either. I thought you Irish were made of stronger stuff; you punch like a fairy!" he laughed, ducking as she feigned swiping her free hand at him. He caught that hand too, gently squeezing them both as he continued to watch her.

"Feeling better?" he said quietly. She nodded, smiling. He nodded back, satisfied that she was.

"You don't need friends like that, Mary. She'll ruin you if you let her."

He stood up and pulled her to her feet, letting go of one hand but holding on firmly to the other. They walked on in silence, hand in hand, through the park towards the street lights beckoning on Main Street. The fuzzy feeling in her head was starting to lift just enough for her to focus on walking in a straight line but her feet felt like lead, making them drag. She was glad she'd not given in to Kelly's nagging about wearing high heels. There's no way she would be able to walk in them now. She glanced down at Richard's hand enveloping hers and her stomach did another flip.

He stopped at the foot of Main Street, deliberating. It was closing time and pub-goers were hurrying up the hill, hunched against the biting cold.

"Let's go the back way to avoid the pubs," he suggested, veering towards the road that ran around Main Street. There wasn't much traffic at that time of night and only one or two dog walkers emerging from the park, who didn't seem to notice the pair taking their time to get home. They walked along the tree-lined stretch of road and every now and then, Mary would stumble and Richard would steady her but they didn't speak. Reaching the top of the road, they turned into the side road that led to the Square at the top of Main Street, in sight of the Black Bull pub and the café. Richard stopped by a street light and leant Mary up against the wall, studying her face.

"Feeling better now?" he asked. She nodded, resting the flat of her hands on the brick wall behind her for support.

"Yes, thanks. My head's a bit … fuzzy … but it's … I'm okay, really," she stammered. The way he was looking at her was throwing her. He touched a strand of hair by her cheek.

"I like your hair, it suits you," he said, watching her reaction. She smiled, hardly able to breathe. It felt like an eternity before his eyes moved from hers, to rest on her mouth. She nervously licked her lips, trying to remain steady on her feet. She leant more heavily against the wall; as she moved, the gold thread in her top caught the light. Richard seemed fascinated by it. She breathed in, pushing her chest out.

"You can touch them if you want," she whispered. His head snapped up and he frowned.

"Don't do that," he muttered. Mortified, she didn't know where to look. He gently pulled her chin up.

51

"Don't throw yourself at me, like you're begging for it. Like all the others round here. You're better than that." He didn't sound cross; more disappointed.

"I'm sorry," she mumbled, not able to look away from his hypnotic stare.

"You don't *need* to do that. I'm already interested." He started to smile at her surprise.

"You are?" She wasn't sure whether he was teasing her.

"I'm here, aren't I?" He was still holding her chin, watching her, waiting for the penny to drop.

"How drunk are you, Mary?"

She gave an awkward laugh.

"I'm not sure. You're saying nice things to me and I'm not sure if ... if it's real or ..." Her voice tailed off.

"Ever been kissed before?" He was staring at her mouth again.

"Yes, of course!" she lied.

"Oh." He let go of her chin and reached for a cigarette. Flicking the match into the road, he leant his hand against the wall and bent towards her. He took a long drag and blew the smoke above her head, regarding her for a moment.

"Close your eyes," he said softly.

"Why?"

He laughed and gave her a challenging look.

"Close your eyes," he insisted. She did as he asked, barely able to breath. She felt his cold hands cradle her face, and the faint heat from his cigarette by her cheek. His cold nose touched hers as their lips met. She was surprised by how gentle his kiss was; not the frantic, face-eating kind of kissing that she had witnessed earlier. The warm pressure of his mouth on hers did strange things to her stomach. She dug her fingertips into the rough bricks behind her, trying to hold herself upright, her legs suddenly like jelly. As he pressed against her, effectively pinning her to the wall, she wrapped her arms around his broad back, and clung on to his jacket. She felt safe and at the same time, weightless. As if she were floating. He slowly pulled away. She opened her eyes to find him watching her, gauging her response.

"Ever been kissed like that before?"

She shook her head. He looked pleased, and took another drag from his cigarette.

"Will you be alright from here?" he asked, nodding towards the café. "I'll watch you."

Mary walked precariously along the slippery cobbles, taking her time. She turned back to Richard.

"See you on Monday," she smiled, still reeling from what had just happened.

"See me tomorrow," he said. "Meet me up by Dimples Lane at ten o'clock."

"Okay." She gave a shy wave, smiling when he winked back at her. There was a small crowd gathered outside the pub and one of the regulars, recognising her, shouted a greeting.

"Night, love!"

She waved and smiled politely, inwardly cringing, knowing that her dad could potentially hear it, announcing her arrival home. Turning at the archway leading to their back door, she looked for Richard. He was standing in the shadows; all she could see was the glowing tip of his cigarette. It gave her a thrill knowing that he had stayed true to his word and watched her walk the short distance safely. She smiled into the inky night in his general direction, and walked carefully to the door, running her hand along the wall for support.

Bridget appeared from the kitchen when Mary reached the top of the stairs. Her expectant smile froze when she saw Mary's hair. Mary nervously smoothed it down, avoiding eye contact.

"Thanks for waiting up, Mam," she whispered.

"Mary, your hair…" Bridget couldn't take her eyes off it. The caramel highlights gleamed in the bright hall light. Mary gave a nervous grin.

"I know. Do you like it?"

Bridget moved to inspect it closer. She smiled in wonder.

"Actually, I do. You look so different, so … grown up." She had been so distracted by Mary's hair that she hadn't noticed her make-up, clothes, or the fact that she was swaying on the spot. Mary shifted her weight and headed for the flight of stairs up to the her room before any questions could be asked.

"I had a great time. I'll tell you about it in the morning," she whispered, pointing towards her parents' bedroom, intimating that any conversation may wake her father. Bridget nodded and headed back to the kitchen. A thought hit her.

"Tie your hair back in the morning before breakfast." Her hushed tone sounded urgent. Clearly it wasn't just Mary that anticipated her father's negative reaction to the change.

She turned the light on in her room and hurried over to the window, hoping to catch a last glimpse of Richard. To her amazement, he was sitting on the church steps opposite her, watching the window. She waved; he stood up and waved back before disappearing into the shadows.

Hugging herself, she sat on her bed reliving the past hour in her mind. She desperately wanted to linger over it but her head felt too heavy. Clumsily pulling her shoes off, she sank back on her pillows and fell fast asleep, fully clothed.

Chapter Four

"What in God's name have you done with your hair?"

Mary hesitated in the kitchen doorway, knowing she would have to face her father's scrutiny. She had done as her mother suggested and tried pulling her hair back into a ponytail but the layers were too short, so she left it hanging loose instead. Kelly's immaculate make-up had proved a challenge to scrub from her face; she had no make-up remover and her regular face cleaner had stung her eyes, adding to her general hung-over demeanour. She tried to avoid her father's indignant stare.

"Well?" he demanded. Bridget refilled his tea cup, shooting Mary a reassuring glance.

"Oh, I think it suits her, Donal. It's good to have a change sometimes."

Donal snorted his disapproval and straightened out the newspaper in front of him, refusing to look at either of them. Mary took the opportunity to address Bridget.

"I'm going to meet up with Kelly this morning, Mam..."

"Did you not spend all day with her yesterday?" Donal interrupted. She looked at her hands.

"Yes, but today we're doing revision."

"For?"

"English." She could feel him bristling as he sat up in his seat.

"Are you telling me that you need help with English, too?" His vitriolic tone annoyed her. She hated how he ridiculed her. Not sure whether it was a new-found confidence or whether she was still affected by the alcohol, but something inside her snapped. She met his glinting stare.

"No, Kelly does. *She* needs *my* help; she's my learning partner." Balking at his reaction to her reply, she lost her nerve and addressed Bridget instead.

"It's a kind of buddy scheme the school are trying to introduce, where the more able ones work with the less able. That way, everybody gets a fair chance. I think it's a good idea," she explained. Bridget nodded her approval. Her smile faded when Donal spoke.

"There you go again, Mary, with your opinions. When you are old enough to have a valid one, then I will listen to you. Until then, I will decide whether something is 'a good idea'; not you."

Mary stared at the table, not moving a muscle. Her breakfast remained untouched in front of her. Knowing he was intimidating her, Donal took his time over his breakfast, tapping his cup for yet another re-fill of tea. The minutes ticked by in silence bar the scraping of butter on toast, and his methodical chewing. Finally done, he folded his paper and stood up.

"If you are going out, I suggest you wear a hat to cover that hair, Mary."

Mary took the familiar footpath along the back of the church up to Dimples Lane and the edge of the moor. She had sneaked out of the house as soon as she could and consequently reached the lane with twenty minutes to spare. Richard was already there, sitting on a bolder, staring off into the distance. His hands were pushed deep into his jacket pockets in an effort to ward off the cold and his set expression gave no indication of his mood. He turned on hearing her footsteps on the stony path, and a smile broke out across his face. Quickly regaining his composure, he stood up to greet her.

"Alright. You're early."

"Says you," she replied, taking his offered hand. He tried not to laugh, nodding.

"Yeah, I've been here all night, waiting."

Mary wasn't sure if he was joking or not, he was so hard to read. His hands were certainly cold enough though, and he was wearing the same black jeans as the night before. She glanced down at her own worn jeans and hoped he wouldn't notice the frayed hems or mud stains that refused to wash out. They started walking along the path through the heather and bracken towards Brontë Bridge.

"I love this place," she sighed, breathing in deeply, feeling instantly calmer. She always made a point of blocking out her father from her mind when she reached the moors. This was her sanctuary and he wasn't allowed to invade it, not even in her head.

"I know," Richard said. Mary looked surprised.

"How do you know?"

"I've seen you up here, loads of times." He tried not to smile at her startled expression. She thought about it for a moment.

"I thought I was invisible," she said quietly. He squeezed her hand, staring straight ahead.

"Not to me."

Her heart soared, not quite able to believe it; could this really be happening?

They veered from the path, Richard leading her towards a rocky outcrop. He started to climb up the steep side, pulling her up behind him. It was only a short climb of about fifteen feet and they quickly reached the top. The panoramic view across the moor was spectacular. Swathes of dark purple hugged narrow footpaths, and in the distance, the deep blue of Lower Laithe reservoir glinted in the low, winter sun.

Richard drank it all in, his face relaxing and a contented half-smile playing on his lips.

"I love it here. Not the village; just up here. *This* is my Yorkshire. *This* is in my blood."

"What's wrong with the village?" she prompted.

"I hate the people. They're all so small. Content to plod on with life; never moving, never wanting more. I want more. I want to stretch my wings. I want to make something of my life."

Mary was more transfixed by him than by the scene unfolding before them. She hadn't imagined him to feel so passionately, about anything. He always appeared distant, detached. And deeply troubled. And here he was, voicing feelings that she too felt.

"I do too," she said softly, wanting him to know she understood but not wanting to hijack his moment of opening up to her. He put his arms around her, drawing her close.

"I know. That's what I like about you. You have ambition." He rested his chin on her head, gazing at the landscape. Mary shivered as a cold wind whipped around them. Spurred into action, he took her hand and started the short descent back to the path.

"Come on, let's keep moving. It's freezing up here."

"Where are we going?" she asked, not really caring; she was just loving being with him.

"Up by Brontë Bridge. I'll show you."

Once they got to the bridge, Richard led her up a thin, barely visible path just past the waterfall. She stumbled, catching her foot on the undergrowth in a bid to keep up with him. He reached behind him and caught her hand, guiding her up the steep path. They gained height remarkably quickly and she stared around her in wonder. It had never occurred to her to climb the sides of the ravine, and the view from a different prospect was breath-taking. The heather appeared more red than purple, and the giant, rectangular slabs of grey rock that she would either skirt around or precariously scramble across, were more noticeably prominent across the moor. It was as if somebody had dropped them from a great height and they had landed like dominoes, in higgledy-piggledy clusters amongst the heather and in the beck. There was no wind; they were completely sheltered from it in that spot, although the sound of rushing water from the falls was amplified. They sat down among the dried heather and stones, both taking in the view.

"Is this what Ireland's like?"

Mary nodded.

"Kind of, I suppose. I grew up in Belfast; that's where I was born. Then we moved to Antrim, which is much more rural. Remote, really. But I didn't get to see much of it, or explore it."

"Why not?" Richard was genuinely curious. She shrugged, thinking about her reply.

"My dad's very protective. It's not the same here. In Ireland, we had to watch our backs all the time, y'know. I grew up with it so it was normal for me. It wasn't until we came here that I realised my childhood wasn't the same as everybody else's."

She reminisced about the excitement she felt coming to Haworth; the freedom of going out to explore the shops, and later, the moors. No longer chaperoned, she had space to think. Richard was watching her, listening. Every now and then, he would pick up a small stone and throw it into the distance, idly following its progress as it bounced to a halt among the rocks below them.

"You talk a lot," he commented dryly when she paused for breath. She laughed.

"Sorry!"

"Don't be; I like it. I'm just surprised, that's all. I've spent the past year staring at the back of your head, wondering what you're like. I'd never even heard you speak until two weeks ago. I thought you were always quiet."

Mary had surprised herself by how much she had enjoyed talking to him. She never opened up to anybody, not even Kelly. Not really.

"I am always quiet," she said. She wanted to add that he made her feel worthwhile listening to, but she didn't have the courage to say that. She was still getting over the shock of him wanting to be with her.

"Even at home?" he wondered.

"Especially at home," she nodded, giving a derisive laugh. "And then when I'm with Kelly, she does all the talking, so..." her voice trailed off as she saw his expression change at the mention of Kelly.

"So why did you leave Ireland?" he asked, changing the subject abruptly. Another stone went flying through the air; this one thrown with more force.

Mary sighed, thinking how to word the answer to the question she had been asked by so many well-meaning people. It was used as a conversation starter; ironically it was the one subject that she didn't want to talk about.

"My granddad died a few years ago. He was blown up. And then, my dad's friend was shot dead two years ago. My dad decided he'd had enough and we needed to get away." She rushed her words, sounding vague.

Richard frowned, cursing under his breath as he took it in.

"Is your dad IRA or something?"

Mary laughed in shock at his suggestion.

60

"No, no! The complete opposite, in fact. He was RUC."
Richard looked blank.

"Royal Ulster Constabulary," she explained. "He was with
the police, in Belfast."

"Oh," he nodded, recognising the name. "I don't know
much about Irish politics, only that it looks a right mess over
there. You're best out of it, I suppose. What does your dad do
now, then?"

"He's head of a security firm in Bradford. And Mam has the
café. When we left Ireland, she said she would only go on the
proviso that she could open a tea shop. It had always been
her dream," she smiled, remembering her mother's face
when it all came into fruition.

They fell silent again, both staring out at the landscape. A
couple of dog-walkers crossed the bridge, completely
unaware of the pair watching them.

"I see what you mean now; nobody can see us up here!"
She wondered how many times she had walked that path, not
realising that he may have been watching her.

"What was *your* dad like?" she ventured softly. He turned
away.

"Don't remember," he replied. She couldn't decide if he
sounded sad or angry.

"Do you miss him?"

Richard snatched up another stone, juggling it in his hand
for a brief moment before launching it like a cricket ball.

"No. He can rot in hell as far as I'm concerned."

Too late, Mary realised she had misjudged him. Sadness
was clearly the last thing he was feeling. He shot her a look,
about to say something, then paused as he read her face.
Getting to his feet, he unzipped his jacket and shrugged it off
before hastily taking his sweatshirt off. As he pulled it over his
head, the t-shirt underneath rode up. Mary blushed when she

caught sight of his chest. She had been right; tattoos snaked across his muscular torso. Seeing her red cheeks, Richard smirked, slowly readjusting his t-shirt before putting his jacket back on. He raised an eyebrow.

"Alright?"

She nodded, looking away, praying for her colour to subside. She could see his expression out of the corner of his eye; amused and challenging. He sat back down and balled his sweatshirt up into a make-shift pillow before laying it on the ground behind them. Lowering her onto it, he smiled down at her.

"So, where were we last night?"

They spent the next couple of hours kissing, talking and watching the clouds. Sunday walkers wove their way across the moor, never once looking up in their direction. That nervous, shaky feeling in Mary's stomach had gone and she felt safe lying in his arms. As the clouds shifted across the sky and the sun began to drop, she looked at her watch, pulling a face.

"I need to get home. My dad will be back from his lodge meeting soon."

Richard propped himself up on one elbow, reluctant to move.

"Lodge? Not church, then?"

Mary stood up, brushing the dried mud and heather from her jeans.

"No. Mam and I used to go to church every Sunday but not since we've been here. She says it's not the same. Besides, she has the café now."

Richard got up and put his arms around her, kissing her one more time.

"We don't tell anybody about this, okay? If people find out, they'll only ruin it for us," he said. She nodded, relieved that he felt the same way.

"My dad would kill me," she said with feeling.

"Yeah, I guessed that. So, nobody has to know."

Mary could tell by that he meant Kelly. She knew for a fact that Kelly wouldn't keep it to herself; far from it. Besides, it felt really exciting to have a secret from everybody. It would be the last thing they would expect of her and that made her feel good.

"Nobody," she agreed.

Mary stirred in her sleep, trying to open her eyes. She thought she heard someone calling her name.

"Mary!" There it was again. The whispered voice was coming from the corner of her room by the door to the spare room. She forced her eyes open and peered into the darkness. Her curtain was open a crack and the street light threw in a shaft of amber light. She could make out a figure in the shadows. Fear gripped at her throat as it slowly made its way towards her.

"Mary!" The voice was urgent, trying to get her attention. Recognising it, she reached across and turned her side light on. Richard was standing in the middle of her room, disorientated in the dark. He grinned at her. He had bare feet and was wearing black joggers and a black top. She stared at him, dumbstruck as he quietly crossed the room to her bed. She finally found her voice.

"What are you doing here? How … how did you get in," she whispered hoarsely.

"Through your back window. You left it open," he whispered back.

She always left it open. It had never occurred to her that anybody could get in. He must have climbed up onto the flat roof of the kitchen but even then, that was two storeys high. Suddenly aware that she was wearing her old, unflattering, rosebud print pyjamas, she gathered the duvet up around her.

"What are you doing here?" she repeated. He pulled his top off and sat on the edge of her bed, silently watching her reaction. Her face turned beetroot and yet she wasn't able to drag her eyes away from his chest.

"I thought you wanted to see my tattoos", he said deadpan. "You can touch them if you want," he added. Her eyes shot up to his and she saw a mischievous twinkle, teasing her. She laughed a little and tentatively touched the tail of the black, scaly dragon that snaked around his upper arm and across his chest, breathing fiery flames. Thorny vines wrapped themselves around his other arm, weaving into a dense, spikey, Celtic knot across his shoulder.

"They're so big. Are they expensive?"

Richard laughed abruptly, amazed by her question.

"Most people ask, did it hurt, but you just ask about the cost. Why is that?"

She felt foolish but hid it well, focusing again on his chest rather than his face.

"Maybe I'm just practical," she shrugged.

"Practicality over pain. I like that. And yeah, they're expensive but I've been working for my uncle since I was fifteen so I reckon I can afford it. Nothing else to waste my money on," he dismissed.

"So, this is your investment plan?" she joked. His eyes narrowed, feigning annoyance at her mocking him. He tugged at her duvet.

"Aren't you going to let me in? I'm freezing out here."
Before she could reply, he climbed into her bed and snuggled
up to her, kissing her.

"You're lovely and warm," he murmured. He smelt of
shower gel and sandalwood, along with the cigarette smell
she had quickly grown to like. It was a familiar, comforting
smell, which was strange as to her recollection, she had never
known a smoker before. Maybe an uncle, in the past, but
certainly nobody she could remember or associate the smell
with. She was sinking in his arms, the butterflies in her
stomach going crazy, when she suddenly felt the flat of his
hand on her waistband.

"Don't," she whispered in a shaky voice.

"I'm not doing anything," he whispered back, kissing her.
His hand moved slightly, pushing her waistband down.

"Richard," she moved away from his mouth to look at him.
He pulled his hand out from under the duvet and waved it in
the air, laughing.

"I'm not doing anything!" He started kissing her again,
sliding his hand back across her waistband.

"Richard, don't."

He propped himself up on his elbow, looking at her.

"What's wrong?"

"My dad might hear us," she breathed, hating how shaky
her voice sounded.

"Where's their bedroom?"

"At the back, downstairs." As she answered, she knew how
pathetic her excuse had sounded. Her stomach was in knots
with nerves.

"Well then," he smiled. She licked her lips and swallowed
repeatedly; her throat was painfully dry.

"It's just … I've never …" Her eyes pleaded with him to
understand. He stroked her cheek, reassuring her.

"I know. It'll be fine, trust me."

Mary looked away, on the verge of tears, She wished she had the confidence to do what he was wanting. She was scared of letting him down and scared of making a fool of herself. Summoning up the courage to give in to him, she turned back to him.

"I'm sorry, I want to but ... I'm scared," she admitted. He nodded, stroking her arm.

"Don't be scared. You're my girl now, not your dad's," he said, misunderstanding what she was scared of. She pushed him away fiercely, triggered by a rush of anger.

"I will never be my dad's girl!" she rasped. Stunned by her reaction, he sat up, his eyes narrowing.

"Oh, really? Is that why you're doing subjects you hate? Is that why you're kicking me out of your bed? Because you're *not* daddy's little girl?" he taunted, frustration coursing through him. He stood up and grabbed his top from the floor, turning his back to her as he got dressed.

"Where are you going?" she asked, regretting her outburst. He shot her a look over his shoulder as he headed for the spare room.

"Home."

"But ... don't go yet," she pleaded. He stopped and sighed heavily.

"Make your mind up, Mary." He stared at her, waiting for a response but she couldn't bring herself to look at him.

"Mary?"

She shrugged and hugged her drawn up knees, fiddling with the duvet cover. He snorted and shook his head.

"See you tomorrow." He disappeared through the door. By the time she'd got out of bed and hurried to the back window, he had vanished into the night.

Chapter Five

Mary had slept fitfully, not able to settle for a few hours after Richard had left her room. As she drank her morning tea, staring out at the street, she was dreading going in to school. She even toyed with the idea of feigning sickness to avoid school altogether but she couldn't face an interrogation from her father, so scrapped the idea.

She studied her reflection. Every time she caught sight of her hair, it still took her by surprise, making her smile with renewed wonder at the transformation. She knew there would be a few comments about it at school. It was the rest of her that she wasn't happy with. She lived in plain jeans and non-descript tops and jumpers; the navy blue, crew neck jumper she was wearing being a perfect example of this. It was shapeless and did nothing for her. Her day of shopping with Kelly had made her realise how staid her clothes were. She craved a change but as always, didn't have the courage to do so. Her mind flitted back to her day with Richard. They had clicked in a way that neither one of them could have predicted, and by the time they left the moor, she felt like they'd been together for ages. And then everything fell apart. She sighed heavily, inwardly groaning as she remembered the look on his face before he had left.

It was no surprise that he didn't acknowledge her on the bus but even so, her heart sank when there wasn't even a glimmer of recognition from him as he passed by her seat. She tried to remain focused on Kelly, with a fixed smile on her face as she listened to her. Kelly had gushed an apology for ditching her at the party, in such an animated way, knowing that Mary would accept it. She didn't once think to ask how the rest of Mary's evening had gone; she was too full of her own news, describing in detail about her night with Marcus. She pulled down the fabric of her polo-neck top, flashing a large, purple-red, speckled mark on her neck.

"My dad would kill me if he saw this!" she crowed, knowing full well that he wouldn't. She rotated her neck round for the small group of girls sitting on the bus with them to see the extent of her love-bite. They gasped and made appropriate noises, agreeing that she would 'definitely be dead' if either one of her parents had caught sight of it.

"I've got another one," she confided in a loud whisper, "but I'm not showing you lot that!" She nodded down towards her chest, cackling as they screeched with laughter. Mary was aching to glance round at Richard, knowing he could undoubtedly hear Kelly, but she didn't have the nerve to.

"I really love your hair, Mary," Tracy said, turning the attention away from Kelly. A round of murmured compliments ensued, buoying Mary's mood. It was short-lived as Kelly piped up,

"Yeah, I arranged it all and told her what to get done. And then I took her clothes shopping. Oh, and you should've seen Marcus's face when he saw my dress – did I tell you what I was wearing?" And the attention was back on Kelly, leaving Mary to feel like her little lap-dog or over-indulged pet. Not able to stop herself any longer, she turned to look at Richard. He was staring out of the window as usual, his stony face devoid of any emotion. It made her uneasy. They had two double lessons together that day and she had no idea how he would be with her. She was right to feel anxious. He made no attempt to acknowledge her throughout their science lesson, not even bothering to offer any help as they worked through experiment results with the class. Mr Platt raised his eyebrows and gave Mary a consoling smile in a bid to acknowledge the frostiness emanating from Richard. Experience had taught him not to push the issue; when Richard was in a closed off mood, he was best left well alone. He silently thanked fate that Josh Higgins was absent that day; his classroom would undoubtedly be a warzone otherwise.

Richard's mood still hadn't lifted by the end of the day; their last lesson being maths. Mary quietly slid into the seat next to him at the back of the classroom. Mr Nelson gave her a nod, eyeing Richard. Word had clearly got round the staff room. She kept her head bent, trying to focus on her work, wishing she were a hundred miles away. As the lesson was drawing to a close, she suddenly became aware that Richard was watching her. She looked up and tentatively smiled. His eyes softened, and she could see he wanted to say something. Instead he reached his hand across the desk and barely touched hers with his index finger, gently stroking her skin. The tender, brief moment was over too quickly and he turned away again to stare out of the window. Mary rummaged around in her pencil case and pulled out her post-it notes, hastily scribbling words before pushing the note towards him. Without a second glance at her, he pocketed it, gathered up his books and headed for the door as soon as the bell went.

"I'm going over to Kelly's for a couple of hours, Mam; is that okay? We have some homework to finish for tomorrow," Mary lied as she helped clear away the dinner plates. She heard the church bells chime half past the hour.

"I'll be back by eight thirty," she added by way of persuasion. Her mother nodded and smiled. Mary glanced at her father, avoiding eye contact. He frowned but made no comment.

"If you're going the back way, take a torch," Bridget prompted.

"Will do," she replied as she left the room to grab her coat and school bag. She picked up the slim torch hanging on the coat rack and stuck it in her pocket. Minutes later, she hurried up the church steps and along the path through the graveyard. The icy cold was biting and the muddy path crackled underfoot where it had started to freeze. Once through the gate at the other end and onto the familiar path that led on up to Dimples Lane, Mary turned through another gate and quietly slipped into the fenced off allotments. She flashed her torch briefly to reaffirm her direction as she slowly made her way along the sloping path towards one of the sheds. The allotment sheds were scattered haphazardly, dropping down the hillside, surrounded by an array of raised beds and chicken coops. Half barrels, rusty oil drums and cracked kitchen sinks were crammed into any free space, filled with frost covered shallots and faded blooms.

The church bells chimed again. Quarter to seven. Pulling her glove off with her teeth, she fumbled about in the dark trying to locate the hidden key under one of the empty terracotta pots stacked up by the shed door. Deftly undoing the padlock, she let herself in and breathed a sigh of relief as she leant against the wall. The shed smelt of damp earth and fox pee, mixed with an equally pungent smell of tom cat. Mary flicked the torch around the shed, familiarising herself with the lay-out. She had been there a few times before but never in the dark. It all seemed very different once the sun had gone in. Stepping over a half filled sack of compost, she perched on the edge of a rickety chair, waiting.

Her scrawled note to Richard had been concise:

'Meet me in Mr Wood's shed at seven. I'll do what you want'.

Below it she gave directions of how to find it. She was sure he knew where it was anyway. Kelly's dad was a keen gardener and spent most of his spare time on the allotment, with his faithful Genevieve by his side. Anybody walking along the footpath would have seen him, and stopped for a chat, at one time or another.

Mary shone the torch on her watch. As if reading her mind, the church bells went into action, chiming seven o'clock. There was no sign of Richard. Mary waited. Her eyes were becoming accustomed to the dark and she whiled away the time by counting the number of plastic seed trays and pots there were piled up in the corner waiting to be reused in the coming months.

The minutes ticked silently by. The pit of her stomach ached with nerves, it was in knots with anticipation at what she was about to embark on. She hadn't really thought it through and now she was beginning to regret her note. She had been so desperate to win back his favour and now that he hadn't shown up, she was left feeling foolish and insignificant once more. The bell chimed quarter past. With a heavy sigh and a small flutter of relief, she stood up and stretched her stiff, freezing body, grabbed her discarded school bag and let herself out. Her hands were numb from the cold and she was struggling to put the padlock back into place. A heavy hand rested on her shoulder making her jump and scream out. She swung round, coming face to face with Richard. Even in the darkness she could see how angry he was.

"What are you playing at?" he demanded, waiting no more than two seconds for an answer. "I thought I told you – you don't throw yourself at me, you don't beg for it. I thought I told you that?" he repeated. Mary stared at him, struck

71

dumb. He didn't scare her but she knew he was barely containing his rage. She swallowed nervously.

"I thought…" she started.

"You thought what? That this would be a great place? You want your first time to be down in the dirt, do you?" He pushed the shed door open, and peered inside, sniffing the air.

"It stinks in there. I wouldn't do it in there, so why the hell would I want you to? What do you think I am, Mary?" He swore as he pulled her out of the way and shut the door, clicking the padlock together.

"Where does the key go?" he asked, following her direction to put it back in its place. She stood motionless, waiting for his next move. He frowned, deliberating what to say. Muttering under his breath, he lit a cigarette and held the match to her face before flicking it carelessly into the mud. She didn't flinch under his brief scrutiny. It seemed to bother him.

"Just go home," he growled.

At a loss and feeling mortified at his derision, she started to make her way back towards the gate, taking care not to slip on the frozen mud. She was aware that he was following her.

"Wait up," he called as she neared the exit. She held on to the gate post and watched him catch up with her.

"I'll walk you home," he nodded, not looking directly at her. She shook her head.

"I'm alright."

"Even so, I'll walk you." His tone had changed and Mary could tell he was calming down. As they reached the church, he grabbed her hand and pulled her round to face him. She stared at her feet, not knowing what to say. He sighed deeply.

"Look, I got it wrong last night." He lifted her chin, forcing her to look at him. "I'm sorry."

"No, I'm sorry. It's just … I'm no good with things like this. I'm not like Kelly," she blurted, relieved that they were finally talking. Richard kicked at a protruding edge of flagstone path.

"I know, that's what I like about you. That's why I'm saying, I got it wrong. You were giving me all the signals all day and I forgot … I didn't think. I realised that, the minute I left you. I've been so angry all day," he admitted, surprising her yet again with his honesty and openness with her.

"Angry with me?" she wondered. He shook his head, giving her a rue smile.

"No, with myself. I thought I'd scared you off. And I was trying to get you back when you gave me that note and … I got angry again."

Mary took a step closer to him, willing him to put his arms around her. Reading her mind, he did just that. She leant against him, listening to the steady beat of his heart. He unzipped his jacket and wrapped it around her too, pulling her in even closer. A satisfied sigh escaped her lips. Neither spoke for some time, content in each other's company without the need to fill the silence.

"Can we start again?" she dared to ask. He nodded. Smiling, she looked up at him.

"Come and see me tonight."

"Maybe we should leave it for now," he started, his eyes searching hers.

"I don't want to leave it," she whispered, pleased at his surprised response. It was a look she had seen in his eye before. She liked to think he didn't bestow that look glibly.

"Come and see me. I want to spend time with you," she coaxed. "In the warm!"

He laughed, nodding.

"Sure?"

"I'm sure," she said with determination. She'd spent the whole day thinking about nothing else. She was tired of feeling left out, of being the 'virgin Mary' that she had been so cruelly dubbed. She wanted to live life and stop being scared, stop dreading the consequences. And more than anything, she wanted to be Richard's girl; not just because she fancied him but because he had chosen her over Kelly. That knowledge alone made her feel euphoric. Remembering his comment about giving signals and not wanting there to be any more misunderstandings, she took his hand and squeezed it.

"I'm sure."

"Okay," he smiled. "And will you be wearing those sexy pyjamas again?"

She groaned at his teasing.

"I was hoping you hadn't noticed them!"

"Oh, I noticed," he replied, laughing softly. Mary glanced at her watch. There was plenty of time before she was expected home but she wanted to go and get ready for Richard's visit later.

"I'll see you later," she smiled, confident that he would show up. He nodded, watching as she walked towards the church steps.

"Mary!" he called in a hushed whisper, "keep a light on, will you? I stubbed my toe three times trying to get across your room in the dark."

She nodded happily, chuckling at his expense. She suddenly felt lifted, alive again. And the cold air no longer cut through her. She felt warm, carrying the heat from Richard with her as she hurried home.

Mary stuck her head round the lounge door, letting her parents know she was back. Bridget smiled, her pen poised above the notebook on her lap.

"That was quick! Everything go well?" she wondered. Mary nodded happily.

"It wasn't as complicated after all. It's funny; when you step away from the situation and look at it differently, it all comes together."

Donal cleared his throat, his eyes glued to the television.

"Did the fresh air clear your head?"

Mary gave him a puzzled look.

"How do you mean?"

He turned his attention to her, assessing her demeanour.

"Well, you looked troubled earlier. I thought you had a headache but now you seem right as rain," he pointed out. The edge in his voice didn't go unnoticed but she refused to kowtow.

"No, not a headache; just focusing on my schoolwork and taking it seriously. Like you said I should." Her eyes met his for a brief moment, defying him to question her comment. His eyes narrowed and he inclined his head, acknowledging her attempt to one-up him.

"Make sure you do just that, Mary," he replied, turning back to the television screen, indicating an end to their conversation. But Mary wasn't quite finished.

"I will, Dad. In fact, I will be doing so much extra revision so I'll just shut myself up in my room from now on. Goodnight, Mam, Dad." She closed the door smartly behind her and grinned into the dark hallway at her own bravery. She knew it was foolish to rile her father but every now and then, it did her good to feel she had a little bit of control, however fleeting it was.

She stood in her doorway, scrutinising her room. She'd never really bothered about the décor before but right now was wishing it was more welcoming, more co-ordinated. What must Richard have thought of it, she wondered as she straightened out her heavy, patchwork bedspread. She remembered what Kelly had told her about Richard's home – or rather, his grandparents' home. They lived on the other side of Haworth, up from the railway station, in one of the rows of terraced houses that hugged the steep hillside, known as Brow. Kelly had remarked how cramped it was and how it smelt like a dirty hamster cage. Thinking about it now, Mary couldn't imagine Richard living like that; he was always clean clothed and smelt of fresh laundry and shower gel. Nothing remotely like a hamster cage smell. She couldn't decide whether Kelly was just being spiteful or whether it was true but he took care of himself despite everything. Either way, she determined that her room would have to do; there was not a great deal she could do to change it in just a couple of hours. She quickly tidied away some books and plumped up the cushions on the sofa before jumping into the shower.

Ten minutes later, smelling of watermelon body butter and wrapped in a faded, worn towel, she had something else to deliberate: what to wear. She stared at her small pile of pyjamas and taking them from the drawer, spread them across her bed. They were all uninspiring, unflattering and, on closer inspection, quite threadbare in places. She wandered in to the next room and flicked through the clothes in her wardrobe. It was the same story. She sighed with frustration and headed back to her bed, picking out the least offending pair of pyjamas. Forget-me-not blue, with a scattering of tiny daisies, they had once been of the softest brushed cotton. Now they more resembled a washed out tea towel.

The minutes ticked by as Mary read and re-read the same page, not able to absorb anything as she nervously waited for Richard to arrive. She had left her back window unlocked and slightly ajar, and turned on the small sidelight on her desk. Her bedside light was also on, casting a soft glow across the room. It was just after eleven when he finally showed up, and Mary was dozing under her duvet. She stirred at the sound of his quiet footsteps crossing the spare room floor and quickly got out of bed to greet him. She took his hand and led him over to her bed and sat down on the edge, encouraging him to do the same. He was dressed in similar black joggers and top as the previous night.

"Aren't you freezing in that top?"

He shrugged.

"I've got a jacket but I took it off with my shoes before I climbed onto the flat roof. It's alright," he continued, seeing the look of alarm on her face, "I hid them under the hedge there."

He eyed her pyjamas, trying not to smile.

"Where's my favourite rose pyjamas? You promised me!" he teased. She gave a derisive laugh, trying not to blush as he looked more pointedly at what she was wearing.

"So I'm guessing that you like flowers," he commented. She sighed heavily.

"My mam buys my clothes. I think I need to get new things and choose them myself. These are embarrassing!" She fiddled with the neck line of her pyjama top.

"Don't do that for me," he said quickly.

"Why not?" She would have bought the whole lingerie department in a heartbeat just for him.

"Because I see beyond all that." He held her gaze, willing her to believe him. She looked surprised.

"Really?"

Richard grinned.

"Yeah. Although you did look great the other night when you went to that party."

"You see! I knew you were just trying to flannel me!" She hit his arm as he laughed at her indignant face.

"So who buys your clothes?" she asked.

"I do."

"And who does your washing?"

"I do, at my uncle's. I go there every Wednesday after school, and at the weekends. He's great." His voice tailed off, and a wistful look crossed his face. Mary had seen his uncle before; he seemed nice enough, a bit quiet but always polite. He lived on the road leading off the top of Main Street towards the local cricket club.

"Is he your dad's brother or mum's?" she continued to push with her questions.

"My mum's."

"So … why didn't you and your mum move in with him when … when your dad left?"

Richard looked away, frowning. He suddenly realised that she knew more about him than he'd told her. It was obvious she'd been talking to others about him and he wasn't sure he liked the idea of that.

"It's complicated, alright. He wanted to help. He wants me to live with him, but …"

"You don't have to tell me, I'm sorry I asked," Mary said hastily, putting a hand on his leg. She could see his mood was changing but to her surprise, he continued his sentence.

"My mum needs looking after. She and my uncle Gary had a big row years ago, about their dad. She never stands up to her dad." He stopped abruptly, looking furtive, and Mary could see in that instant that he was comparing *her* to his mother. She swallowed a lump in her throat.

"Sometimes it's impossible to do that. Nobody really understands what goes on," she mumbled. He stared at her, his mind racing.

"What does that mean?"

Realising she had said too much and seeing the rash conclusions he was already drawing, she tried to change the conversation.

"Nothing. I'm sorry I asked." She straightened up and forced herself to smile. "I just want to know you."

Taking her lead, he quickly dropped the conversation, flashing her a devilish grin.

"You want to 'know me'? Okay Mary, but give me a chance, I've only just got here and you're dragging me into bed already!" He laughed as she elbowed him, then elbowed her back and pushed her down against the pillows.

"Enough questions, alright? We've got plenty of time for that later. First," he hesitated, his grin disappearing. "About last night."

Mary shook her head, trying to stop his words.

"It didn't happen," she insisted.

"But it did, Mary. I was wrong to rush you." His steady gaze watched her reaction. "Are you sure you want this now?"

She nodded, the colour rising up her neck. He was staring at her in such a way that made her back tingle.

"Yes," she reiterated. He nodded slowly.

"Because if we do this, there's no going back, okay. You can't kick me out of your bed again, that wouldn't be fair. Say 'no' now, not later." He waited for her to respond. A thought crossed her mind and she cleared her throat, feeling awkward.

"Have you … got anything?"

He gave a short laugh.

"I forgot you're Miss Practical. Yes, I have. Don't worry, I'll take care of it," he said patting his pocket. He thought he saw uncertainty flicker across her face.

"Look, we can wait if you want," he started. Mary pulled him towards her with a shy smile.

"Can we just do it, Richard. You're making me nervous!"

"Sex is just a lot of awkward poking and shoving, and fumbling about, and then it's all over really quickly but it makes you feel good sometimes, y'know," Kelly had reliably informed Mary during one of her many animated conversations. As Mary lay in her bed next to Richard she had to disagree with everything she'd been told. For her, time had stood still, there was nothing awkward about it and the intense feeling that engulfed her was like nothing she had ever experienced or even imagined she could feel. Waves of contentment washed over her and she had an urge to cry with happiness. She had the biggest grin on her face, so much so it made her cheeks ache. How could Kelly not have felt any of those things, she wondered. She rolled over when Richard sat up and swung his legs out of bed.

"Where are you going?" she asked, touching his arm. He turned to smile at her.

"I just need a smoke." He reached for his joggers, feeling in the pocket for his cigarettes.

"Richard?"

"Yeah?" He stared at her, his eyes widening before his face creased into a grin.

"I know, I can't smoke in here," he said it for her, "I'll be back in a minute." He quickly pulled his joggers and top on and headed for the window in the spare room. Mary propped herself up, watching him leave. She frowned. She had seen a look in his eye that she couldn't fathom. He almost looked scared. And he was trying to hide it behind that smile. Was it fear of being caught by her dad? Or worried that she could fall pregnant? Neither of those seemed to fit; they had been conscious of not making any noise and he'd taken care of things, as he said he would.

Richard returned, breaking her train of thought. He leant over the bed and kissed her.

"Get some sleep. I'll see you in the morning," he whispered. She clung to his arm, disappointed.

"Are you leaving already?"

He nodded.

"I need to get home. I can't exactly sleep here, can I?" He smiled and kissed her again, telling her to stay where she was in the warm as he headed once again into the other room. Mary could barely hear him leave, he was that agile and adept at creeping about. She got up just to check he had in fact left. She peered through the window into the darkness but once again, he'd disappeared from sight. Feeling dejected she crawled back into bed and cocooned herself against the cold. She was asleep within minutes before she'd had a chance to deliberate any further.

Chapter Six

It was the usual story on the bus the next morning; Kelly talking far too loudly, showing off to her clutch of hangers-on, and Richard blanking Mary as he boarded the bus. She closed her eyes for a brief moment, willing herself not to be bothered by it yet again but she was feeling vulnerable that morning and could have done with just a hint of recognition from him. The bus trundled along the winding road, the chassis rattling with every pot hole and bump, and Kelly's brash voice droned on and on. Mary had the urge to stand up and scream until everything fell silent but instead she swallowed her mounting frustration and turned to look at Richard. To her immense surprise, he was staring straight at her, his customary stony face not giving anything away. They held eye contact for several seconds before he gave her a very subtle wink and turned away as a smile started to spread across his face. He cleared his throat and rubbed his nose with his hand as if trying to rub the smile away. Mary's heart skipped a beat and she let out a little laugh, looking down at her feet to hide her happiness from her friends. She could feel he was watching her again but she didn't trust herself to look at him; instead she focused on Kelly's monologue and joined in with the sycophantic laughter, pretending her broad smile was for Kelly's benefit.

Richard crept into her room every night for the rest of the week. By day, they would talk in lesson but other than that he wouldn't acknowledge her in school; by night she had his undivided attention. As the church bells chimed midnight signalling the end of Friday, they lay in each other's arms, listening to the wind whistling and rattling at her windows. She traced the outline of his chin with her finger, her skin rasping on his light stubble. He gave her a lazy smile, not wanting to move.

"How come you never smile at school?" she asked. He shrugged dismissively.

"I've got nothing to smile about."

She thought about it for a moment.

"You smile when you're alone with me."

He propped himself up on his elbow to look at her, smiling.

"That's when I've got everything to smile about."

She grinned. He still surprised her with his contrasting emotions.

"Am I any good?"

He looked puzzled.

"Any good?"

A sheepish look crossed her face.

"You know, at this," she waved a finger between the two of them. "Am I … okay … at it?"

Richard laughed, shaking his head.

"Are you fishing for compliments, Mary?"

"Maybe," she smiled coyly. He laughed again, pulling her towards him.

"Yes, you're okay."

Not satisfied, she pushed further, her voice a notch higher, teasing.

"Just okay or … more than okay or …"

Playing along, he spoke into her hair.

"More than okay."

"How much more?" she tried not to giggle. He moved away from her, studying her face, his smile fading. He stared at her for what seemed like an eternity.

"You're perfect." His guard completely down, he looked vulnerable. Younger. How she imagined he looked before he took on all the troubles of his complicated world. She should have let it go there but not able to stop herself, she posed a tentative question.

"So, if I'm perfect, why do you look scared?"

"I'm not scared."

She felt him tensing up yet she persisted.

"But you look it."

He frowned, shaking his head a little.

"When?"

"When we've … y'know … when we've finished, you always look scared. Why?"

"I'm not scared," he insisted, lying back against the pillows. She realised she had said the wrong thing but it irked her that he wouldn't admit to it. They fell silent for a while; he, not wanting to pursue the subject, she, not able to let it go.

"I thought we were going to be honest with each other about things," she said quietly, reproaching him.

"We are," he said, staring at the ceiling.

"So?"

"Just drop it, Mary," he warned. She turned away, not impressed with his response. He sighed heavily and rolled her back to face him. She waited as he deliberated his words. She could feel his turmoil, sensing he was struggling with something. He sighed again.

"I've fallen for you. That's never happened to me before."

Her eyes widened as she took in what he was saying.

"You have?"

He nodded, a shy smile meeting her ecstatic grin.

"That not scary!" she squealed wrapping her arms around his neck, "that's great!"

He laughed lightly, feeling self-conscious and overwhelmed by her spontaneous reaction. He hadn't enjoyed being forced to show his hand yet at the same time, felt relieved to have opened up to her. He held her for a while longer before sitting up on the edge of the bed.

"Are you going for a smoke?" she asked softly.

"In a minute." He glanced round the room, and picked up the book on her bedside chest of drawers. It was her latest second-hand bookshop find; a blue, cloth bound, worn copy of *North and South,* by Elizabeth Gaskell.

"You read a lot," he commented, taking in the small stack of books on the other side of her bedside lamp, overflowing from the bookcases.

"It's my escape," she admitted simply. He nodded, understanding what she meant.

"What's your escape?" she asked. He shrugged, not giving it much thought.

"Smoking."

"Weed, you mean?"

He nodded, staring at his feet.

"Isn't that bad for you?" she pressed. He shrugged again.

"Can I try it?"

He turned to look at her. She was serious.

"No."

"Why not? You do it."

She sat up next to him, leaning her head on his shoulder. Instinctively, he put his hand on her bare thigh.

"I don't care about me," he said. She put her hand on top of his, weaving her fingers through. She was still reeling from his earlier admission, not quite able to believe somebody like him could fall for somebody like her. On the surface, they seemed such polar opposites but she was quickly discovering that underneath, they were very much akin.

He spied her small, portable record player, a tan-coloured throw-back from the 60's, next to the television on the pine unit.

"Do you have many records for that thing?"

"A few," she nodded. "Some good ones too. What do you like?"

"What have you got?" He strained his neck, trying to recognise any of the titles neatly piled together, wedged between the television and record player.

"Sugar Minott's my favourite," she said, pulling her pyjamas back on and crossing the room. Hurriedly following suit, he crouched by the records, studying them.

"Who's Sugar Minott?"

"*How* have you never heard of Sugar Minott?" she exclaimed. "He's a really famous reggae singer, from Jamaica." She swiftly tipped the record from its case, put it onto the deck and carefully placed the needle on the spinning vinyl disc. Turning the volume right down, she beckoned for him to move closer to hear it through the speakers on either side of the case. He smiled, listening to the lyrics and watching Mary mouth them. When he heard the refrain, 'We've got a good thing going, a real good thing going, that girl and me," recognition dawned and he nodded. Mary turned it off.

"Sorry," she whispered, "I wish I could play you the whole thing but," she pointed to the floor, "they might just hear it."

"Good choice, I like it," he nodded his approval. He stood up, pulling her to her feet.

"I can't see you tomorrow night." He sounded sorry.

"That's okay. Why not?"

"Saturdays I usually spend with my uncle. We work all day and then sometimes go out in the evening."

Mary thought for a moment, frowning.

"But I saw you up on the moors the other Saturday. Did you have the day off then?"

He nodded

"Kind of. He went to a car auction in Huddersfield. I didn't fancy it. But tomorrow we've got a lot of work on."

"What are you doing tomorrow evening then?"

He gave an embarrassed laugh, scratching his head.

"My uncle is a Karaoke king! Simply put," he inclined his head. Mary's mouth dropped open in exaggerated shock.

"What? Oh my goodness, I would never have guessed that!" she laughed, then covered her mouth as she realised how loud she was being.

"Where do you go?" She couldn't imagine it was anywhere local; Richard wouldn't be seen dead in a karaoke pub nearby, she felt sure.

"Halifax. His mates all go there. I'm the designated driver." He did a mock bow.

"Because you don't drink?" she rightly guessed. He nodded.

"It's alright; I get a free meal out of it, usually an Indian, and then his mates club together and give me twenty quid for the lifts home."

"Twenty quid! If you ran a taxi service you could make a fortune!" She was aware her voice was rising but she was suddenly seeing yet another side to him.

"That's the plan," he said with a definite nod. Mary caught her breath.

"Seriously? You've never said."

"You've never asked."

It was most likely unintentional but his abrupt reply racked her with guilt. It was true, she realised, that she very rarely asked any questions; not since their first day together. She knew that he worked for his uncle, Gary Swales, a car mechanic that ran his business from home. She also knew that Gary would buy vintage cars to renovate and sell on to collectors. She had just assumed that if Richard wanted to tell her things, he would. Now she realised, that may not be the case. He may be waiting for her to show an interest. She indicated for them to sit on the sofa, took his hand and gave him her full attention.

"So tell me; what's your plan?"

He took a moment, deliberating how to put into words something he had so far kept to himself.

"I'm saving to buy a couple of cars, a Bentley and a Rolls - ideally a Silver Shadow or a Phantom three - then set up a chauffeur business, y'know, weddings, functions, that kind of thing. Eventually I'd love to have a small fleet, with a few vintage cars and a couple of Limos on top of the others." He watched her eyes widen in awe as she took it all in; could see her visualising it in her head.

"That's my plan."

She smiled widely, nodding encouragement, caught off-guard by his drive and passion.

"That sounds incredible! Where would you base it? Here?"

He shook his head.

"No, I'm thinking more of York."

"I'm going to York!"

He looked at her steadily.

"So you are," he nodded slowly, his stillness indicating he had already thought of that. In fact, she was the reason he had decided on York. Mary smiled as she read his thoughts, trying to ignore the butterflies that were playing havoc with her stomach.

"How about Sunday? A walk in the morning?" he suggested, watching her face drop.

"Oh, I can't! I've already promised a dog walk with Kelly. Sorry. Sunday night?" she asked hopefully. He nodded.

"I think I can last til then."

She chuckled. She knew he was joking but a glimmer of jealously in his eye when she mentioned spending time with

Kelly hadn't gone unnoticed. She opted to ignore it, wanting him leave on a good note.

"Well then, you go and enjoy your lads night out. Don't work too hard! And I'll spend the evening with John Thornton."

"Who?"

She snatched her book up from the side.

"He's one of the main characters in my book!"

He looked at it again, more closely this time.

"Oh, Elizabeth Gaskell," he nodded, recognising the name. She was surprised.

"You know her?"

"Listen, when you grow up in Haworth, you learn everything about the Brontës from the word go. We did a big project in primary school and I remember that Elizabeth Gaskell was Charlotte Brontë's best friend – right?"

Mary nodded, delighted that he was sharing a part of her world, however minor the detail. She followed him into the next room, hanging on to his hand. She hated this part; him leaving in the dead of night. But at the same time, it gave her a thrill, watching her lover stealthily sneak out through her window.

"Enjoy your book … and keep playing our song," he whispered, giving her a brief kiss before dropping noiselessly down onto the roof below. She carefully pulled the window to, watching for a last glimpse of him but as always, to no avail. She shivered, clutching her hands to her chest and hurried back to bed.

"Our song." She grinned as she repeated his parting words, her mind still spinning from all that had taken place that night. Life was just getting better and better.

"Did you ask your parents?" Kelly demanded as Mary approached the bus stop the following Monday morning. Waiting until she drew level with her before replying, Mary shook her head. Kelly tutted with exasperation.

"Why not?"

"It's okay, I kind of mentioned it to my mam and she's fine but I am not telling my dad," she insisted.

"Mary! When are you going to listen to me; your dad is fine, he'd do anything for you, I bet. I really wanted them to come. My parents are," she coaxed, eyeing Mary, hoping her disappointment would sway her. Mary shook her head again.

"Look, I can go halves but please, do not expect me to invite my parents! Where would the fun be in that? My dad would watch me like a hawk, Kelly. Like a hawk," she emphasised, widening her eyes dramatically to make Kelly laugh. It worked and Kelly dropped the badgering, flashing a smile at the young driver as they boarded the school bus.

The two girls had spent the previous day discussing plans for their upcoming birthdays; Mary's being three days before Kelly's. Originally, Kelly had planned a house party but her father had managed to hire the Social Club for February 12th - Saturday - the day after Kelly's birthday. He got a good deal by calling in a favour, and one of Kevin's friends had offered to do the disco for the price of a pint or two. So Kelly had suggested to Mary that they make it a joint 18th party.

"Let's make it really classy!" she had said, reeling off a list of paraphernalia needed to make it exactly that. Buzzing with excitement, they had just under three weeks to plan everything.

"You wear that outfit you wore for Adam's party. Nobody from school saw you and you looked amazing," Kelly gushed. "But I'll need something new to impress Marcus. It needs to be something really 'wow', y'know? Something that'll make his eyes pop!"

Kelly carried on talking about the party for the duration of the journey to school, feeding titbits of information to their friends, telling them that formal invites would be handed out later in the week.

"I love a good party, me," she announced, pulling out her pocket mirror to re-apply her lip-gloss and admire her reflection.

"What was all that about a party?" Richard wondered as he sat down next to Mary for their first lesson, confirming that he had been listening to Kelly on the bus. She told him briefly of Kelly's plans.

"She's invited most of the village so I only added one more name to the list. Yours." She shot him a look but couldn't gauge his reaction. He stared at the board, watching Mr Platt write on it.

"Why didn't you tell me last night?"

Mary floundered, not sure what to say.

"I don't know, I forgot really. You were distracting me," she ventured. He sighed, seeing right through her. He turned to look at her, his tone insistent.

"Mary, why didn't you tell me?"

She hung her head, blushing.

"Because I knew you wouldn't like it. You don't like anything to do with Kelly."

He took his time responding, mulling it over in his mind.

"But you're going?"

"Well yes; it's my birthday party too." She wasn't expecting to have this conversation at school; if they had been at home she could have been more tactile as she spoke. Keeping this pretence up at school was hard enough as it was.

"I'd rather be somewhere else just with you though," she added quietly, her eyes pleading with him. "But it's all been arranged and I can't change it. It's my 18th," she reasoned.

"Okay."

"Okay … you'll come?"

"Okay, I'll come," he nodded.

She tried to hide her grin, glancing at his set expression.

"I wish I could make you smile in class."

"Oh, trust me, Mary, you do but I keep it inside." He leant towards her, lowering his voice to a barely audible whisper.

"I just don't want to let on to these tossers that I *am* human after all." His eyes creased at the corners with the merest hint of humour at his self-mockery.

The week flew by and they grew closer with each passing day, and night. He had even started to acknowledge her in the mornings when he got on the bus. Just a brief nod and a mumbled, 'Alright', but it meant the world to her. Her friends noticed and Kelly was quick to comment.

"See, Mary. I told you; invite him to the party and he'll think you're his friend." She had been extremely put out when Mary had insisted on inviting him, as a 'thank you' for his help in lessons, and didn't miss any opportunity to voice her disapproval.

"Like we'd want to be friends with *him*," she sneered. Mary wanted to respond and jump to his defence but common sense stopped her. Instead she just grimaced and shrugged it off, mumbling,

"It's okay, I can live with that!"

Richard got off at her stop and lit up a cigarette while she said goodbye to Kelly, then started to walk up Main Street with her. She grinned at him.

"Why are you walking this way? It's Friday."

He smiled, acknowledging the break in his routine.

"Yeah, I know. I just fancied walking you home, that's all."

She stared at him, surprised.

"Really? I thought maybe you were going to your uncle's again."

He shook his head.

"So tell me, what's on your mind?"

"How do you mean?" she asked, confused. He stopped walking to look at her.

"You've been trying to say something to me all afternoon in maths. What is it?"

An awkward laugh escaped her lips and she looked up and down the street, avoiding his face.

"I was wondering … do you still want to come round tonight, erm … it's just … I'm on." She stumbled over her words wanting to get them out in a hurry. He tried not to smile.

"Yes, of course I do. I want to see you. Besides, you keep me warm in this weather. I like holding you and listening to you talk. For hours," he laughed.

"Really? You still want to, even though …"

"Even though. It's not just about the sex, Mary; I thought you'd know that by now." He started walking again, at a slower pace. She laughed lightly.

"By now! You make it sound like we've been together for ages."

"We have. At least, it feels like we have. Doesn't it?"

"Two weeks tomorrow," she told him. He stopped again, his eyes searching hers intently.

"Is that all?" He seemed transfixed by her, his face softening. The face she had so quickly, and so completely, fallen in love with.

"I know what you're thinking," she said softly. He raised his eyebrows.

"Yeah? Go on then," he challenged. She knew he was teasing her.

"You're wishing we were a million miles away, where we don't have to hide. Where you can hold my hand in public and nobody would bat an eyelid."

He blinked in surprise at how accurately she had read him, not even attempting to mask his feelings from her.

"I'm going to do it, y'know. I'm going to leave this place and make a success of my life."

Mary had no doubt that he would, her smile encouraging him further.

"I'm leaving for York when you do," he nodded.

"But I need to pass my exams to get a place. It's only a conditional offer from the uni. What if I fail them? I'll slow you down." She voiced the thought that had been nagging at her all week since he had confided his plans in her.

"You *will* pass. I know you will. Just keep doing what I'm showing you and you'll pass. I believe in you, Mary." They had reached the top of the hill and stopped just before the café.

"I believe in you too," she replied, hugging his words in her head. She could tell he wanted to say more, wanted to linger, but instead he just gave her his customary nod of his head and carried on walking, not before murmuring,

"See you tonight."

He arrived shortly after eleven, producing a bar of chocolate from under his black jumper. Mary accepted it, chuckling quietly.

"You're my very own Milk Tray man! Although, was he ever bare-foot?"

Richard inclined his head, pleased with her response.

94

"Yeah, except it's Galaxy, not Milk Tray. Sorry."

Mary hugged the chocolate to her chest, shaking her head.

"I don't care! It's chocolate! You are literally a life-saver." She broke a piece off and offered it to him, tucking her foot under as she sat back down on her bed. He sat next to her, watching her face radiate childlike joy as she stuck a square of chocolate into her mouth and let it melt on her tongue.

"Remember my cousin I told you about, same age as me?" he asked.

"Lizzie? The one that lives in Oxenhope now?" she mumbled, the chocolate sticking to the roof of her mouth.

Richard nodded.

"Yeah, her. Well, she's always a right moody mare when she's on and I remember my aunt used to say, oh just give her chocolate so we can all have a bit of sanity back!"

Mary laughed, nearly choking on her mouthful.

"Are you saying I'm a moody mare?"

"No, not at all. I'm just saying, I'm not going to take any chances," he laughed, ducking from her poorly aimed, half-hearted punch. She snuggled in to him, swinging her legs across his lap. He put a protective arm around her, pulling her close.

"She taught you well, your aunt. Always bring chocolate," she smiled.

"I'd bring you the moon and stars if I could," he uttered. Something in his tone of voice made her chest flutter, making it hard to breathe. Reaching behind him, he pulled the heavy, patchwork bedspread towards them. He caught her eye, seeing how she had reacted to his words. In truth, he hadn't meant to say it out loud but she had such an effect on him that he couldn't stop himself. She was drawing him out, opening him up, stealing her way into his heart and making herself at home there. He had always vowed never to let

95

anybody in but she had taken him completely by surprise and he had to admit, it felt good.

"I'd even give you the world but if chocolate is all it takes to make you happy, then chocolate it is." He wrapped the bedspread around them both and tucked it in to keep her back warm. Satisfied that she was comfortable, he took in a decisive breath and fixed his eyes on her.

"Now, talk me through this week's revision sheet for science and tell me what you didn't understand."

The church bell chimed half past midnight, stirring them from their cosy state. Mary cocked her head towards the window, her instinct telling her something was different. The wind had dropped; her window was no longer rattling. She detached herself from their tangle of arms and legs, and quietly padded over to peer out through the curtains. She let out a hushed gasp of wonder.

"Richard, it's snowing," she whispered, beckoning him to join her. The heavy snowflakes were silently falling at a speedy rate, quickly blanketing everything in their path and bathing the street in a luminescent glow. It looked like a Christmas card scene or a classic jigsaw puzzle that could be found in most charity shops. Mary sighed with delight, sinking her weight into Richards arms that were wrapped around her. He peered through the window up at the sky, resting his chin on her head and letting out a resigned sigh.

"It's not letting up; I need to go before it gets too heavy."

Mary twisted round in his arms and leant her head against his chest.

"Why don't you stay here. I'll wake us up early in the morning," she tentatively suggested.

"Are you mad? We could be completely snowed in by morning or, if it settles by then your dad would have no trouble spotting my footprints in the snow. They'd lead him right to my door!"

Mumbling apologies, she stuck her hands inside his sweatshirt and stroked his back, pressing her hands against his warm skin, not wanting to let him go. He kissed the top of her head.

"Soon," he whispered. "This time next year when it snows, we'll be tucked up in our bed in York, not caring about the weather outside. Just caring about keeping each other warm."

He reluctantly pulled away from her and headed for the spare room window, swearing softly as he braced himself against the icy gust of snow that blew about his face. Mary watched his swift descent. He retrieved his coat and shoes from the heavily laden bush, and shook the snow from them before hurrying down the path, head bent against the swirling flurry of white.

Mary quietly closed the window but lingered for a while, hypnotised by the falling snow. She loved winter. She loved the cold, biting air and the smell of log fires and coal smoke that pervaded the street. She loved curling up in her warm bed and hearing the wind at her window, rattling to get in. And since she had fallen in love with Richard, she loved everything about the season even more keenly. Cold noses and numb fingers would always remind her of their first kiss. Feet so frozen that it hurt to walk would always remind her of their windswept trek across the moors. And now, midnight snow storms would always remind her of his promise for next year; of his determination to make a life together. The thought of that prompted her to break the hypnotic trance and return to her bed, pulling her school bag onto her lap. She sorted through her revision cards and laid out ordered piles on her bedside chest, ready for the morning. She was

97

filled with a renewed drive to succeed. Richard believed in her; it was high time she believed in herself.

Chapter Seven

The snow was still thick on the ground in places by the following Sunday and the heavy sky offered an indication of more snow to follow. Mary pulled her cable-knit hat further down about her ears and buried her chin deep in the collar of her padded jacket as she tramped along the crunchy footpath to Dimples Lane. Richard was already there, waiting. Like Mary, he too was dressed to ward off the elements but pulled off his gloves to cradle her face as he kissed her.

"How far shall we walk?" he wondered. "Brontë Bridge?"

"How about Top Withens? I'd love to go there with you. We could be Heathcliff and Cathy for the day!" She grinned at the prospect, not at all abashed by her romantic fantasy. Richard eyed the clouds.

"It's a bit far. It's going to rain."

Mary looked up, shaking her head.

"No, I think that's snow on the horizon but we can get there and back before it starts, don't you think? Please," she begged. He gave a resigned shrug, putting his gloves back on before taking her hand.

"Okay but I warn you, it's going to rain!"

Mary laughed, squeezing his hand.

"I don't care! It doesn't matter if we get a bit wet, does it?" She eyed the dark water of Lower Laithe Resevoir in the distance as they walked briskly along the footpath, occasionally slipping on the patches of snow that had turned to ice. It was a far cry from the glinting blue jewel bathed in sunlight that they had spied two weeks previously on their first walk together. But she marched on undeterred.

By the time they had passed Brontë Bridge, climbed the steep incline and were on the relatively flat path on high ground to Top Withens, the sky had turned black and the temperature plummeted. The wind battered their faces and whipped about their legs, and then the heavens opened. Not a slow drizzle or a build-up; it was as if somebody had tipped a never-ending bucket of icy water over their heads. Drenched within seconds, they debated turning back but decided they were so close now, they could shelter somewhat in the old ruins until it passed. The black silhouette of the isolated pair of trees at the head of the ruins grew tantalisingly closer with every sodden step. The snow quickly turned to muddy slush and rivers of red sediment ran down the well-worn grooved path, as it did with each frequent downpour. Mary bent her head against the driving rain and held on to Richard's coat as she walked in his footsteps. He had insisted on walking ahead of her to shied her from the worst of the weather. Her earlier enthusiasm had quickly turned to exhaustion and she stumbled and slipped on the uneven path.

"Watch out!"

Mary could barely hear Richard's warning above the howling wind but followed his lead and abruptly swerved from the path onto the uneven boggy tufts of grass. As they passed the obstacle in their path, Mary paused to look, wiping the water from her eyes. It looked like a soft toy that had been put through the wash and lain out to dry but on closer inspection, she could see it was a rabbit. It had been shot, in mid leap it would seem judging by the way it lay on the path, stretched out. It had been pounded by the rain and wind, and its fur was transparent over its pale skeleton, its eyes wide open staring at Mary. Richard pulled her away.

"Is it dead?" She was sure it was but those eyes seemed to fix on hers.

"Of course it's dead!" he shouted back, striding on. He could see an end in sight as the low, bulky outline of the building loomed ahead. As if by magic, as they reached Top Withens, the rain stopped as abruptly as it had started and the wind dropped to a low whistle. A tantalising ray of light broke through the black clouds and a pack of grouse took flight from their scratchy gorse shelter. Weak sunlight continued to push the clouds, dispersing them across the grey-streaked horizon.

They sat on the wet stone walls, catching their breath and watching the clouds scuttle across the sky. Richard pulled his soaked gloves off with his teeth and wrung them out. He shot Mary a look.

"So, next time will you listen to me?" He was teasing but that was of little comfort to her as she followed suit, wringing out her gloves and hat before begrudgingly putting them back on again. Her teeth were chattering and her whole body shaking with cold.

"Well at least we've had the full Heathcliff and Cathy experience!" she feebly joked back. Richard grunted, putting his arms around her in a bid to warm her up.

"I'm getting straight in a hot shower when I get back," she said with feeling.

"Fine, if you want to pass out!" he retorted. "You need to warm yourself up first. Everybody knows that, surely?"

Feeling foolish, she changed the subject.

"What happened to that rabbit? Why was it shot and then just left?"

Richard shrugged.

"Poacher may have missed one. Target practice. I don't know," he dismissed it, checking his watch and mentally calculating how long it would take to get back to Haworth.

The clouds were on the move again, rolling towards them, growing darker by the minute.

"Target practice? Is that a thing?" she persisted. Richard sighed, wiping his nose on the back of his wet glove.

"Does it matter?"

"It matters to me. I hate animals being hurt, especially for 'fun'". A thought crossed her mind. "You don't shoot, do you?"

He laughed abruptly.

"No! Why would I?" He was about to change the subject when he caught a look in her eye. Sighing again, he asked,

"What's Kelly said about me now?"

She faltered, shaking her head.

"Nothing much … just …"

"Just?"

"She said, when your granddad's dog had puppies, you drowned them in a bucket. Then you bragged about it at school." She didn't quite meet his eyes, hating herself for even voicing her thoughts. He swore and jumped down from the wall. Mary eased herself down, not sure what to say next.

"Sorry, I shouldn't have …"

"Is that what you think? What she said?"

Mary vigorously shook her head.

"Then why say it?"

She shrugged, not sure how to respond. She was wet and tired and not thinking straight. Richard glared angrily into the distance.

"She's always going to be here, isn't she! I can never be shot of her. Some 'mate' she turned out to be!" He paced about, kicking at the wet heather, then leant against the solid wall beneath the commemorative plaque, refusing to look at Mary. She closed her eyes. This was not how she had envisaged their romantic walk; none of it had gone according

102

to plan and she wasn't sure how to proceed from that point. She had two options; argue it out now or walk back to Haworth in silence and let it fester. The answer was obvious.

"What *did* happen between you and Kelly?" She moved over to him and took his hand. He snatched it away.

"Nothing. I don't want to talk about it."

She stood her ground calmly.

"Fine. But if I have to keep guessing because you won't talk about it, you can't really blame me if I get it wrong. I don't want to draw the wrong conclusions but I only hear one side of it and even though she's my friend, I know for a fact that she's not always truthful. So, help me out here, Richard. Please." She watched him for a moment, his set jaw twitching and his frown deepening. With a heavy sigh, she turned away and went back to the low wall they had been sitting on. She didn't have to wait long for him to join her.

"Kelly's problem is she's still mad at me because I turned her down. It bruised her ego." He could tell by her lack of reaction that she'd heard the story before.

"She was my mate, y'know. My best friend from primary school; we were always there for each other. And then one day, she threw herself at me, full on, and expected me to jump into bed with her. But I couldn't do that. You don't sleep with your friends – that's not right. Besides, I never fancied her."

"*We're* friends," she smiled brightly, "You sleep with me."

"We were never friends before, Mary. I made sure of that."

She stared at him as it dawned on her.

"You planned it? Is that why you never spoke to me out of class, why you ignored me? Because you wanted to …"

He shrugged, smiling; his smile telling her she'd caught him out. She laughed.

"I'm your friend now though, right?" she prompted. He took her hand.

"You're my everything."

She saw that look again, that vulnerability in his eyes. She knew him to be true, she knew he wouldn't lie to her about his feelings. Her heart soared knowing that he trusted her enough to be so honest. She remembered his words two weeks previously, 'I don't trust anybody. It's easier that way'. How things had changed in such a short space of time.

Her mind flitted and before she had time to consider her words, she carried on questioning.

"And what about Josh?"

He tensed up.

"What about him?"

"Why do you two hate each other so much?" She half expected him to walk off again but he didn't. He thought about it for a moment.

"He used to rub my nose in it that his mum had come back but my dad was gone. For good."

"That's so mean!" she exclaimed, although knowing Josh, she could imagine exactly how he would have taken pleasure in saying just that.

"Yeah well, his mum's a right slag. She only came back because she had nowhere else to go after my dad died. If Josh is happy with that, good luck to him." He looked at Mary. "Can we drop this now. This is our day and I don't want to think about them, any of them." He jumped down from the wall, offering his arms out for her.

"And just so you know, I don't shoot rabbits or drown puppies, or go lamping or any of that stuff. Don't believe any of it, Mary. I told you, there's too many people that'd want to ruin it for us."

"I won't let them," she replied forcefully. "I know you."

"Yeah, you do." He squeezed her hand. "Shame you didn't trust me earlier about the weather though, and if you look now, they are definite rain clouds," he said pointing to the heavy clouds speeding towards them. "And we are definitely going to get soaked again. Come on!"

As predicted, they were on the receiving end of another downpour during their brisk walk back to Haworth; the gale-force wind helped speed them along but also cut through their icy bodies, sticking wet denim to their legs. Mary had barely warmed up by the time the church bells woke her for school the next morning and it was a subdued, lethargic pair that sniffed their way through lessons.

"Bless you!" Mr Nelson looked up as they sneezed in unison. He did a double-take. There was something - a look - that passed between them but when he glanced up again moments later, they were working quietly together with their usual, slight reserve, their body language giving nothing away. He had been incredibly pleased, and surprised, with Mary's progress and had said as much to Richard the previous week when he called him aside for a chat. He had sensed a change in Richard too and put it down to him being given a responsibility, a challenge, and forming a new, unlikely friendship. Yes, he thought, that had been a good move on his part; pairing the two of them up was having a positive effect on the both of them.

Saturday dawned bright with no hint of cloud in the fresh, blue sky. Mary reluctantly got herself ready for work. Ordinarily she would have been rushing to get over to the parsonage but all she kept thinking was how Richard had a day off and it was perfect weather for an escape up onto the moors. She would have to contend with daydreaming about it instead.

It didn't take long for her to perk up; as she took the church steps two at a time and hurried along by the old school rooms where Charlotte Brontë used to teach the local children, her colleague Maureen spotted her and slowed down so they could walk in to work together. In her late forties, Maureen had been the one to show Mary round when she started her weekend job at the museum, and had taken her under her wing, encouraging her and showing her by example how to talk to the numerous visitors. Mary had learnt a great deal from Maureen; not just about the Brontë sisters and the Parsonage but about life in general. She quickly realised that she talked with Maureen in her first two months there more than she had talked with her own mother in her entire life.

The Parsonage, a solid, detached brick house, had endured thousands of visitors over the years since it opened as a museum in 1928. The Brontë family moved from the nearby village of Thornton to the Haworth parsonage in 1820, forty-two years after it was built. Maria Brontë and her two eldest children had died within five years of arriving but Patrick and his four remaining children lived out their lives there. After Patrick Brontë died in 1861, the contents of their home were auctioned to make way for his successor, and then in the preceding years many items were bought back again by The Brontë Society. Once they had acquired the Parsonage, they set about restoring it to how it was during the Brontë family's occupation. The surrounding graveyard however, had irrevocably changed. Once a barren, windswept hillside cemetery, it was later extensively planted with trees among the tightly packed graves to improve drainage, changing the landscape from the one the sisters would have known.

Mary knew these facts off by heart; they were something she had memorised and developed into her routine patter for visitors. Most that came to the Parsonage were avid lovers of the books but not all knew of the history behind the sisters home, or indeed, the village, and arming herself with those facts fuelled her confidence and stopped her from stuttering when she spoke as she initially had. It hadn't taken her long to settle in and become part of the museum team.

It was after midnight when Mary was awoken by the familiar sounds of Richard climbing through the back window. He called for her in a hushed voice. She hurried through to find him perched on the window sill, holding a plastic bag in his hand. He silently handed it to her and disappeared back through the window. Before she'd had a chance to inspect the heavy bag, he was back; this time carrying a small pet carrier.

"For you," he announced, handing it to her and simultaneously relieving her of the heavy bag. A faint meowing emanated from the grey carrier. Mary stared at him, lost for words. She hadn't expected to see him until the following evening and she certainly hadn't expected this. She peered in through the slits and spied a ball of ginger fluff.

"It's a kitten!" she gasped, walking slowly through to her room. She put the carrier down on her sofa and sat next to it, waiting for Richard before opening it up. Carefully plucking the tiny creature from a scrunched up blanket, she held it to her face, grinning.

"It is a 'he' and he's about eight weeks old," he told her. "I got him tonight, from Halifax. Here's all the stuff you'll need," he continued, showing her the contents of the bag. "Litter tray, food, bowls, everything. If you need anything, I'll fetch it for you." He watched her reaction, smiling at her surprise. She kissed the kitten's bony head and buried her nose in his fur. He squirmed a little before starting to rumble and pummel the air, flexing and retracting splinter thin claws.

"He's gorgeous," she cooed, grinning at Richard. "I'm going to call him Richard."

"Don't do that! Everybody will put two and two together," he said quickly. Mary nodded.

"Okay then; what's your middle name?"

Richard shook his head,

"No, that'd be cruel to him. I hate my middle name so let's think of something else." He should have known she wouldn't let it go and without much persuasion, told her what it was.

"Rodney!" She tried not to laugh but stifling it just made it worse.

"Yeah, see? It's a stupid name," he muttered. She shook her head.

"No, it's perfect. If nobody else knows it, then I can call him Rodney and only I will know who he's named after." She said the name out loud a few times, then started laughing again.

"You're right. I can't call him Rodney; all I keep hearing is, 'Rodney you plonker!"

Richard muttered under his breath, saying he knew that would happen. Mary tried to appease him and tried to stop her mounting fit of giggles. Just then, he jumped up, suddenly remembering something. He disappeared through the window once more, returning a few moments later with yet another bag.

"Here. It's your birthday present. I thought you could have it a few days early."

Mary took the bag from him, handing him the purring kitten to hold.

"I've decided," she whispered, watching the ginger kitten sink into Richard's lap and close his eyes, "I still want to name him after you, so how about Roddy? It's not quite Rodney," she reasoned. He nodded, gently stroking the now sleeping kitten with his finger.

"Go on then, open it," he prompted, nodding at what she was holding. She stroked the parcel, appreciating the shiny, pink paper with '18' embossed in silver all over it. A large, silver bow added the finishing touch. She carefully ripped it open, already guessing by its shape and size that it was a book. In fact, there were two books wrapped up together. The first: a bottle green, gilt edged copy of *Wuthering Heights*. The front of the book was decorated with a wood engraving that she instantly recognised to be the work of Fritz Eichenberg. The iconic image of Heathcliff, leaning against the skeletal tree of Top Withens, his head raised to the heavens in agonising torment, was one she had long since loved. She hugged the book to her chest, laughing with joy before flicking through the pages, marvelling at the engravings throughout and holding the book up to her nose to smell. Richard shook his head in mock despair.

"You actually sniff the books." Secretly, he was more than pleased with her reaction to it. It had taken a day of rifling through second hand shops to find the perfect copy. The second book had been a lucky find in the process, an added bonus. Again, in immaculate condition considering its age, it was a 1908 edition of *The Complete Poems of Emily Brontë*, edited by Clement King Shorter. Mary mouthed his name, turning to the first page to check the copyright date. That's when she spotted the inscription, 'Forever'.

"Was this … already here?" she stuttered. Richard shook his head. Her grin widened.

"Check the other one," he urged. She did so, turning to the first page. Her heart fluttered as she read his words.

'The moors belong to us. That's where our hearts will always be.'

Unable to hold back, tears trickled down her face as she chewed her lip in a bid to stop them.

"You know I mean it, right?" he whispered. She nodded, smiling, her throat aching from wanting to sob. Putting the books down, she flung her arms around his neck, taking him by surprise. Roddy didn't stir.

"I love them! Thank you *so* so much!"

Mary hovered by the lounge window the following morning, watching her father's car as it disappeared out of sight. Running up to her room to fetch Roddy, then sneaking back downstairs unnoticed, she hurried across to the churchyard. A few minutes later, she returned, blatantly clutching Roddy tucked under her jacket. She hurried into the café where Bridget was busy getting things ready for the day. Hannah, one of her three members of staff, was the first to spot him and rushed over to take a look.

"I found him yesterday," Mary told them. "At the back of the Parsonage. Apparently there was a feral cat who had kittens recently and he must be one of them. Anyway, I went back to check this morning and he was still there, all alone. And frozen, poor little mite."

Roddy blinked, enjoying all the fuss after his confusing morning. His loud, tinny rumble delighted his group of admirers and so he rumbled a little more.

"Surely you don't expect to keep him, Mary?" Bridget piped up, already knowing the answer. Mary pleaded with her.

"I'll look after him in my room. He can have his litter tray in my bathroom and he's got no end of window space to sleep and watch the world. Dad won't even notice him, I promise." She looked to Hannah for support.

"Aw, Bridget, you can't turn the poor little scrap out in this weather. Look at him," she cooed, having the exact effect Mary wanted. Bridget sighed, smiling as she stroked his head.

"Okay, but … no shirking in your duties looking after him. You are solely responsible for him. Keep him away from your father," she warned before waving her away with an affectionate laugh, shaking her head at how easily the 'little scrap' had stolen their hearts.

"Happy Birthday, Mary!" Bridget placed the customary cup of tea by her bedside, accompanied by an elaborately decorated cupcake, with a diamanté '18' cake topper. Mary stuck her finger in the swirl of pink and purple frosting, scooping up a generous amount into her mouth, making appreciative noises. Left alone to enjoy her blueberry cake, she watched the rain splash on the cobbles below, deep in thought. Roddy, smelling something delicious, abandoned his own breakfast and clawed his way up her pyjama leg to settle on her lap and crane his scrawny neck in the cake's direction. He eagerly licked her finger, sticking his nose in the sweet butter and sneezing before continuing to lick every last bit on offer. He then settled down to clean himself; a lengthy process that he had already been through that morning.

She knew it was silly but she was feeling quite down about her birthday. Turning eighteen was such a big deal apparently and yet she felt no different. What bothered her though was not being able to share her big day with Richard. She knew that Kelly would make a fuss and consequently so would the other girls, but the one person she wanted a fuss being made by, would be forced to ignore her or at best, mumble 'happy birthday' as they sat together in lesson. And the party was only a few days away and it would be the same scenario. He would be there, in the same room as her, pretending that they weren't a couple. Initially, she had found it exciting, keeping him a secret, but the novelty was wearing thin. He had quickly become the only good thing in her life and she was hungry for more time with him. Not in eight months when they would be in York; she wanted it all *now.* And she deeply resented the one person who was stopping it.

"Good morning, Mary," Donal nodded curtly, pushing an envelope across the table towards her before returning to his paper. She opened the card, read the stark message inside penned by her father and put the twenty pound note on the table.

"Thank you." She glanced at her mother who patted her apron pocket and gave a secretive smile. As soon as Donal had left, she came back into the kitchen and placed a blue jewellry box in front of Mary. She stood back and watched her open it.

"Oh, Mam, it's beautiful," Mary gasped. A dainty teardrop opal, offset with a solitaire diamond at the top, and suspended from a sterling silver box chain, nestled on the navy foam pad. They had spied it a few months previously in the jewellers shop along Main Street and Mary had instantly set her heart on it.

"Let me," Bridget offered, taking the necklace and fastening it around Mary's neck. She smoothed back her hair and rested her hand on Mary's shoulder. She wasn't a very tactile person – it was the way she had been raised – but she sometimes wished she could give in to spontaneous gestures of affection. Watching Mary approach adulthood and seeing her change and develop into a young lady filled her with a sense of pride but also one of panic. Eighteen years had flown by and she still didn't feel that she had got to know her own daughter. There was always a reserve, a disconnection from each other. She knew she should try to fix it, to rectify the absence of affection, but something was always holding her back and she could never get beyond that. Sighing, she eyed the kitchen clock and hurried Mary along.

"Happy birthday!" Kelly cheered as Mary reached the bus stop. She pulled a party popper behind Mary's head, shooting colourful streamers into her hair. She pulled another two before Mary insisted that was enough. Then followed a raucous rendition of 'Happy Birthday' before she planted a noisy, lipstick kiss on Mary's cheek. As a final gesture, she pinned an '18' badge, the size of a side plate, to Mary's coat.

"That'll get you plenty of birthday kisses," she winked. "Try the driver," she added as they boarded the bus. Mary shook her head, laughing. Kelly roused the girls into another rendition of the birthday song and they were all giggling by the time they reached Richard's stop. He looked surprised at Mary's flushed face and hair full of coloured paper, and his face creased into a smile – but only for a moment.

"Happy birthday, Mary," he said gruffly, aware that he was being watched by her friends. He swung into his usual seat at the back, silently looking out of the window. The girls stared after him.

"Did he smile at you?" Tracy turned from Mary to Kelly, dumbfounded. "He smiled at her!"

Kelly scowled, clenching her fists.

"Yeah well, I'll wipe the smile off his face on Saturday, don't you worry!"

Mary looked alarmed.

"Why, what are you going to do? I really don't mind him smiling at me," she said meekly.

"Yes, you do! Besides, I've got big plans for you on Saturday. You can thank me later," she grinned, shooting at look at Richard. Mary sensed what she was planning.

"*Please* don't fix me up with anybody."

113

"Did I say that's what I'm going to do? You'll just have to wait and see but trust me, it's going to be fan...tas...tic!" She put her hand up to stop Mary's protesting and changed the subject, talking about the latest scandal with her cousin's best friend's wayward sister. Mary subtly pulled the streamers from her hair and rubbed the lipstick from her cheek. Tight knots were twisting her stomach as she fretted over Kelly's plans for Saturday.

"I bet she gets you drunk. She'll spike your drink, I reckon," Richard said later that night as they lay in bed discussing Kelly's motives. Mary wasn't so sure. There had been a glint in Kelly's eye that she didn't like. She was beginning to realise that there were many things about Kelly that she didn't really like. Funny how she hadn't noticed them before.

"Thank goodness you'll be there to look after me," she reassured herself, settling her head on his chest. He kissed her hair, grunting agreement.

"I can't do much though, can I? Not with the whole village there, watching." He was as concerned as she was but didn't want to let on. He was dreading Saturday as it was. The thought of being in a small room with all his peers who he despised, made him want to put his fist through a wall. He was doing this for Mary.

"York can't happen soon enough," he muttered, voicing his thoughts out loud.

Mary woke with butterflies in her stomach on Friday, a mix of trepidation and excitement about their party the following day. Initially, Kelly had been cagey about her threats and had then backed down, saying she'd only been joking.

She could feel the tension in the room as soon as she walked into the kitchen for breakfast. Bridget shot her a warning look before bustling about with tea and toast. Donal

114

shifted in his seat and cleared his throat to address her, without taking his eyes off his newspaper.

"When I was your age, Mary, if there were unwanted kittens around, do you know what we did with them?" He didn't expect an answer and Mary didn't offer one. She fixed her eyes on the tablecloth in front of her, barely able to breath. She had been found out and she feared for Roddy.

"We would swing their heads against the wall to bash their brains and then throw them in the river."

Mary's eyes flew up towards his set face, partially masked by his paper.

"That's cruel! That's so barbaric!"

He sniffed and shook the newspaper to straighten it.

"It may be cruel but better that than be overrun with flea-infested vermin." He lowered his paper, fixing angry eyes on her.

"You bought a kitten into my house without asking my permission. I understand you care but I warn you now, if I ever catch sight, or sound, or *smell* of it, I will throw it out of your window. Do I make myself clear?"

Mary nodded, her head bent. Her insides were trembling. She knew from his comment that her mother had stepped in to back her up, defending her caring nature but she also knew that she was sailing very close to the wind. She was harbouring too many secrets. As if reading her mind, Donal continued his monologue.

"I am *aware* when something is going on. I have a nose for these things. If something changes, it changes for a reason."

Mary held her breath, shaking almost uncontrollably now. He carried on reading for a minute longer, folded his paper and placed it on the table. Without looking at her as he rose from his chair he said,

"Your hair has grown out, Mary. Almost back to normal." He headed for the door.

"She's getting it cut again today, Donal. As a birthday treat. From me."

An icy silence filled the room. Mary couldn't believe how her mother was challenging him. He clearly couldn't believe it either. He glared at her and marched out.

"Do you have your eye on somebody? Is there somebody at school?"

Mary looked up from her frothy hot chocolate, surprised at her mother's abrupt question. She started to blush.

"No. Why?"

They had met up in Keighley after school and once Mary had finished at the hairdresser's, they found the nearest teashop before embarking on dress shopping. She had been surprised at Bridget's offer of a shopping trip; it's not something they had ever done before, other than the obligatory school uniform shopping when she was younger, but this felt nice. It made her feel like an adult.

Bridget noticed the colour rising and felt a pang of disappointment. She wished Mary would confide in her more readily. Smiling, she stirred her tea trying to act casual to cover the awkward pause.

"You just seem different lately. Happy." She eyed her daughter, sensing the reluctance. "It's okay. I wouldn't have told my mother if I had my eye on a boy when I was your age."

Mary gave a little laugh, feeling bad for not being truthful.

"I don't really. I'm just wanting a change, that's all."

Bridget nodded, accepting her explanation but Mary felt she needed to say more. She couldn't resist mentioning Richard.

"Listen Mam, I can't say this in front of Dad but … I'm happy because I'm finally understanding my work at school. Richard has helped me so much - he has been amazing - and I can *finally* see a light at the end of the tunnel. It doesn't seem so scary any more. Uni is within touching distance now," she gushed, eyes sparkling. Bridget reached across the table and grabbed her hand, squeezing it.

"Good, I'm glad. I really want you to get there. I *really* want you to. Work hard, Mary. Make sure you get what you want out of life."

"I will, Mam," she nodded, still grinning. Bridget straightened up and drained her teacup.

"And you're right; let's not mention that boy in front of your father."

Chapter Eight

Mary practically skipped to work the following morning. Her shopping trip had been successful, her hair felt and looked amazing and, despite his threats, she was quite relieved that her father now knew about Roddy. It was one thing less to keep secret. Her mind flitted back to her new dress and she couldn't wait to see Richard's face at the party.

The hours ambled by as she impatiently clock-watched although she had enjoyed her day at work, particularly after being serenaded by her colleagues and presented with a chocolate cake and some presents. Smelly bath oils: a cute pair of pale blue, knitted gloves with a darker blue, faux fur cuff, and a matching scarf with faux fur pom poms. Not forgetting the book token that had been tucked inside a beautiful, magenta coloured, clothbound journal. Waving happily to her work friends, she hurried the short distance home, clutching her gifts to her chest. Stopping off briefly in the café to show Bridget her presents, she hurried upstairs and jumped into the shower.

Kelly had been more than a little put out that Mary was getting ready at her own home alone rather than together, and had complained bitterly about it for the entire journey to school the previous day.

"But your whole family will be getting ready too," Mary had insisted, "I would be in the way. You know it." What she really meant was that she didn't want Kelly to ply her with drink, or dominate her in any way. She wanted to do her own hair and make-up, and she didn't want Kelly to see her dress and try to convince her to wear something different.

Carefully applying the make-up she had bought for Adam's party, and remembering Kelly's tips, she soon looked older, more sophisticated and less freckly. She took a bag from her drawer and laid out her new underwear on the bed. She had feigned going to buy a present for Kelly and had left Bridget looking at saucepans while she had snuck into the lingerie department. The dove grey, lacey bra and knickers were a far cry from her usual supermarket purchase, and far too pretty to actually wear, she thought. She picked up the pack of nude coloured, hold up stockings she had bought and studied the blurb. Twenty denier, shimmer leg, wide lace top, and offering ' sophisticated glamour'.

"That'll do the trick," she chuckled, shaking her head in amazement at her own bravery. She had to steel herself to look at her own reflection in her new lingerie and stifled a gasp of wonder. It was exactly the look she was going for; elegantly sexy. She had steered clear of the black and red combinations that seemed to dominate the department, deciding she wasn't quite ready for that look just yet. But this look was perfect.

Padding on tiptoe through to her wardrobe, she pulled out her new dress that hung in protective wrapping. A perfect find in the designer range at Debenhams, she had masked the price tag from her mother's watchful eye. Yes, it was expensive and put a dent in her university fund but she consoled herself with the knowledge that she could wear it again, many times over, during Freshers week. The square-necked, sleeveless, cobalt blue sheath dress was 'this season's colour', the assistant had assured her. Not too figure hugging and not too low cut, it came to just above knee length, showing off her toned calves – or, walker's legs, as Bridget would say. Deciding that her trusted ballet pumps wouldn't go with the ensemble, she had opted for a pair of steel grey, kitten heels. As she slipped them on, she pulled a face and stuck her pumps into her handbag for the walk home. Fastening her new necklace, she carefully aligned the opal pendant while scrutinising her outfit from every angle in the mirror. Donning her long, winter coat that covered up everything, she had a last minute change of heart and swapped her shoes for her pumps, planning to swap back again once she had reached the Social Club.

Although they had planned the party together, Kelly had taken charge of shopping for everything and, as Mary was working, she had organised her family to help set up the hall. Their colour scheme was fuchsia pink, black and silver. Balloons and banners hung from every wall and huge, helium filled balloon hearts with '18' on them, bobbed about. Trestle tables were laid out with food along one side of the room, close to the bar. Kelly's mum had surpassed herself with the food. Plates of sandwiches, sausage rolls, cocktail sausages, crisps and cakes were crammed onto the table, leaving little room for the soft drinks and glasses. Anything alcoholic would be available from the bar although Kelly's dad had no doubt that half the guests would sneak their own bottles in nevertheless.

By the time Mary arrived, Kevin and Steve were doing a sound check and testing the lighting. Kelly stopped in mid step, two errant balloons in her grip, and stared open-mouthed at Mary. She swore loudly.

"You look amazing!" she held her arms out and as Mary hugged her, she could feel how tensed up Kelly was. She stepped back and looked Kelly up and down.

"You do too," she replied. As ever, Kelly had overdone the hairspray, the eyeshadow and the fake nails, although Mary had to admit, the effect was certainly eye catching. Her fuchsia pink dress was basically an elongated vest which clung to every inch of her, ending just below her thighs. The shoestring straps did nothing to cover her glossy black, satin bra and in turn, the bra did little to cover her boobs. Her backcombed bun was secured with a silver bow and she had sprayed the ends of her hair pink.

"I thought we agreed: pink and black. That's blue, Mary!" Kelly tried to hide her envy by scolding her. Despite all her efforts, she was being outshone by Mary's understated, classy outfit, and it didn't sit well with her. Nothing rankled Kelly more than not being in control, and she definitely felt that Mary was slipping out of her control.

"I'm sorry, Kelly. I was going to find something pink but my mam bought me this dress and she really wanted me to wear it tonight, especially as she can't be here." She shrugged, pulling a mournful face. Kelly sighed, begrudgingly accepting her excuse and taking her arm, ushered her to the bar.

"Right. First legal drink for you. What will it be?"

Mary shook her head.

"I can't drink, sorry."

Kelly opened and closed her mouth, her eyes narrowing.

"Why not? It's your birthday!"

"I know, but I'm on anti-biotics and …"

"What for? Since when?" Kelly demanded, not happy at the turn of events. Mary floundered.

"Since yesterday. I have … I have an infected wisdom tooth," she said quickly, gingerly patting the side of her mouth. Kelly's dad looked up from behind the bar where he was helping to stack the glasses.

"Ouch, that's nasty, love. Poor you, but you're right; no alcohol for you tonight." He gave Kelly a look that warned her not to push the issue, then gave Mary a reassuring wink. She smiled her gratitude. She really liked Kelly's dad, he was a gentle giant who had all the time in the world for anybody.

The hall quickly filled up and the two girls were greeted with noisy hugs from the other girls and awkward grunts from the boys. Loud music thumped and reverberated off the walls, and flashing strobe lights distorted the room. Most of the guests had arrived shortly after seven but by half past, there still was no sign of Richard. Mary kept glancing towards the door, waiting.

"Where is he?" Kelly snapped, looking at the clock above the door. Mary blinked.

"Richard? I don't know."

"Not Richard, you idiot. I mean Marcus!" Kelly shot her a look. "Why the hell would I care about Richard? And why do you?"

"I don't care," Mary replied calmly, "but as he's the only person I invited, I was half watching out for him, that's all."

Kelly turned on her heel and headed back to the bar, shouting angrily at her sister about Marcus.

It was nearly eight by the time Richard turned up. He hovered in the doorway, scanning the room, looking for Mary. She spotted him first and slowly made her way towards him, as if she happened to be going in that direction. Her insides were shaking, she had no idea why. Seeing him just sent her stomach into a spin. He was wearing smart, black jeans and a tailored, wide striped, black and white shirt with a button down collar, under his black leather jacket. He turned when Mary gently tapped his arm and stared at her, lost for words.

"Hello," she smiled. "Thank you for coming." She tried to sound non-committal, although the effort was killing her. She nodded and smiled at the people around her, then glanced back up at Richard who was blatantly staring at her. She tried not to laugh; it was exactly the reaction she had wanted. He bent his head towards her.

"You look amazing! Walk away before I kiss you and blow our cover."

"I dare you," she whispered back. His face dropped.

"I'm joking!" she giggled quietly. "You look amazing too, by the way." She turned and sauntered across the room towards Tracy, knowing that he was watching her. Her mood lifted the minute he had walked through the door and she couldn't stop smiling. She was getting compliments left, right and centre, some from people she didn't even know but vaguely recognised from school. She certainly was the centre of attention and she lapped it up in her quiet way.

"Alright, gorgeous!"

Mary turned to find Josh standing right behind her. She smiled and nodded and made to move away but he stepped in front of her.

"Hey, what's the rush? I haven't had a chance to talk to you all night," he said, eying her up and down. He smelt of alcohol and his eyes were bloodshot.

"Well, you're a dark horse. You scrub up nice," he winked, touching her shoulder. She laughed, embarrassed by his cringey chat-up line, and excusing herself, pushed through the crowd to escape him. She headed for the tables of food. Richard was on the other side of the room and she could tell by his expression, that he had seen Josh talking to her. Two girls were stood either side of him, both leaning in to him and giggling as they sipped at their drinks. Mary noted that they had gone for the same look as Kelly and it irked her that Richard wasn't moving away from them. He was just letting them lean all over him, their boobs practically falling out of their dresses. He caught her eye and looked away, taking a long drag of his cigarette. She knew him so well now that she could gauge his mood by the way he smoked; he was clearly riled. She checked the clock, squinting through the dark. Half past nine. Only another hour and a half to go before she could escape to her room and wait for Richard.

"Where did you get to?" Josh put a heavy hand on her shoulder and turned her around. Hemmed in by the tables and the hungry drunks gathered there, she anxiously looked for Kelly for support. But Kelly, humiliated by being stood up by Marcus on her big night, was pouring her attention all over Steve the DJ.

"So," Josh leant towards her, sliding his arm around her waist. "A little bird tells me you fancy me."

Mary's eyes widened, following his gaze. Just then, Kelly looked up and grinned, toasting them with her empty glass. Panic dried her throat and she swallowed frantically, trying to worm out of his grip. He pulled her towards him with both arms and forced his mouth onto hers. She tried to push away but that just encouraged him further and he pushed his fingers through her hair, grabbing hold of a handful so she was unable to move her head. His other hand remained firmly on her back in a vice-like grip. Just when she thought she was going to gag, he broke away, smirking.

"Not bad, little virgin Mary. I reckon I could teach you a thing or two. Fancy going outside for some fresh air?"

Shaking and trying to catch her breath, she knew he wasn't going to take no for an answer.

"I need the loo first," she mumbled, still breathless. He released his grip on her and she hurried towards the bar, straight for Kelly's dad.

"Mr Wood," she pleaded. His smile faded seeing her distress.

"What's up, Mary?"

"Can you help me?" Her voice started to break. "There's a boy that won't leave me alone and..."

"Right, stay here with me." He lifted the bar and pulled her through to the other side, pointing to a small stool in the corner.

"Sit there, Mary. Who was it?"

Mary was frantically searching through the sea of faces for Richard. He wasn't by the wall where she had last seen him. He wasn't by the door or sitting down on the row of chairs that hugged the room. There was no sign of him. Or the two girls. Distracted, she turned back to Kelly's dad.

"It was Josh Higgins."

He tutted, shaking his head.

"Ah, Josh. Thinks he's God's gift. Don't worry about him, he's all show really. But you stay here with me, that's fine." He turned back to the customers at the bar, chatting loudly and laughing. Pulling pints at the Social Club was one of his many little jobs around the village. It didn't pay much but he didn't mind. Occasionally he would look back at Mary and give her a little wink. He felt sorry for her; she was so out of her depth in that crowd of rowdy, testosterone-fuelled teenagers.

Ten minutes passed and Josh hadn't ventured towards the bar to find her. She stood up slowly, checking to see if the coast was clear. There was still no sign of Richard. She couldn't believe that he had left her in the lurch like that, after all they had said about the party; he was going to be there for her in case anything went wrong. She desperately wanted to go home but there was still another hour to go before it finished.

"I've got the car outside; do you want me to run you home?"

Mary smiled weakly at Mr Wood, nodding, not trusting herself to speak. He guided her outside and dropped her off outside her door two minutes later. He watched as she unlocked the door and let herself in. Waving, he slowly reversed and headed back down the hill.

Bridget heard the door and greeted her at the top of the stairs.

"You're early!" she whispered, nodding towards the lounge. "We were just about to go to bed. Everything okay?" she wondered, taking in Mary's pale face.

"Fine, I have a headache though so Kelly's dad drove me home."

They chatted in hushed tones for a minute longer then Mary hurried up to her room. She flicked on the light, kicked off her shoes and went through to open the back window, hoping that Richard would turn up soon. She caught her breath as she walked into the spare room. Richard was sitting at her desk, in the dark. He stood up slowly, glaring at her.

"What the hell are you playing at?" he rasped, his eyes glinting with rage.

"I couldn't stop him!"

"Yes, you could."

She snorted with frustration at his ridiculous retort. She still felt sick from the taste of Josh's mouth, and she was still angry that Richard had deserted her.

"Well, you had those girls – they were all over you!" she hissed. He widened his eyes indignantly.

"Yeah, *they* were all over *me*. And if you'd bothered to notice, I left."

He paced up and down, fuming. Mary leant over and flicked the side light on; she didn't like them arguing in semi-darkness. She spotted that his fist was grazed and bleeding. He glared at her again.

"Anybody else, Mary. You could've had anybody else! But … Josh?" His voice was rising as his temper grew. She needed to calm him quickly. She kept her voice hushed, hoping he would copy.

"I didn't *want* it! I hate him! But he had a hold of me. I couldn't get away."

He swore, pacing again.

"He knows I fancy you. He's doing this to wind me up," he growled.

"How? How can he know you fancy me? Even I don't know that when we're at school!"

Richard wasn't listening, he was focusing on his own thoughts and growing more incensed by them.

"He knows me. He sees us in class and he knows that getting with you would wind me up. That's why he did it!" He punched his bleeding fist into his other hand. Mary stared at him, annoyed with his ranting. He hadn't once asked if she was okay.

"Right, so he did it to wind you up. Not because he fancies me then?" she goaded.

"You're not his type."

"I'm not *your* type either, judging by what you picked up tonight," she retorted, her voice rising again. He carried on swearing angrily.

"What's wrong with you? Do you *want* him to fancy you? Is that it?"

"No, of course not but could you not make me feel quite so plain and insignificant." She watched him process what she was saying, not liking what he was hearing. Unable to stop, she continued goading him.

"Maybe he does fancy me. Is that so ridiculous?"

"Why the hell are you even debating this?" He pointed an accusing finger at her. "You shouldn't wonder whether anybody else fancies you. You're *my* girl. End of." They glared at each other, neither one backing down.

"Yes, I'm your girl but even so, it's actually pretty great to think somebody else might fancy me too. Girls like to feel wanted; like to be noticed."

He went deathly quiet, not moving a muscle.

"You sound like Kelly."

She knew she'd gone too far, said things she didn't mean and didn't believe herself. The thought of anybody else wanting her made her feel physically sick but she was so angry with him for not defending her, for just walking away.

"Have you been drinking?"

"Of course not!" She breathed on him; her breath smelt of cherry drops. "Why would I drink? You don't like it so I don't." She had shifted her pitch, softening her tone to calm him down. She gave him a tentative smile. He sighed.

"If he ever touches you again, I'll kill him."

"So will I!" she tried to laugh. He paced about again, slapping his head with his hand in a bid to get the images out.

"But you *kissed* him, Mary!"

"No! No, I did not!" she defended. "He kissed me. He came over and stuck his tongue down my throat!" She ignored his expletive. "But I did *not* kiss him back. If you had hung around long enough, you would have seen that. How I tried to fight to get away from him. But you disappeared with those … whores!"

His eyes widened angrily.

"You reckon? You think I'd do that? *You're* my girl. I wouldn't do that to you."

She blinked, brought back down to earth by his honest words.

"Good. Because if anybody else touches you, I'll kill them," she said quietly, echoing his sentiment. His shoulders slumped as he exhaled slowly. She edged closer, her voice barely a whisper.

128

"I didn't *want* his attention. I didn't *ask* for it. All I want to do is tell the world about us. But we can't do that." She held her hand out for him as she moved closer and stroked his arm.

"You're the only one I want, Richard." They stood in silence, looking at each other, both calming down. She tugged at his shirt, pulling it free from his jeans.

"Come to bed."

He frowned, not moving.

"You think that's going to win me over?"

She smiled .

"Yes."

He started to laugh, letting her lead him into her bedroom. Turning, she rested her hands on his chest, leaning into him.

"Do you like my dress?"

"Yes. You look great," he nodded. "You looked amazing tonight."

"I bought it just for you." She put a finger to his mouth to stop his protest.

"I know what you said, that it doesn't matter what I wear, but I want to look pretty for you."

"You do."

She looked into his eyes.

"And when I was trying it on, I imagined you taking it back off."

He glanced down at her dress then back at her face.

"Take my dress off," she breathed. He tensed up and frowned. She smiled.

"I'm not throwing myself at you. I'm not begging for it. I'm just saying, take my dress off."

"Are you telling me what to do, Mary?"

"No," she gave a little laugh.

"It sounds like it," he said, taking a step back, steely faced.

"I'm not. I'm *asking* for you to undress me." She stood on tiptoe and whispered in his ear, "I've got new underwear too. I want you to see it."

His face darkened, his brow furrowed. She sighed lightly, undeterred.

"Why do you look so cross? Do you think that scares me?"

"Doesn't it?"

"No. You can look as mean as you like but I trust you. I feel safe with you. You would never hurt me." She looked at him. "Would you?"

His fixed stare faltered and he shook his head.

"No, I'd never hurt you."

"Well then," she coaxed. "Look, I do everything you want but for once, let me take the lead."

He gave an involuntary laugh of surprise. She sighed again and moved away.

"Okay, you don't want to undress me; fine. I'll do it myself. You can watch." She lifted her arm to undo the side seam zip.

"No, let me." He pulled the zip and carefully lifted the dress over her head, catching his breath at the sight of her underwear. Elated, she grinned and pulled him towards the bed.

"Now tell me you don't want me dressing up for you," she teased. He shook his head, not able to take his eyes off her.

"Just so you know: this here," she gestured to her body, "is strictly reserved for you. Nobody else. Ever." Placing a hand on his chest, she pushed him down onto her bed and straddled him, slowly unhooking her bra. There was no hint of self-consciousness, no stain of colour rising from her neck; just an alluring smile on her face.

"What have I done to you?" he murmured, bewitched by her. She scrunched her nose up.

"A bit late for regrets now," she teased.

"I regret nothing," he said, sticking his hands behind his head, watching her. A slow smile spread across his face, transforming his features.

"Me neither!" she giggled, carelessly dropping her bra to the floor.

Chapter Nine

That night had brought about a marked change in their relationship. Already close and comfortable with each other, they became closer still, on a much deeper level. Richard was besotted with her, desperate for her company every minute of every day. He had taken to sitting closer to her on the school bus: lining up behind her in the corridor before class, and had gradually changed his routine so that he could walk her home from the bus stop each day. He crept into her room each night, arriving very late on the nights he was out with his uncle, and stayed until dawn started to break.

They spent so much time together that they became as one person, each knowing exactly what the other was thinking or feeling. They had taken on each other's traits; he became less volatile and more able to step back from his anger, and she grew in confidence and self-belief, determined to get where she wanted in life. Their mutual love of Roddy was the icing on the cake; he completed their little unit. Although if truth be told, Roddy had decided that Richard was his master and Mary was merely the one who fed him and provided him with a comfy bed. He would sit by the back window each evening, waiting and watching, and with his gift of sixth sense, would alert Mary of Richard's arrival before he was even in view of the building. He paraded back and forth on the window sill, chirruping ecstatically and waving his tail in the air, then as soon as Richard eased his way through the open window, Roddy would proudly lead the way into the bedroom.

Mary reflected on the past two months since her birthday party as she strolled up the path to their rendezvous on Dimples Lane. So much had happened and time had sped along and yet, she felt like she had already spent a lifetime with Richard. At first she'd thought it was jealousy that had changed him but now she knew it was simply because they both felt deeply that they were destined to be together for the rest of their lives. It was the one thing that spurred them one each day.

It was the second week of their Easter break; just two months to go before they left school. She had sailed through the mocks - thanks to Richard's support and patience - and was confidently working towards the final exams, with the finishing line and York University plainly in sight. She was in a good place and the changing season lifted her spirits even more. Tufts of emerging daffodils lined the path, intermingled with drifts of purple and yellow crocuses. Tight, white buds lit up the dark Hawthorn branches, with a promise of a fantastic display of heavenly scented blooms to come. Chunky stone troughs of spring bulbs sat on doorsteps and hanging baskets were bursting back into life. The sun warmed her back as she walked and the smell of dew on fresh grass filled the air. Her contented smile widened when she caught sight of Richard waiting for her. He wrapped her in his arms.

"I've missed you," he murmured into her hair.

"How have you missed me!" she laughed. "It's ten o'clock; you left me at five."

"Five hours, Mary. Five long hours," he said dramatically, pulling her along the heather clad path.

"Come on," he urged, I've got something to show you."

Once they had reached their usual spot overlooking Brontë Bridge, he pulled out a small book from his jacket pocket and handed it to her. She gasped, grinning.

"Where did you find this?"

"Down the road in that bookshop you always go to. It was only 50 pence and look, almost brand new! I'm getting your eye for a bargain," he grinned back.

It was a guide book entitled, 'City of York', with a city centre street map and a list of all the museums, shops, restaurants and places worth visiting. Richard took the book from her and opened up on the map.

"See here?" he said, pointing to a little road near the National Railway Museum, on the opposite side of the River Ouse to the university. Mary nodded, peering at the map, trying to get her bearings.

"There's a garage there that has a workshop and garage space to let. They're also looking for a trainee mechanic."

"How do you know all this?"

"Because," he pulled a letter from his pocket, "I have an interview with them. This Thursday."

Mary stared at him, open mouthed.

"But ..." She couldn't finish her sentence, at a complete loss for words. He laughed at her stunned expression.

"He knows my uncle; I've met him a couple of times at car auctions. So when I heard he had some space to let, I phoned him and that's when he mentioned the job. I'd work for him four days a week, go to college one day a week and in my spare time, do up my own cars and start to set up my business." He waited for her response. "Didn't I tell you it would all work out, Mary?"

She flung her arms around his neck.

"This is brilliant! When would you start though?"

"Well, that's the thing. I could start end of June but college wouldn't start until September so he said we can discuss that on Thursday. I'd rather wait until September when you leave for York too. Don't you think?"

She nodded, suddenly feeling very emotional. He took her hand.

"Mary, what do you think?"

Unable to stop herself, she started to cry. He frowned; she very rarely cried. Seeing his concern, she shook her head, apologising.

"I think … I think I love you," she laughed through her tears. He wiped tears away from her cheeks with his finger.

"I think I more than love you," he replied.

It had taken him quite some time to say, 'I love you', and she had quizzed him about it shortly after Valentine's Day. He had surprised her with a box of chocolate hearts, each one beautifully wrapped in red foil, and a single red rose, but avoided saying the 'L' word.

"Why do you never say you love me? I know you do."

"How do you know?" He looked sheepish and a little defensive; uncomfortable with her direct question.

"The way you look at me. The way you are with me. When you're lying in my bed, I know you're thinking it," she replied. He nodded, sniffing; something he always did when he felt awkward.

"Well then. Why do I need to say it, if I show you anyway." He paused for a moment. "It's only words, Mary. Anybody can say words and not mean it."

"I know, it's just …"

He interrupted her, continuing his train of thought.

"My dad used to say he loved me. He told my mum he loved her. I believed him."

"Well, that's the thing," she replied quietly, "Nobody has ever said they love me. Not my Mam; certainly not my dad. Grandparents," she shook her head. "Nobody."

Richard looked at her for a long time, his heart aching at the thought of a young Mary craving to be loved, to be told she was loved.

"I'm sorry, I had no idea." He hated how inadequate his words sounded.

"It's okay. How could you know," she smiled.

"No, I've been selfish. The thing is, Mary, saying 'I love you' doesn't even begin to describe how I feel about you. You're all I think about, day and night. You're the air I breathe. You keep my heart beating. You're beautiful, inside and out. 'I love you' doesn't seem to cover any of that." He watched the shy, pleased smile spread across her face, her eyes sparkling with happiness at his words.

"I *more* than love you, Mary. And I shall tell you *that*, every day."

And that's exactly what he did.

They sat on the heather studying the guide book, heads bent together, planning their future and visualising what life in the city would be like from the plethora of photos throughout. Mary yawned and stretched out on the ground. Richard lay down next to her, watching as she closed her eyes.

"Tired?"

"Mmmm."

"You should get more sleep," he teased. She laughed softly.

"You should let me!"

He chuckled, sticking his hand inside her jumper, stroking her stomach.

"Never!" he whispered with a possessive growl. She laughed again, feigning snoring. They lay in silence for a while, basking in the warmth of the early spring sunshine.

"Your boobs are bigger. Are you due on this week?" he wondered. He knew her body so well and she revelled in that. She opened her eyes, squinting at the sky as she mentally calculated. Her whole body froze as she turned to him, wide eyed.

"Two weeks ago. I was due two weeks ago!"

"Really?"

She sat up, re-calculating, using her fingers as counters.

"Oh, my God – am I pregnant? And why are you smiling?" Her voice was squeaky.

"Because … your voice! You sound like Minnie Mouse! Don't panic, you've probably got your dates wrong."

"No, no I haven't. We've been careful, haven't we?"

He nodded but she thought she saw a look, a flicker in his eyes.

"Haven't we?" she insisted.

"Well, yes but it's not a hundred percent is it." He got to his feet and held his hands out to help her up.

"Where are we going?"

"To get you home. Then I'll go and get a tester." He was serious now, taking control. She nodded, her stomach lurching from a sudden rush of nausea.

"What do we do? If I am." She was starting to tremble, a thousand thoughts running through her mind.

"Do? What do you mean, 'do'? You're not getting rid of it!" He stared at her, trying to fathom what she was thinking.

"Of course not!"

"Is that what you want? To get rid of it?" He held her shoulders, demanding an answer. She shook her head frantically.

"No, absolutely not. I meant, what do we do about my dad? If I'm pregnant, he would kill me. And you." The certainty of it was etched in her face. He rubbed her arms, reassuring her.

"One step at a time. Let's find out if you are actually pregnant before you plan our brutal deaths." He tried to joke but he could see terror in her eyes. It had always irked him how wary of her father she was, how she would tiptoe around him, but this was genuine fear he could see. He started to think there was more to Mr O'Shea than people actually knew.

They sat side by side staring at the tester in her hand.

"Are you angry?" she asked, breaking the silence.

"No! Not at all. Are you?"

Mary shook her head.

"No, but this changes everything."

Richard took hold of her trembling hand.

"It doesn't. The job is as good as mine anyway so I can look after you. You knew that, surely?"

"Yes, but … a baby. How can we look after a baby?" She put the tester on the low table in front of them and pressed her clammy hands against her flushed cheeks, feeling sick again.

"We've already got a kitten; how much harder can it be?" he joked. She shot him a look of despair.

"How can you be so calm about this?"

He shrugged, smiling.

"Because I can look after you. I can do this, Mary, and so can you. Just focus on your exams, and we'll leave for York at the end of June. I'll find us somewhere cheap to rent – I was going to do that anyway."

"My dad …"

"Won't know about it. We'll leave before he finds out," he reassured her. She nodded meekly, glancing around the room. They had gone to Richard's uncle's house; she'd not been there before. It was a typical Haworth stone cottage; cosy, small rooms with large windows that overlooked the road on one side and the Brow on the other.

"Why did she leave him?" she asked, nodding towards the family portraits on the fireplace. A smiling couple and two grinning girls posed for the studio photographer. They radiated a picture of happiness.

"He was a drinker. Like my mum. I don't blame her for leaving."

"And now? Does he still drink?"

Richard laughed, shaking his head.

"No, now he has Karaoke. He's a better person for it so who knows, maybe one day she'll come back." He could see she was getting emotional again and pulled her to her feet to hold her.

"We'll be fine, Mary. This is perfect, trust me," he whispered, his mind racing ahead, mentally noting how to plan the next few months, a satisfied look in his eye.

For the next few days they spent every moment together talking and planning, and for every question and scenario she threw at him, he had a solid and reassuring answer. The more Richard took control, the calmer Mary felt and she started to believe it could actually work. She stared at herself in the mirror after a shower, scrutinising her body for any tell-tale signs. Her boobs were definitely heavier and they ached; her eyes seemed luminous, almost doe-eyed but apart from that, nothing else to indicate the explosion of activity going on in her womb. She smiled at her reflection as she spread her hands across her stomach, protecting the miracle secret buried deep inside her.

Richard picked her up by their usual spot at nine o'clock on the day of his interview, driving his uncle's distinctive, midnight blue Rover V8. Mary had told Bridget she was off for a full day of revision with Kelly and warned her that she may be home late, as they planned to nip in to Keighley for a couple of hours afterwards.

"Nice car!" She flashed him a smile as she settled into the seat next to him. "I could get used to this."

"Yeah well, in a couple of years, I'll be driving you to do the weekly shop in one of my Limos. You can get used to that too!"

He opted for the scenic route to York, avoiding the road through Haworth, which gave Mary a chance to marvel at a part of Yorkshire she hadn't seen before. Rolling green hills and stretches of purple moorland shimmered as the gentle spring breeze swept through the new growth. Spring lambs dotted the landscape as if somebody had tipped a bag of cotton balls on the lush fields. The hedgerows and verges were festooned with nodding daffodils, white blooms and vibrant green buds. New life was emerging at every turn. Mary absently stroked her flat stomach, her eyes drinking in the passing scenery.

"Alright?" Richard glanced at her, eyebrows raised. She nodded, smiling.

"Any more sickness?" he wondered. She nodded again.

"This morning. I thought it was psychosomatic at first but no; proper vomit."

He grimaced, making a disgruntled noise.

"I'm sorry, did I share too much?" she teased, laughing at him.

As they approached York city, Richard quickly ran the plans by her again.

"So, I'll drop you off as near to the Minster as I can, then I'll come and meet you there after my interview. It shouldn't be more than an hour, I reckon." He shot her a concerned look. "Are you going to be okay?"

"I'll be fine." She eyed the crowds of Easter tourists milling along the road. "I'll stay put in the Minster so we don't lose each other. Good luck!" She leant over and kissed him before getting out, waving as he drove on, before heading towards the spectacular towers of York Minster.

Stepping in to the cool Norman cathedral from the warm April sun, she found the sheer size of the interior quite overwhelming and let out an involuntary gasp of surprise. She quickly moved to the side of the vast nave, clutching her guidebook, and sat down to avoid the volume of people thronging by the entrance. Most were armed with packed agendas and hungry, tired children; those of which with a little energy left wielded long, wooden swords from their visit to the popular Jorvik Viking centre as their parents hurried them along, determined to take in all the sights in as little time as possible. Mary settled back in her seat, reading up on the history of the ancient site. Built on the foundations of a Roman fortress, the Minster evolved from a wooden chapel, to a stone church, to the splendid magnesian limestone gothic cathedral that had taken two hundred and fifty years to complete. Everything was so symmetrical and grand; ornate carvings, pillars and arches stretched the entire length of the sixty-three metre long nave (the longest nave in the country, her book reliably informed her) and light flooded in through the many stained glass windows, bathing the floor in a kaleidoscope of colours. The height rose twenty-nine metres from the stone floor to the vaulted roof; the lattice pattern reminding her of her grandmother's fruit pies that she made for special occasions. She sat for a while longer, taking in the splendour and feeling comforted by the distinctive smell that pervaded any place of worship, regardless of size. The steady volume of tourists didn't wane. Those without children in tow took their time, sauntering along with heads facing upwards to admire the craftmanship, whereas some wandered a little faster, deep in conversation, totally oblivious to their surroundings. Mary surmised they were local to the Minster and wondered whether she too in time would become blasé to its ornate beauty. Despite the number of people and the acoustics of the building, it was remarkably quiet. Voices carried up to the roof and dispersed sending faint echoes into the stillness. The most prevalent sound to be heard was that of shoes squeaking as they caught on the worn, stone floor.

Moving on, Mary followed the crowd towards the east end of the building and stopped to admire the magnificent organ. It was a fay cry from the tiny, aging organ her uncle used to play in their local church. Below a large crucifix was a memorial to the fourteen boys of the Minster Choir who had been killed during both world wars; thirteen in the first world war, and one in the second. She noticed two had the same surname. Brothers? Or cousins, maybe. Either way, it meant a double heartache for the family left behind. Her mind flitted back to the day her grandfather died. The shock, the grief, the outrage. The retribution. Mary had such conflicting emotions when it came to war. Planting a bomb was such a cowardly act. If she were angry enough or believed passionately enough in what she was fighting for, she would fight face to face. Not plant a bomb that could take innocent lives along with the targeted one. She stopped short, suddenly aware that she was echoing opinions voiced by her father. She had vowed never to think like her father. She loathed him as much as she feared him. She couldn't wait to escape him.

Richard found her sitting quietly listening to the choir practice. He gently touched her shoulder. An expectant smile broke across her face as she stood up to hug him.

"So?"

He shrugged, trying not to smile.

"So … I got the job!"

Mary squealed and hugged him again.

"I knew you would! I'm so proud of you." She took his offered hand as he headed for the exit.

"Do you not want to look round the Minster?" she wondered. He shook his head.

"Another time. I really want to be outside; I want to look round the city that's going to be our new home." He was buzzing, telling her everything about the garage, the workshops, his new boss.

"And he knows of quite a few flats and small houses going for rent. He said he'd keep his ear open for anything suitable for us."

"Did you tell him about the baby?" She felt a twinge of panic at that thought but Richard shook his head.

"No. I need to break it to my uncle first. But not yet."

They followed the crowd into Stonegate, strolling along to take in all the different sights and to look at the array of shops that filled the old, Medieval street. Mary pointed out familiar high street names, peering into shop windows.

"I can see where all my wages will be spent!" Richard laughed, being dragged along.

"No, not at all," she replied hastily. "My priority will be our home, making it perfect for us. But I won't be paying these prices!" She pointed to a cushion; pretty, but nothing so special that could possibly justify the steep price tag. She'd never really been interested in home décor before but now she had a strong urge to make a home with Richard and she was itching to get started. They had agreed not to focus on baby plans until their exams were over but she couldn't stop herself from visualising them decorating the nursery, or pushing a pram through York's maze of little streets.

Richard paused outside a pub, drawn by its black and white timbered front, and cascade of plants hanging above the door

143

and leaded windows. The *Punch Bowl* was one of the oldest pubs in York and consequently, popular with tourists. Lunchtime smells wafted out through the open door, beckoning them in.

"Do you want to go in? Pub lunch?" he suggested. Mary peered through the door, hesitating at the volume of customers overflowing towards the street.

"I'm not really a pub person. Shall we try and find a tea shop instead?"

Richard took in a sharp breath through his teeth, looking regretful.

"I'm not sure if we'll find a tea shop in York," he teased, dodging her playful slap.

"Actually, can we scrap that idea. What I'd love to do is grab a meal deal from somewhere and go for a picnic in …" She hurriedly consulted their guide book, her finger hovering over the map page.

"In the Museum Gardens. Which is that way," she pointed down the street. "I think," she added, handing the book to Richard. They stopped at a bakery and while Richard went in to buy some warm pasties, Mary peered through the neighbouring gift shop window, and idly flicked through the assorted bracelets on the revolving stand by the shop door.

"What do you think?" She rotated her wrist for him to admire the bracelet made up of two strands of small, soft jade coloured stones. She studied the brown label attached to it, reading aloud.

"Aventurine. Promotes a sense of emotional safety and security. A good companion for the pioneering spirit, someone who is pushing themselves to places they have never been before. An all round healing stone that brings you wellbeing." She grinned at Richard's nonplussed expression. "It is literally made for me!"

"You really believe in all that rubbish?"

"Well, I didn't until now. Do you?"

He shrugged, watching her carefully hang the bracelet back on the stand. She sniffed the paper bags he was holding and let out a satisfied sigh.

"They smell good! Shall we find that park? I'm starving now."

Richard thrust the paper bags in her hands and, picking up the bracelet, headed into the shop, returning minutes later to present her with a purple and white gift bag.

"For you. You don't need all that stuff it says but if you think it'll help you then I think you should wear it."

She grinned, slipping the bracelet back on her wrist.

"I feel calmer already," she joked, reaching up to kiss him. They both glanced round at the passers-by.

"Our first kiss in public and nobody has batted an eyelid. I love this place!"

The Museum Gardens hugged the River Ouse and backed on to the City Library. It was originally the site of St Marys Abbey, the ruins of which glowed in the bright spring sunshine as light bounced off the pale stone. The Yorkshire Museum, built alongside the Abbey ruins, housed a vast collection of Roman artefacts, from old perfume vials to carved stone coffins – found complete with skeletons carefully encased in gypsum. The more non-descript coffins unearthed were dotted about the gardens in amongst the plants; ancient relics giving shelter to teeming wildlife. Squirrels darted across the lawns, scampering up the thick trunks of oak and sycamore. Pigeons paraded along the path in wide groups, hopefully eyeing the lunch time visitors for discarded morsels. Smaller birds darted in and out of the colourful rockery plants and purple acers; equally hopeful but far less brazen than their plump counterparts. Mary looked for a secluded spot in amongst the trees but Richard opted to sit in the sunshine on the wide stretch of grass by the ruins, in full view of everybody.

"No more hiding," he said, draping his arm across her shoulder and pulling her in close when she sat down next to him. They ate their lunch, idly watching the steady stream of people pass them by; an even mix of workers on their lunch break and tourists making the most of the warm, Spring sunshine. Mary read snippets out from their guide book and with each nugget of information, their excitement grew at the prospect of their new home. Full from their pasties and sleepy from the sun, they leant back against the warm stone wall, contented smiles stretched across their faces. Mary idly fiddled with her new bracelet.

"What made you choose me? I've seen the girls that go for you and I'm nothing like them. I'm not your type."

Richard gave a surprised laugh, straightening up and shaking his head in mock despair at her.

"They go for me; I don't go for them. You *are* my type. I just never knew what my type was until you came along." He ripped up blades of grass and threw them beyond his feet, thinking about his answer. He shot her a look, trying not to grin.

"I'm not going to lie, the night I met you from that party," he paused, clearing his throat and sniffing, "I fancied you yeah, but my intention was to get you into bed." He laughed lightly when she feigned indignance.

"I know, I know," he held up his hands in defence. "The thing is, I was getting to know you and then the thought of somebody else beating me to it, did my head in. I had to get you first. And then ..."

"You fell for me," she finished his sentence. He nodded, squinting at her.

"So when did you first think you fancied me?" she asked.

"Not sure. I think the day you gave me that cake. No, wait; the day you wanted to throw something back at Josh." He paused, casting his mind back. "You know what; I first fancied you that day we walked up the hill and you told me you wanted to be a teacher. And by the time you talked your socks off on our first day up by Brontë Bridge, I was hooked." He loved seeing her smile the way she was right then. He loved making her feel wanted and loved.

"You make me feel things I didn't think I'd ever feel, Mary. I didn't know I could feel like this about anything or anyone. It's you; you've done this to me."

"We're going to have the best life together," she said, feeling so elated.

"We are." He lightly touched her stomach. "I don't want you to give up your dreams though."

She shook her head, growing serious. She had already planned it out in her mind.

"I won't but my priorities have changed now. I can defer my place for a year, get settled here and have our baby, then next year go to uni. We'll have to work out child care. But for now," she sat up and cast an appreciative eye around the grounds, "We're here. You have a job. We have our plans. That's all we need. Now, let's go explore some more."

They walked the cobbled streets, constantly referring back to their guide book, and made some unexpected discoveries along the way. By the time they were heading back to Haworth, they had made a long list of places they wanted to visit and had a rough idea of the area they wanted to live in.

"There's just one thing missing," Richard mused, staring at the road ahead. "The moors. I'll miss that." There was an undeniable crack in his voice.

"We'll come back. To visit, go for walks," she encouraged. He shook his head.

"No, when I've left, I don't want to come back. I want to move on but I know a piece of me will always be hankering for the moors."

"Me too," she murmured. She knew she was nowhere near as attached to the moors as he was but she knew what he meant. It had become a very special place to the pair of them and she couldn't visualise anywhere else like it that could take its place. But she also felt that once they had left she wouldn't want to come back either. A pang of nostalgia swept over her which quickly disappeared when she imagined the disapproving faces of her friends; once news broke about her relationship with Richard, she doubted that they would have anything kind to say about it. Sighing, she determined to focus on the future and not look back. Leaning her head on the padded head rest, exhaustion took over and she fell fast asleep as the car purred along the country roads back to Haworth.

Chapter Ten

The next two months raced by in a whirlwind of revision and, in their private moments, making plans for the immediate future. Mary had successfully excused her exhaustive state on exam nerves and blamed the sickness that she was unable to hide, on a stomach bug. She had reached her sixteenth week of pregnancy without her parents being any the wiser. Richard was fiercely protective of her, demanding to know every detail of her changing body. He rubbed her back when it ached, he held her hair out of the way when she threw up, he brought her a constant supply of whatever foods she was craving and all the while, reassured her that everything would be okay. She needed to hear it. Often. As her stomach swelled and rounded, and her face changed shape, the fear of being found out increased.

Finally, the day of their last exam dawned, exactly two weeks before the end of the month and the start date of their tenancy on the little flat in York that Richard had secured. It had been a struggle not to dwell on that rather than on the exams but somehow they had kept each other going and on track. Thankfully, her exhaustion had been replaced with a sense of wellbeing and a surge of energy, and the sickness that had plagued her through the early weeks had since subsided. As she took her seat in the school hall, elation rather than nerves coursed through her. She turned to look at Richard, seated two rows behind her, smiling when he winked at her.

"Good Luck, Mary," Mr Platt whispered as he passed her desk, doing a final check that all was in order before delivering a few words of encouragement to them and handing over to the invigilator.

Mary watched the minutes tick by on the invigilator's large clock, her paper completed, read and re-read. She had answered every question, even the ones she was unsure of, and was finding it hard to contain the mounting grin of relief that was itching to erupt across her face. The atmosphere on the bus home was electric. Realisation that their exams were over superseded any sadness that their school days were also over. For most, they would carry on seeing each other, hanging out at the park or pubs but for Mary and Richard, it marked the beginning of their life away from the village. Kelly's exams were already over so in her absence on the bus, Mary sat as close to Richard as she could without being too obvious. As the bus neared Haworth, a noisy plan was hatched to all get off at the park, get some alcohol and have an impromptu celebration. As they piled off the bus in high spirits, Richard instinctively held his hand out to help Mary off. It didn't go unnoticed.

"I wouldn't let him touch you, love," Josh jeered loudly from behind her. "He'll have you knocked up in no time. He's good at that!"

Mary stared wide eyed at Richard, watching his face darken with rage.

"Shut up!" he hissed. Josh jumped off the bus and swaggered towards them, his arms outstretched, inviting trouble.

"What? Have you forgotten my cousin?" He turned to address Mary. "Fourteen. She was only fourteen when that skank knocked her up." He could see the stunned expression on her face, the fear in her eyes, like a startled rabbit. That's when he realised she had a thing for Richard, and that meant he had the upper hand.

"Shut up!" Richard growled, trying to walk away but Mary was rooted to the spot, her eyes fixed firmly on Josh. The crowd had formed a ring around them, waiting, watching. He grinned, goading Richard further.

"Yeah, she couldn't wait to get rid of it. I mean, who'd want that skank's baby growing inside them?"

Richard's breath came out in short, sharp snorts, his fists clenched. He stared at the ground growing dangerously still.

"I said, *shut up!*"

"What, you don't think you're a skank? Have you seen your mum lately? She's worse than you, that skank whore."

He would have said more but Richard charged at him like a bull, ramming him against the brick shop front, narrowly avoiding the glass window. He pulled Josh's head back and slammed it against the wall, simultaneously kicking the back of his legs, causing him to buckle to the ground. Bending over him, he pulled Josh's head up again and smashed it against the cobbles before delivering a swift kick to the side of his face. It happened so fast that it took a moment for Mary to snap out of her stunned trance. She pulled Richard's arm, screaming at him to stop. He blindly shook her off and continued to kick Josh's crumpled body. Blood trickled through the grooves, curving round the cobblestones and pooling as it flowed down the incline. She pulled at him again, stumbling in her effort, shouting at the on-lookers for help. They too stood trance-like until her screams fired them into action. Furious at being man-handled, Richard lashed out, swearing and kicking until he caught sight of Mary's stricken face. She didn't need to ask if it were true; she could see it in his eyes, in his whole demeanour. He wiped his mouth with the back of his hand, glaring at his peers as two of them approached him, then hesitating, backed away. Somebody was helping Josh to sit up as others crouched around him. Mary still couldn't move; her legs felt like jelly and her head was swimming. Richard took a step towards her, uttering her name. That was enough to unglue her feet and send her hurrying up the hill without a backward glance. She willed herself to keep moving, angrily blinking away the tears that burnt her eyes. She heard someone – it sounded like Angela - jeering at Richard,

"Leave her alone, tosser!" Not wanting to turn to see who it was, or how he had reacted, she carried on, with her head bent to avoid eager faces ready to greet her as she passed by their shops.

Back in the safety of her room, she leant heavily against the door and sank to the floor, every inch of her shaking. Josh's words played over and over in her head; she couldn't unhear them. How could it be true? And yet, she knew it was. The look in Richard's eye spoke volumes, and judging by his reaction, it was clearly something he'd had no intention of telling her about. How could he do that to her? She angrily snatched the bracelet from her wrist and threw it across the room, wanting it as far away from her as possible. It caught the edge of the coffee table and dozens of beads spilled across the carpet. A whimper escaped her lips; she crawled across the floor to scoop them up, then seeing how far they had scattered, let out a defeated sob and gave in to the tears that clogged her throat.

She sat for a long time in the patch of afternoon sun that hit the middle of her room, her tears slowly subsiding and her mind slowly rebooting. Roddy had taken the opportunity to settle on her lap, purring dutifully to ease the distress he could sense in her. The shaking tapered off and numbness took its place. She barely stirred when Bridget knocked on the door, calling her down for dinner. Blaming a migraine, she skipped the meal and curled up in her bed begging for sleep to claim her, to give her a break from the panic that was crowding her brain. But sleep eluded her, so she had to contend with lying in the dark, listening to the street slowly wind down for the night. The last pub-goers scraped their heels against the cobbles, their laughter fading as they made their way home and the street fell silent. Roddy stirred from his spot in the crook of her knee and jumped off the bed, padding into the spare room. Mary heard him meowing at the window, the pitch causing her stomach to twist into tight knots. She knew Richard was there, on the other side of the glass. She had made sure the window was shut tight before she'd gone to bed; he had no way of getting in. She buried her head under the duvet, not wanting to hear the quiet knocking, or the scratching as Roddy tried frantically to dig his way through to his master.

The knocking stopped after a few minutes. She imagined him walking back down the hill, heading home. Would he be angry at not being let in? Frustrated at being found out? Or would he be full of remorse, armed with an explanation? Not that she'd want to hear it; she couldn't bear the thought of hearing anything he had to say. She felt completely betrayed and completely trapped. And yet, it irked her that he hadn't been more persistent with trying to get her attention at the window. Punching her pillow into shape, she pushed her face into it, trying to muffle the sound of her tears. Roddy didn't return to keep her legs warm, he stayed on the window sill, staring out into the dark. Mary had forgotten what it was like to have her bed to herself. The sheets, usually crumpled and warm, felt like smooth, icy steel against her skin. Cold and empty, and without the warmth of Richard's body, it felt like a different bed.

Another hour slowly passed before she finally drifted off, only to be woken again by Roddy's scratching and persistent meowing, followed by a knocking. She heard Richard rasp her name against the window. He sounded desperate, defeated.

A smile crossed her face; he hadn't given up on her after all. She lay listening to his knocking for a little while, then pulling the duvet tightly around her, fell asleep, strangely comforted by the knowledge that he was just outside.

Grimacing at the pain in her head, Mary fumbled with the snooze button on her alarm. Sleep had briefly allowed her to forget the previous day but reality hit the minute she opened her puffy eyes. Her lips felt swollen and sore, and the skin on her face was taut from tears. Bridget couldn't hide her surprise when she came in with Mary's morning tea.

"You look awful," she frowned, holding a cool hand against her brow. "What's brought this on, do you think?"

Shrugging, Mary forced herself to drink the tea and attempt a smile. Despite Bridget's protests, she insisted on going to work, wearily getting into the shower as soon as she was left alone. She didn't doubt that Richard would try to see her later in the day; he may even be waiting for her when she finished work. He did that sometimes. What she didn't expect, was to find him waiting in the archway by her back door as she left for work. Startled, she stopped and stared at him. He was deathly pale from lack of sleep, and she noticed he was still wearing the same clothes from the day before. His eyes were heavy and scared when they met hers.

"Mary," he pleaded, his shoulders hunched, anticipating rejection. She shook her head and hurried past him onto the street. He didn't follow her.

To her relief, she was sent to work upstairs in the Servant's Room, keeping an eye on the exhibits and answering any questions visitors may ask. It was one of the quieter rooms, which suited her perfectly. Ordinarily, she didn't mind talking to visitors but as she listened to her colleagues downstairs chatting and laughing as they greeted people at the front door, she was glad to have escaped upstairs. A prickly sensation crept up the back of her neck making her shiver.

"Somebody just cross your grave?"

Mary laughed lightly, nodding to the middle-aged woman who smiled quizzically at her.

"Probably," she smiled back, then turning, looked out of the window that, ironically, overlooked the graveyard. Richard was there, standing among the horizontal, heavy tombstones, staring up at her. She turned away, her heart starting to race. Unable to resist, she turned back to the window but he was gone. Moving closer, she scoured the graveyard to no avail; he had vanished.

Minutes later, she heard familiar footsteps on the stairs. He stood in the doorway, silently pleading with her. The woman smiled and nodded a greeting to him as he stepped aside to let her through. Mary watched her cross the landing to the next room, before turning to Richard, not quite making eye contact.

"What are you doing here? How did you get in?" she whispered urgently.

"Through the front door."

She looked surprised.

"But .. you have to pay!"

He nodded.

"I know; I did." He moved towards her, frowning when she backed away.

"Mary, I have to see you. I have to talk to you." His insistence was edged with tiredness and desperation. She refused to look at him, fixing her eyes on the door frame behind him instead.

"I don't want to hear it," she dismissed him quickly.

"Yes, you do," he snapped, then trying to calm himself, sighed heavily. He moved into her eyeline, determined for her to look at him but she didn't give in.

"Please, Mary." His voice cracked, his shoulders slumped and he pushed his hands deeper into his trouser pockets. A couple wandered in, smiled and quietly read the information cards on the wall. Richard crossed over to the window and leant against the old, cast iron radiator, watching Mary chat brightly to the couple. Once they had left, she glared at him.

"Leave me alone! I can't believe I trusted you. I let you sweep me off my feet and then you betrayed me. We've got nothing to talk about," she hissed, her eyes flashing angrily. He straightened up, growing very still. He looked pointedly at her stomach.

"You're carrying my child. We've got plenty to talk about," he countered.

"Yes, *I'm* carrying it; not you." She swallowed nervously when his eyes darkened but she refused to budge. He crossed to an antique spindle back chair in the corner, pulled it towards the doorway to block it, and sat down. Mary's mouth dropped open in dismay.

"You can't sit there!" She knew that any minute now somebody would try to come in, and she couldn't be sure of how Richard would behave.

"Richard!" she urged in a strangulated tone. He fixed her with a cold stare.

"I'm not moving until you agree to listen to what I've got to say." His earlier vulnerable face was now stony and dangerous. She conceded, nodding.

"Okay. Meet me outside when I finish."

"No, meet me in the field round the back," he instructed, standing up. She nodded quickly, breathing a sigh of relief when he put the chair back and left the room without a second glance at her.

As it was, she was allowed to leave fifteen minutes early. The afternoon sun warmed her face as soon as she stepped outside. She hesitated; a part of her wanted to turn right and head home but another part of her knew she had to face Richard. It was easier to hate him when she was alone in her room but just seeing him earlier undid all that. She knew she could never hate him. But she was certainly going to make him realise how much he had hurt her. With a determined sigh, she turned left and headed for the field.

Richard was already there on the other side of the long, dry stone wall, waiting. He jumped up from the ground when she approached, and sticking his hands in his pockets, nodded at her.

"Thanks," he mumbled.

"What for?" She tried to sound aloof but her words came out as a hoarse croak.

"For coming. I know you don't want to see me." He squinted at her, hoping she would tell him otherwise but all he could see was anger in her eyes.

"Shall we walk?" he suggested, nodding towards the path. She shook her head, deciding to get straight to the point.

"Was she like me? Was she a virgin?"

He shrugged, looking past her. Infuriated, she snapped, "Don't shrug at me! Was she?"

Taken aback by her aggression, he nodded.

"Yeah, she was."

Mary stared at him, her mind racing. She had already known the answer but had to hear him confess it. She let out an unsteady breath, trying to keep it together.

"So this is it then. You've got me pregnant too. Now what? Move on to the next one?"

157

"No! Don't be stupid. That was in the past; *you're* my future!" He matched her defiant stare.

"Don't count on it," she retorted. "You have a lot of explaining to do."

"I know." He hung his head, not sure what to say next. She watched him dislodge embedded stones from the path with his foot before kicking them into the rough grass. The silence grew unbearable, each waiting for the other to speak. Mary finally broke the silence.

"Why didn't you tell me?"

"Why would I? It's not something I'm proud of or want to remember." His dismissive tone infuriated her. She needed him to open up, to be honest with her. Surely he could see that the only way they could move forward was to talk this out; so why wasn't he?

"What else have you done that you haven't told me about?"

"So much." He glanced at her then looked away across the moor. She breathed a heartfelt sigh.

"You have to tell me. I need to know everything."

"Why?" He flashed her a look of frustration. She held her hands out, shaking her head in despair.

"Because. That's why. Because I need to be able to trust you and right now, I don't. I don't know anything about you, clearly, and I thought I did. So tell me. Help me to understand what's happening here. Please." She choked on her last words. He sighed and leant against the wall, lifting his head up to the sun while deliberating his words.

"I used to steal money for fags, for weed. When there was no money to steal, I'd just steal the fags from the shop. I stole things to sell. I smashed things; vandalised fences, walls. Windows. I broke bones, I hurt people. I was always fighting and I always won. I smashed car lights, car windows. I stole

158

cars, drove them too fast and smashed them up. I torched a couple." He reeled off the list, pausing to glance at her reaction. Her eyes were wide but she didn't flinch or make any comment.

"That's when my uncle stepped in. He gave me a paid job at his garage and said, 'you can vandalise as many walls as you like but don't you ever total a car, *ever* again'." He let out a derisive laugh at the memory. Reaching for his cigarettes, he stopped himself, glancing at her. She gave him a weak smile.

"You can smoke. It's okay." She stroked the side of her stomach. He shook his head, sniffing, then stared at her defiantly.

"Now, why would I be proud of any of that? I did it because I was angry, not because I wanted to build a reputation. I was so *angry*! Why would I tell you any of that? That wouldn't impress you; and if it did, then I wouldn't have gone for you in the first place. You wouldn't be what I was looking for."

They held eye contact for a long time, both slowly calming down, both digesting what he had just confessed to. She joined him in leaning against the wall, inches away from him.

"How did you never get caught?"

He shrugged.

"The stealing was easy, even the cars. I'd ride them around then ditch them. The ones I totalled were my uncle's. He didn't press charges."

Mary was too shocked to say anything. She remembered how he'd told her there was a family feud some years back. His uncle could obviously see that it was a cry for help, for recognition.

"People are so unforgiving, Mary. You make a mistake once and they never let you live it down. They never let you move on. There's no room to grow."

"To be fair, I think you made more than just one mistake," she smiled, reaching for his hand. He grabbed it, turning to her.

"You guide me. You're my star guiding me through all this shite in life. I don't want to be that angry idiot but it's always there. Somebody is always ready to remind me, to hold me back. Don't be like them. Don't judge me on what I did. Judge me on what I do *now*; who I am *now*." He looked at her with earnest eyes, waiting. She took his other hand, nodding slowly.

"I ..." she paused, swallowing hard. "I want to see you for who you are now but ... but what really hurts is finding out that this," she let go of his hand and clutched her swollen stomach, "this isn't new for you. You've been a dad before. You've had these feelings before. I thought this was our moment, our first baby. You and me, creating a life."

"It is!" he insisted, interrupting her. She shook her head.

"You told me that you'd fallen for me and that had never happened before."

"Yeah," he sniffed.

"But you got another girl pregnant!"

"I didn't feel anything for her. I didn't love her. I didn't even know she was pregnant until she'd been sent away to get rid of it and her dad came, threatening me with the police."

Mary blinked.

"So, you were just using her?" she uttered.

"Yes." He defied her to argue. She gasped at his bluntness.

"Yes. I wanted to ruin her. I wanted to ruin her family." He was growing angry again, not liking that she was continuing to question him.

"Did you mean to get her pregnant?"

"No. I didn't mean to but I didn't care that I had," he snapped.

"But she was fourteen!"

"So? Look, I was angry then. I hated everything and everyone. I wanted to destroy Josh and his perfect family – the lot of them – like they had destroyed mine." He turned away, swearing, kicking at the path. Mary watched him, not sure what to say next. She had one question left, one burning question. She led up to it.

"Are you using me?"

He turned abruptly, dismayed.

"No!"

She nodded, seeing he wasn't lying.

"Did you mean to get *me* pregnant?" There it was; the burning question. He looked away.

"Richard, did you mean to get me pregnant?" Her voice rose with panic as she realised the truth. He nodded, squinting at her.

"Yes."

"But why?" Her throat felt constricted and her heart was pounding in her ears.

"So that you'd stay," he mumbled.

"Here?"

"No. With me."

He was making no sense to her. She held her head in her hands, her mind running wild.

"I don't understand. Surely you knew I would stay with you anyway. I thought we were planning a future together. When in your head did you think, 'oh, I must get her pregnant before she runs off'?"

He sighed, knowing he couldn't hide from it any longer. He wanted an end to all the questions.

"You're eighteenth birthday party. That night, I saw you with Josh and I realised … I panicked … I had this vision…"

"What of?" Mary was listening intently now, things were starting to make sense to her.

"Of the future. Of you with somebody else. And I realised that ..." he paused, carefully choosing his words. "That I'd taught you about ..." He looked at her, pained by his own doubt. He reached out to touch her face. She leant towards his hand, pressing her cheek against it.

"You're beautiful, Mary. You know what you're doing and you could have any blonde haired, blue eyed bastard you want."

An involuntary smile lit her face.

"I could, but I only go for *black* haired, blue eyed bastards," she joked. He smiled briefly at her teasing, cupping her face with his hand, pulling her closer towards him. He stared into her eyes, sensing her forgiveness; her anger gone, nothing but warmth and love radiated from them. He gently kissed her lips. She responded by wrapping her arms around him, grabbing hold of his t-shirt, not wanting to let him go.

"I'm sorry, I'm so sorry," he murmured, barely audible through his remorse. Mary stroked his face, shaking her head.

"You look so tired," she remarked softly. He shrugged.

"I was out all night waiting for you."

"You mean, you didn't go home at all?"

He shook his head.

"I couldn't leave. I wanted to be near you, I wanted to see you first thing."

"I'm sorry too," she said quietly. "I should've trusted you more. I should've let you in to talk last night."

He shook his head again. He looked at her for a long time, letting the silence envelope them.

"I was scared last night, Mary. Nothing good in my life stays. I idolised my dad. And then he left. It took me ages to come to terms with that, and then he died. I lost him all over again.

My mum … it broke her when he left. But instead of focusing on me and the future, she chose to blot life out. Blot me out. She may as well have left too; she did in a way. I feel so cheated, so robbed of good things, of solid things. Something I can rely on. And then I met you."

Completely mesmerised, she couldn't tear her eyes away from his. They had never seemed so intensely blue, so open and honest. She felt like she had at long last unlocked the final key to him. He had laid himself bare and she loved him all the more for it.

"I can't lose you, Mary," he whispered.

"You won't. You're stuck with me – with us – forever." She placed his hand on her bump, smiling up at him.

"Now I have to go and make my peace with Roddy," she grimaced. Richard frowned.

"Why, what did you do?"

"He was so put out that I wouldn't let you in last night, he ignored me completely!"

"That's my boy," he chuckled, firmly taking her hand as they walked back towards the gate.

"What time will you be round?"

"The usual. If I'm not there by midnight you'll know I've fallen asleep somewhere," he joked, stretching his aching back. Before they were in view of the parsonage, he pulled her towards him and kissed her passionately.

"See you tonight," he winked as she walked on ahead of him. He stood and watched her, waiting until she was by the church and nearly out of view before following in her footsteps. She turned and gave him a subtle wave, grinning. He nodded, grinning back. They were so wrapped up in each other that neither of them noticed a figure lurking in the shadows of the churchyard, watching them.

Chapter Eleven

Mary woke with a start the next morning when the church bells chimed seven o'clock. She rolled over and stroked the cold pillow next to her, wondering about Richard. He hadn't showed up which was completely out of character for him, but she assumed he had indeed fallen into a deep sleep at home. She had gone to bed exhausted from the previous night's disturbed sleep herself and even slept through her quarter to seven alarm. A quick look at the blue sky behind the curtains brought a satisfied smile to her face. Perfect weather for their usual Sunday walk. She used to worry about bumping into somebody she knew – Kelly mainly – but in all the time they had been escaping to the moors, they hadn't met anybody who knew them. It was such a vast place and they tended to walk off the beaten track, exploring new ground, finding new nooks to lie back and watch the clouds from. Richard had been right; they certainly would miss the moors when they moved to York.

The thought of York kept her smiling through breakfast and once Donal had set off for a day of golf and his Lodge, she got her things together and hurried out; not before sneaking a couple of chocolate chip muffins into her bag. Hurrying along the familiar path through the churchyard and up to Dimples Lane, she spotted a figure halfway along the lane, leaning against one of the tall trees that flanked the path. As she drew nearer, she recognised it was Josh. Slowing down, she wondered if it was too late to turn round and head back without being too obvious. He made the decision for her.

"Alright, Mary! Where are you off to?" He walked slowly towards her, limping slightly. As she drew level, she could see the extent of damage done to his face by Richard. His eye was puffy and bruised, his nose swollen and he had a dark swelling on his temple where a scab was forming. There was a gap in his teeth where one of the bottom incisors had been lost, and his lip was split and still speckled with blood. She eyed him nervously, not knowing whether to remark on his injuries or just ignore them. She opted to ignore them.

"I'm going for a walk, that's all," she replied, slowing her pace but not wanting to stop. He stood in front of her forcing her to stand still. He ran his tongue along his split lip, watching her.

"He's not up there."

She tried not to show her surprise at his statement.

"Who?"

"Dickhead White," he snorted. She shrugged her shoulders.

"So?"

"So," he nodded. "He's hung over somewhere. I saw him in the park last night, off his face. So drunk." He raised his eyebrows waiting for her response. She kept her voice level.

"He doesn't drink."

Josh snorted again, shaking his head.

"Well he did last night. And he was shagging some girl in the bushes. I didn't recognise her but that's him all over – shags anything." He looked pointedly at her, hardly able to contain his disgust. She bent her head and made to walk on but he blocked her again.

"No, wait, I want to talk to you."

"What about?" She was itching to get away but he made her nervous.

"Oh, y'know, this and that." He glanced at his watch, then proceeded with small talk about exams and their teachers.

"So, Kelly's your best mate, yeah?"

Surprised, she nodded. He nodded with her.

"Yeah, she's a good girl that one. Does what she's told," he winked. Mary cringed inside. She made to move again but again, he stopped her, grinning.

"So about your birthday party. I know we didn't ..." he clicked his tongue twice, "But I thought, well she doesn't know what to do. Y'know, being a virgin." He gauged her reaction, enjoying seeing her squirm. He took a step closer and bent his head towards her.

"I thought I'd be doing you a favour. That was the plan. But ... you *do* know what you're doing, don't you?"

Her eyes flew up to his.

"What?" she barely breathed. His eyes narrowed, his smile gone.

"How come you put out for that skank but you didn't for me?" he spat angrily. She flinched.

"What are you talking about?" she tried to bluff.

"I've seen you. With him. I saw you yesterday."

She shook her head.

"Don't deny it! I watched you in the field, with him." He ran his tongue around his mouth and spat on the ground, staring at his saliva, deliberating his next move. He sighed, feigning pity as he eyed her, then rubbed his cheek, gingerly feeling the bruise on his jaw bone.

"Thing is, he's not allowed to have a girlfriend; not since he knocked up my cousin. His granddad wasn't impressed when I told him about you."

Mary stared at him, fear quickly creeping over her. Josh smirked seeing the look in her eye.

"He was livid. So angry. And I know for a fact that first thing he planned to do this morning, was go see your dad. I bet he won't be pleased either." He looked pointedly at his watch, drawing in breath through his teeth. "Yeah, I wouldn't want to be you right now. Should've stuck with me, love. Not that wanker." His derisive laughter coupled with a growing concern for Richard's safety made her snap. She squared up to him.

"You know what your problem is? You're just jealous!"

"Of him?" he scorned.

"Yes, of him. He's a hundred times better than you, and you know it. And if his dad was anything like Richard, no wonder your mam chose him. She chose *him* over you. Your own mother chose *him*. She only came back because he died. That's the only reason." She spat her words angrily, not caring if they hurt, her thick accent becoming more pronounced with rage. He swore loudly at her, raising his hand, wanting to punch her. She turned smartly on her heel and marched back down the lane. Josh shouted angrily at her back.

"He's a dead man walking. You tell him I'm waiting! I'll make him pay." He carried on cursing and shouting until she was out of earshot.

Heading back towards the church, she tried frantically to think where Richard would be. She knew Josh was lying about him being drunk in the park with a girl but if he was telling the truth about the rest of it, she doubted very much that Richard had spent the night in a peaceful sleep. Deciding he would go to his uncle's if there had been any trouble, she headed that way. As she cut through the churchyard, she saw him coming round the far side of the church, head bent as he hurried along, unseeing, towards her. She called to him, emitting a horrified gasp when she saw his face.

"Oh, holy God, what happened?" she choked. He hung his head, not wanting to look at her. She gently lifted his chin, holding back tears as she took in his injuries. One eye was almost closed over and the skin around it a dark shade of red and blue. There was a cut on his cheekbone just below the swelling, and another an inch below it. They looked like they'd been inflicted by something metal; she guessed at a ring. His ear was swollen and bruised too and there was further red bruising along his jaw line and chin. His lip had split open in the corner and the wide gash was still wet with blood. At a complete loss for words, she just stood and silently held him, feeling him sink into her.

"I was looking for you," he said quietly.

"I was looking for you too. Where were you? What happened?" She matched his quiet tone, not wanting to upset him or show how distressing it was to see him like that. He took a while to answer.

"You can't go home, Mary. Somebody told my granddad about us."

"Did he do this to you?"

He nodded.

"I just have to take it, y'know. If I hit him back, I'd kill him. I wish I could just kill him," he muttered. He shot her a quizzical look. "You're not surprised. You knew, didn't you?"

She nodded and briefly told him about Josh. His face twisted with rage and he started pacing up and down, swearing. She tried to placate him and taking his hand, led him to the back of the churchyard amongst the ancient tombstones where they were out of sight. She sat down on an old tree stump, watching him pace, kicking at the tree roots.

"Where were you last night? Why didn't you come to me?"

"I was so mad. When I'm that mad I'm best left well alone. I slept in Kelly's dad's shed for a bit. My granddad's kicked me out and even if he hadn't, there's no way I'm ever going back there. He can go to hell!" He stopped pacing, his mind flitting. He was trying to think practically.

"We have to leave today. If he does see your dad, you can't possibly go home. You know that, right?"

Mary nodded. She'd already determined that in her head. She checked her watch. She'd seen Donal leave for golf and she knew he wouldn't be home until around four in the afternoon. It was only just after ten. They hastily drew up a plan. Richard's uncle would be out of the house by midday; that's when they could take his car to leave. Against his better judgment, Richard agreed to Mary going home to fetch Roddy and her bank card.

"It'll be fine, he's not there," she assured him. "And we can't leave without Roddy."

They had no idea of where they would go other than to York, and find somewhere to stay for two weeks before their flat was ready for them to move in to.

"Wait here. I'll be as quick as I can." She gingerly kissed the side of his mouth, avoiding his cut lip, and swiftly walked the short distance home.

Peeking in through the café window undetected, she could see two of the staff, Marie and Gemma; Hannah had phoned in sick, so Mary knew that Bridget would be busy in the back to make up for being short-staffed. She quietly let herself in through the back door and climbed the stairs, two at a time, coming to an abrupt halt on the last step. Bridget was standing in the kitchen doorway, ashen. Donal appeared from behind her and ordering her to move aside, silently indicated for Mary to join them in the kitchen. His glacial expression bore through her as she walked past him into the room. He closed the door firmly behind them. Not wanting to give him the satisfaction of seeing how shaky she was, she sat down on one of the cold, kitchen chairs and tried to subtly regulate her breathing. She could see the tell-tale red spots on his cheeks of barely-contained fury. Closing her eyes for a second, she wished she had listened to Richard. She knew this wasn't going to end well. Pulling at her loose t-shirt so it didn't cling

169

to her stomach, she steeled herself to meet her father's accusing face.

"I was on my way to play golf this morning when I was flagged down by Ted Swales." His tone was slow and calculated. "Do you know Ted Swales?"

Mary shook her head.

"But you know his grandson, Richard White."

"Yes," she nodded, her steady gaze unwavering. It seemed to infuriate him.

"Ted Swales tells me you have been seeing his grandson." He leant his face towards hers, piercing eyes defying her to lie. "Is this true?"

"Yes. You know he's been helping me with maths and science. You know that because Mr Nelson told you. Months ago!" Surprised at her own courage, she let out an exasperated noise, a cross between a strangled laugh and frustrated snort. He stepped back, incensed by her response but determined to keep the upper hand.

"I see. I thought that arrangement was just for school. Where else have you been studying?"

Trying to think on her feet, she stumbled over her reply.

"Nowhere, it's just … we live in the same village. I can't just ignore him out of school, can I?"

Donal turned away to stare out of the kitchen window. Mary shot a look at Bridget, who gave her a concerned half-smile. Still staring at the distant view, he fired his next question at her.

"So, who's been smoking in your room?"

Her stomach plummeted.

"What?" she stammered. He swung round.

"Who has been smoking in your room, Mary? I found cigarette ends on the flat roof underneath your window. How did they get there?"

Her mind racing, she tried diversion tactics, annoyed.

"Have you been in my room?"

Donal's eyes widened at her reproach.

"Yes, I've been in your room! This is my house and I demand to know what goes on in it. So," he straightened up, squaring his shoulders, "Who has been smoking up there?"

Her head started to spin. She clenched her clammy hands together on her lap. Bridget stepped forward, her tone insistent.

"Mary, you have to own up. Have you been smoking out of your window?"

Swallowing hard, she nodded and hung her head.

"Why?" Bridget pleaded. Mary looked up at her, seeing her disappointment.

"Everybody does it, Mam."

"You mean, Richard White does it!" Donal interjected.

"No, I mean *everybody* does it," she replied steadily. He pointed an accusing finger at her, millimetres away from her nose.

"*He* has had a bad influence on you. I knew this would happen. You are not to see him again, and if you say you cannot avoid him because he lives in the same village, then you will not be allowed out any more. You will not be seeing *anybody*."

"But Donal, he was only helping her with maths," Bridget defended. "You can't stop her from …"

"Do not tell me what I can and cannot do, Bridget!" he snapped. "I do not *care* about her maths. I do not *care* if she fails." He turned to Mary. "In fact, I hope you do fail. Put an end to this nonsense now." The tip of his nose had turned white, his piercing eyes like granite. That look used to scare her but for some reason, she was ignoring all the warning signs.

171

"What nonsense?" She scowled, shooting a questioning look at Bridget. He snorted, mocking her.

"This ridiculous notion of going to university. Your mother did not go to university and look at her; running her own business. A business we expected *you* to continue." He smirked at her stunned face. "You cannot possibly expect to survive in the world with your attitude, Mary. You know nothing."

Reeling from the turn of events, she realised this wasn't about Richard; this was about her wanting to make something of her life. Her wanting to be independent. To no longer be controlled by him. She saw red.

"What, so I'm expected to stay here – with you two – and serve cake for the rest of my life?"

"You guard your tongue, young lady!" he snarled. Realisation dawned. She looked from Donal to Bridget, stunned at how naive she'd been.

"Is this why you made me take maths and science? Because you knew I'd fail? Well, you can go to hell!"

With lightning reflex, Donal slapped her face with such a force that her head flew back.

"How dare you swear at your mother like that. Apologise this instant!"

Suppressing the instinct to clutch her smarting face, she glared at him.

"I was swearing at you, you stupid bastard!"

He lunged at her, grabbing her arm just below her shoulder, his bony thumb digging into her arm pit, and hauled her up from the chair.

"Donal, don't, " Bridget uttered, too fearful to move.

"Stay out of this, Bridget. You have made her soft and this is the thanks you get. I warned you." He frog-marched Mary out of the room and pushed her roughly towards the stairs. She could feel how he shook with a violent fury.

"Get up to your room!" he barked. She steadied herself with her hands on the stairs as she stumbled up them. He pushed her into her room and slammed the door shut behind him. She was aching to rub her arm where his fingers had dug into her skin but refused to give him the satisfaction of seeing her pain.

"Turn your back and face the wall," he ordered. Mary did as she was told.

"Hands up!" He waited for her to respond, his breathing quickening when she didn't comply. He pushed her roughly against the wall, bellowing at the back of her head.

"I said, hands up!"

She held her hands up, rocking slightly as he pulled her top up, flipping the hem up over her head, covering her face and trapping her arms in the material. She felt him undo her bra and fold the back straps in, to reveal a bare expanse of skin. He reached his hand round and tugged at the button of her jeans, undoing her zip and pulling her jeans and knickers down to her thighs. She heard him unbuckle his belt, her stomach twisting at the familiar sound. Firmly placing his hand on the back of her head, he pressed her face into the wall. She could feel his breath on her neck, as he hissed in her ear,

"You have no-one to blame but yourself."

She swallowed hard, bracing herself. She knew what was coming. She bit down on her lip as the first lash cut into her back; her back arched, recoiling from the agony. She heard him counting under his breath,

"One ... two ... three." And another lash. He always counted to three. He was always methodical, always controlled, when dishing out his punishment.

'He will not make me cry. He will not make me cry,' she chanted in her head, focusing on her words to block out the agony. By the sixth and final lash, her shaking body was begging to slump to the floor but she fought against it. She refused to let him see her weakness. She knew it frustrated him beyond belief when she didn't shed a tear or beg for mercy; it probably spurred him on to beat her more but she couldn't let him win. She used to, and he ridiculed her for it. That was almost more painful than the whipping. Not letting him see her cry was the only bit of control she had over him. That thought helped her to cope.

Donal stepped away, his breathing laboured from his exertion. She could hear him wipe the blood from his belt with his handkerchief before feeding it back through his trouser loops and doing up the buckle. She could feel him staring at her, she could sense his cold contempt. He reached forward and pulled her top back down, grazing her raw skin. She tried not to flinch.

"I can see why you're worried about serving cake for the rest of your life; you're getting fat, Mary." He left the room, pulling the door firmly shut behind him. She heard him turn the key in the lock. Letting out a strangled sob she hobbled to her bed and lay face down, bunching her duvet up like a nest to bury her head in and cry.

It was some time before she found the strength to move and when she did, she cried out in pain. The blood on her back had dried, the split skin starting to harden, and moving only served to aggravate it. The caked blood cracked and pulled on the tiny hairs; the sensation not unlike ripping a plaster off. Mary gingerly eased her clothes off and slowly crossed to her wardrobe in the back room. She pulled out her loosest fitting summer dress - a yellow cotton t-shirt dress -

that barely touched her skin. Wincing as she did her bra up on the loosest hook, she studied her reflection in the mirror. She looked decidedly pregnant in the shapeless dress. Remembering an old pair of elasticated, cotton jersey shorts, she tried those on along with a sleeveless, mint coloured, swing top. The fabric and cut was not too painful on her skin, unlike the jeans she had been wearing earlier. Her old blue, fisherman's rib, handknitted cardigan lessened the bump; she would just have to tolerate its weight across her shoulders.

Peering through the keyhole, she could see that the key hadn't been twisted round; it should be easy to push out. Sliding a piece of paper under the door, she poked at the key with a thin pencil until it thudded to the floor. She then carefully pulled the paper back towards her at the same time as pressing the carpet fibres flat with her hand. The key wasn't on the paper; it must've bounced off as it landed. Grunting with frustration, she knew her only other option of escape was through the window. Richard made it look so easy but then again, he was adept at climbing. And he wasn't four months pregnant. Mary picked Roddy up from her bed and squeezed him, burying her face into his fur.

"I'm sorry, my baby, you'll have to wait here. I'll be back in a bit for you. I promise." With that, she put him back on her bed and shut the door between the two rooms so he couldn't follow her. Throwing her bag out first, she eased herself out of the window, ungainly dropping to the flat roof below. She could hear Roddy scratching at the door, his plaintive meowing becoming frantic. Pausing to catch her breath and allow the searing pain across her back to subside a little, she nervously eyed the next drop to the ground below. There was no way she could do it. Looking round for something to hold on to, she spied the drainpipe running down the side of the wall and realised that must be how Richard climbed up.

175

Testing its stability, she took her life in her hands and clumsily slid down, banging her knees and scraping her arms in the process. She squatted on the ground, steeling herself to crawl past the café kitchen window. It was open, and sounds of crockery and chatter wafted through. It had been her intention to let herself in through the back door, retrieve the key to unlock her room and fetch Roddy, but a sudden clatter from the kitchen startled her and she ran through the archway towards the church steps as if her life depended on it. She didn't stop running until she was in amongst the tombstones and out of sight from the street.

"Where the hell have you been? I've been worried sick – it's nearly midday!" Richard grabbed her shoulders, relieved to see her. A high pitched howl escaped her lips and she crumpled to the ground, every inch of her shaking from spent adrenaline. His instinct was to pull her up and hold her tight. She whimpered, moving away.

"Please … don't touch me."

"What's happened?" he demanded, dropping his hands from her. "Mary? What's happened?"

She shook her head, not able to speak for a moment. She could sense him growing impatient.

"My dad was there."

He swore angrily, cursing himself for letting her go home. "And?"

"And your granddad had spoken to him."

"What did he say? Why were you so long?"

Mary faltered, not able to look at him.

"He locked me in my room. I had to climb out of the window." She tried to laugh but it caught in her throat.

"Did you hurt yourself?" He gently held her arms, seeing the grazed skin where her elbows had caught the stone wall. She shook her head. His eyes narrowed.

"What then?" Waiting for a response, he brushed her fringe back from her face and froze.

"What the hell's happened to your face? You've got a bump on your forehead." He pulled her chin up, forcing her to look at him. "Did he do that?"

She nodded.

"Your dad hurt you?" he repeated. Being hurt by his granddad was second nature to him but he seemed to be struggling with the concept of Mary's father hurting his own daughter. Seeing the doubt in his eyes, she turned her back to him and carefully lifted her top, exposing her back. She expected him to swear but instead he was deathly silent. She looked at him over her shoulder. He was staring in horror at where the thick leather had lacerated her soft skin, and at the angry, red welts where the belt hadn't quite cut through. He couldn't tear his eyes away. She let her top fall back down and turned to him, wanting him to say something, anything, but he just stared at her, completely dumb struck. She saw that look again - that vulnerable child within him – and felt guilty.

"It's alright, it's not that bad. I've had worse," she tried to dismiss.

"He's done this before?" His voice was barely audible. She nodded.

"In a couple of days, it'll sting like sunburn but I'll be fine."

Astounded by her courage, he turned her around and lifted her top to look at her back again. He gently traced faint scars across her shoulders from old wounds.

"How come I've never noticed these marks before?" His voice cracked.

"Probably because you're too busy looking at my boobs," she tried to joke, turning back to him. Her smile faded at the look on his face; a look of absolute despair at the thought of

177

her enduring such a beating. He gave her a long, searching look, trying to digest what had just happened, and what had clearly happened to her many times before. His features hardened as despair turned to anger to white rage, his eyes glinting dangerously and body tensing.

"I'm going to kill them! Your dad. My granddad. Josh. I'm going to kill the lot of them!"

"No, leave it. It's done. Just take me away from here," she pleaded. "We've got the money; let's just leave now. If my dad finds out about the baby, I'm scared he will actually kill me." She tried to reason with him. "Please, Richard."

"They've got to pay for this, Mary. They've got to!"

"Why? Why give them the satisfaction of showing them how they've hurt us? Let's just get to York and start a new life." She gripped his shoulders, willing him to listen. He frowned, glaring into the distance, sighing heavily.

"Okay but the minute we get to York, we're getting married. That way your dad can never touch you again. He'd have to go through me and I will never let that happen, trust me."

She stared at him, reeling from his words, his cack-handed proposal.

"What?"

He sniffed, giving a derisive laugh when he realised what he'd just said.

"Yeah, not quite how I'd planned it, sorry." His eyes scoured the ground by his feet. He grabbed a piece of rye grass and, pulling it through his fingers to dislodge the seeds, twisted the stem into a loop.

"Will you marry me, Mary?" He offered her the makeshift ring with an awkward smile. She stuck her left hand out, splaying her fingers for him to put it on, grinning at him.

"Of course I will! You even have to ask?"

He slid the ring on her finger; it was far too big and oozed a little sap where his nails had scored it, but she held it up to admire it as if it were a sparkling diamond sitting on a band of gold.

"I'll look after you, Mary, I promise."

"I know you will, and I'll look after you too," she smiled, twizzling the green stalk ring as she spoke.

"I don't need you to …"

"Yes, you do," she interrupted. She touched his bruised face, smiling at his defensive frown. "Yes, you do. I'll look after you for the rest of my life and I know you'll do the same for me."

He nodded, knowing there was nothing more to say. Squinting at the church clock, he took a decisive breath.

"Right, it's nearly half past twelve. My uncle will be gone by now so you wait here and I'll go get the car. You stay out of sight until I come back for you. Got it?"

"No, I have to fetch Roddy!" Caught up in the emotion of the moment, she had momentarily forgotten that she'd left him behind.

"You can't go back now!"

"Yes, I can! We can't leave him there, can we!"

"You are not going back there," he stated firmly, then snorted with frustration, trying to think quickly of a solution.

"Is there anybody you know that can fetch him and look after him for a bit?"

"Like Kelly, you mean?" She pulled a face. "I'm sure she knows about us by now, so no. She wouldn't do anything for me, I know that for certain." She could see his anger mounting again as he battled with his conscience. He was as loathe to leave Roddy as she was but he wasn't going to run the risk of either of them bumping into Donal O'Shea.

"How about, erm, what's her name? Works for your mum …
Hannah! How about Hannah?" he suggested. Mary nodded.

"Right, we'll phone her when we get to York. Ask her to
fetch him. Have you got her number?"

"Yes," she lied, watching him nod with relief. He cupped her
face and kissed her, promising to be as quick as he could. She
watched him hurry away and just when he thought he was
out of sight, she heard him kick the metal bin by the
churchyard entrance, and let out a guttural scream of
frustration. Her stomach lurched at the sound but she wasn't
surprised. She could tell he'd been holding it in. She knew he
was beyond angry, beyond reasoning. She had been
impressed by how rationally he had been able to think and
plan their next move. But she knew, deep down, that he was
livid – absolutely fuming - at having his hand forced by Josh.

She waited a few minutes, visualising how far he had got
before she headed swiftly back home. She caught a glimpse
of Bridget in the café as she snuck past the window. Letting
herself in, she crept up the stairs, heart pounding and on high
alert. There was no sign of her father but even so, she didn't
hang around. Retrieving the key, she unlocked her door.
Roddy was asleep on her bunched up duvet. He blinked
sleepily at her as she scooped him up and put him in the
carrier. Grabbing his bowls and food, she stuffed them into a
plastic bag, and the empty litter tray into another. With a final
look around her room, she shut the door behind her, leaving
the key in the lock. She tried not to think of everything she
treasured that she was leaving behind. The only things she
had taken in her bag were the books that Richard had given
her for her birthday. She hoped that one day she could come
back and fetch the rest of it, but she couldn't dwell on that
now.

Roddy meowed as he bumped about in the carrier, peering out anxiously through the slatted sides. Mary knew she couldn't take him with them now; if she did, Richard would feel she had gone against him. She knocked on a door near the bottom of Main Street.

"Mary!" Hannah looked surprised, then seeing the cat carrier, ushered her inside.

"I'm sorry to disturb you – I know you're not well," Mary stammered. "But could you please look after Roddy for a bit?"

Hannah gave her a knowing look.

"Is you dad on the war path?" She didn't like Donal O'Shea, she didn't trust him.

"Yes. It's only for a couple of weeks," Mary said tentatively.

"A couple of … Mary, what's going on?" She placed a maternal hand on her shoulder, pulling back when Mary flinched. Her heart broke a little and she nodded.

"Of course. As long as you want. He'll be fine with me."

Swallowing the lump in her throat, Mary put Roddy down and turned to the door.

"Mary, are you running away?"

Not trusting herself to look at Hannah's concerned face, she bent and whispered 'goodbye' to Roddy.

"Thank you, Hannah," she mumbled and bolted out of the door, hurrying back up to the church.

The bell chimed quarter past one and there was still no sign of Richard. Exhausted and hungry, Mary ate one of the muffins intended for their walk. It seemed like days ago that she had woken in high spirits and planned their sunny walk; not just a few hours. Her life had been turned upside down so abruptly and she wondered what they would do next; where would they sleep that night, or for the next two weeks? She

181

let her mind wander, not able to think clearly, as she waited for Richard. The bell chimed half past. He'd been gone an hour. The walk to his uncle's would've only taken ten minutes at best, so where was he? A cold shiver went down her spine, not unlike the previous day and she stood up abruptly. A sudden flash of her father's face gripped her with panic. What if he had intercepted Richard? What if Richard was trapped at his uncle's by him? What if Donal was 'teaching him a lesson'? She didn't have Gary's number so she couldn't even go to the phone box and call to see if Richard was okay. Not stopping to consider her own safety, should her father be there, she headed for Gary's house. She avoided the café by taking one of the back alleyways but stuck to the route she thought Richard would take, just in case he'd been delayed and was in fact on his way to her.

A small crowd were gathered by the top of the street that ran on from Main Street; four women and a teenage girl, all with their arms folded and all with concerned expressions. Spying her, one of the women crossed over to her.

"Excuse me, love. Mary, isn't it? You haven't seen Jodie have you?"

"Jodie?" Mary looked at the other women, recognising one of them but couldn't quite place her.

"Yeah, Jodie Higgins."

Mary shook her head, none the wiser.

"No, sorry. What's happened?"

"She had a sleep over last night at our house and left nearly an hour ago. She only lives up the road, y'know," she stressed, pointing in the direction that Mary was headed. She went cold.

"Higgins?"

"Yeah, love. You know her brother, Josh, don't you. She's only nine, a little dot. Looks a bit like Josh. That's her mum."

She pointed to the blonde woman Mary had recognised. "Sure you haven't seen her?"

Mary shook her head, her mind racing.

"No, no, sorry. But I'm going that way so I'll keep my eye out for her. Have you tried the park?"

The woman shook her head, crossing the road again to where the others were knocking on doors, asking for help.

"Gail, let's try the park. You lot, carry on knocking on doors."

Mary stole a look at Gail Higgins. Always immaculately dressed and made up, and always looking younger than her years, she was now drawn and pale, eyes wide and frightened. Mary felt sick. She had a bad feeling in the pit of her stomach.

The blue Rover was parked down the side by Gary's house. Mary went round to the back door, the same way as she had before with Richard. She knocked and waited. There was no reply. She knocked again and peered in through the frosted glass pane. She tried the door handle; it was locked. She knocked again and called Richard's name. Eventually, he came to the door.

"What are you doing here? I said, *wait* by the church." His tone was urgent yet he looked annoyed with her. "Mary, you have to leave. Now."

"But …"

"You shouldn't be here. Did anybody see you?" He was ashen, more so than earlier.

"Is that blood on your shirt?" She stared at the red smudge on his chest.

"Yeah, I cut my hand. Wiped it on my shirt," he shrugged. He was being evasive and she couldn't understand why.

"The car's outside; is your uncle here?"

He shook his head.

"Then let's go," she urged, pushing the door open to encourage him to leave. She caught sight of a pink backpack by the side of the door.

"Whose is that?"

"Nobody's." He looked as if he wanted to shut the door on her but he didn't move.

"Richard?"

"You shouldn't be here, Mary."

She stood still, her feet like lead, staring at his shifty expression.

"Oh God, you've got her here, haven't you? You've got Jodie!"

He pushed her away from the door, following her outside.

"I don't want you here. You can't touch anything. You can't …" The desperation in his voice made her blood run cold.

"What have you done?" she breathed.

"Nothing."

"Richard, is she here? Please, tell me!"

He closed his eyes and nodded, his shoulders dropping in defeat.

"What have you done?" she reiterated. He kept his eyes shut, taking in a shaky breath.

"I was driving to the church when I saw her walking up the street. I thought … I just saw red. I wanted to scare them. I thought if she went missing, just for a couple of hours …"

Mary licked her lips nervously. She could see he was teetering between remorse and red hot rage. She needed to tread carefully.

"Okay, well … her mum is frantic, so you've done it; you've scared them. Just let her go and we can leave before the police start looking for her." She touched his arm, trying to gain eye contact. He opened his eyes, fear pouring out.

"She's dead."

184

Chapter Twelve

"Did you hear me?" Richard stared at her, waiting for a response. She nodded, staring back wildly. She was nodding but her brain was refusing to compute the information.

"I don't understand. How can she be dead?"

He looked away, his expression hardening as he swallowed his fear.

"Richard, what … what are you telling me? How is she dead?" She was shaking again and it was an effort to speak but she needed to understand what was going on.

"She just is," he shrugged. That shrug frustrated her; it always frustrated her how he would dismiss things with that shrug.

"So … did you just grab her from the street and … and beat her to death?" Her voice rose, mirroring the panic rising inside her.

"No!" He glared angrily at her.

"Then what? What have you done?"

He growled with frustration, clenching his fists and tensing his whole body before taking a deep breath and exhaling sharply. He looked at her, his eyes challenging.

"I just offered her a lift and she jumped in. I couldn't believe how easy it was. Then I said, 'I've got something for your brother. Let's pick it up before I drop you off'. And she said, 'alright'. So we got here," he gestured to the house, "I took her up to Lizzie's old room and shut her in. I was going to leave her there; let my uncle find her when he got home. But she started to scream and throw things about. I went up and tried to shut her up." He swallowed hard and rubbed his hand across his forehead, swearing under his breath.

"How?"

186

He shook his head. Mary took a step towards the back door, her mind racing.

"Maybe, you're wrong. Maybe she's okay; you just hurt her a bit, that's all."

Richard grabbed her arm pulling her back.

"Aren't you listening to me? She's *dead*, Mary! I killed her! I didn't mean to – I just wanted to shut her up. I put my hand over her mouth and the little cow bit me." He held out his palm, showing a livid bite mark, and pointed to the blood stain on his shirt. "Then she started calling me names, y'know, 'tosser', 'wanker', 'loser'. A little kid like that with such a big mouth. Just like her brother!" He grew more incensed as he re-lived the moment, slapping his temple with his hand.

"Why couldn't she just be scared, just cry. Like a little girl should. She just kept pushing me, y'know. 'Loser, loser, you're a loser', like a football chant. So I grabbed a pillow and covered her face, and pushed really hard until she shut up."

Unable to speak, unable to move, Mary just stared at him in complete shock. She didn't see remorse in his eyes; she saw determination.

"That should've been Josh. Or your dad. My granddad. I'm going to kill them all!" He moved swiftly to the back door and pulled it shut, then headed for the car, snatching up Mary's hand. He opened up the passenger door for her.

"Get in."

She stumbled into her seat, fastening the seatbelt with an unsteady hand. She watched Richard's set expression as he reversed off the drive and roared down the road.

"Where does your dad work?"

Mary stared wide-eyed at him.

"We're not going there! Richard, please! Stop the car."

"He needs to pay for what he did to you. I can't let him get away with it. Tell me where he is, Mary!"

"Stop the car!" she screamed at the top of her voice, grabbing at the wheel. The car swerved across the road, careering down the hill. Richard swiftly gained control of it, narrowly missing a zebra crossing barrier by the park. He pulled sharply into the side road and stopped the car, turning to Mary. He held his hands out in disbelief, his mouth open, waiting for her to explain.

"I can't let you do this, Richard. Please, stop this. Turn the car round and let's just leave for York, like we planned," she pleaded, barely able to support her trembling voice.

"Leave? In case you've forgotten, I just killed a kid. I'm going to prison for a very long time, so I might as well finish the job and make it worth my while. Starting with your dad and ending with Josh."

"Oh, holy God," she whimpered. "You need to stop. You need to stop! We can make this right, it's not too late. We can go to the police and tell them what happened. It was an accident! They'll know that, they will."

He sighed heavily.

"Mary, I have a police record so big, they will never believe me. It's no use." He looked at her, his heightened anger subsiding.

"What about me? What will I do without you?"

He leant over and touched her cheek.

"You'll wait for me. And I'll wait for you." He choked on his words and started to weep. "I'm so sorry," he spluttered, "I'm sorry."

Mary unstrapped and leant across to hold him, hastily devising a plan of action.

"Maybe … maybe my dad can help us," she ventured. Richard frowned at her, quickly wiping his face with his hands, and sniffing repeatedly.

"How? And why would he?"

"Well, he was in the police, so he knows how things work. He could back you up. Despite everything, I think he would see how you've been victimised. He would see it was an accident."

"Seriously?" Richard clearly didn't believe her. She wasn't convinced herself but was trying to placate him, although a small part of her was hoping that, when push came to shove, her father would step up and help them.

"He's been in situations before. From his own experience I think he would understand what happened with you. And her." She couldn't bring herself to say her name out loud. Doing so would make it seem too real and she wasn't sure she would cope with that just yet, and keep Richard calm. They fell silent for a moment.

"Okay," he nodded. "So what do we do now?"

She squeezed his hand.

"We go to the police. Before they start looking fo…"

Just then Richard's car door was pulled open and he was hauled from his seat and slammed against the side of the car.

"Where's my sister?" Josh rasped, his eyes flashing dangerously as he stood nose to nose with Richard. Mary jumped out and rushed to Richard's side. He put his hand out to protect her, telling her to stay back. He squared up to Josh.

"How the hell would I know?"

"Because somebody saw her get in your car."

"Oh, really?" Richard smirked. "Well, whoever told you that, needs their eyes testing. That was Mary getting into my car."

Josh shot her a look; she nodded.

"It was me," she muttered. He snorted.

"You again, Mary. I told you he'd shag anything. Looks like I was right, eh?"

Richard pushed Josh away from him and straightened up.

"Jealous, are you?" he goaded. Josh's eyes narrowed. Richard pointed to his mouth, where his lip was fat and swollen around his missing tooth.

"That looks sore, Josh."

"You don't look great yourself, mate."

"Yeah, well, I owe you one for that and here you are. Back for more." He clenched his fists and stepped forward.

"Yeah, and you're going to wish I wasn't." He grabbed Richard's shoulder with his left hand, pulling him towards him and plunged a knife deep into his chest. Mary let out a guttural scream, catching him as he slumped to the ground. He clutched at her arm, staring at her, a strangled moan escaping his lips.

"What have you done?" she screamed at Josh. He stared at the dark patch spreading rapidly across Richard's shirt, as if somebody had just burst a water balloon on him. Dropping the knife, he turned tail and ran. Mary screamed at the top of her voice for help, cradling Richard in her arms. He was limp and deathly pale, his laboured breath rattling as he tried to draw air. She rocked him, shaking him as she did so.

"Stay with me, Richard. Stay with me." She screamed for help again, looking round frantically for anybody to see them. Somebody came running.

"I need an ambulance! Quickly!"

The stranger took one look at Richard and ran towards the nearest house, banging on the door. Richard grew heavy in her arms, his eyes flickering shut.

"Don't close your eyes, don't you dare close your eyes! Richard, don't leave me," she sobbed, shaking him more urgently. His hand slipped from her arm. She caught it, willing him to hold hers. He didn't respond. She let the lifeless hand fall again and grabbed at his face, clutching his cheek.

"Richard," she begged. "Richard?" She stared at his deathly pallor, waiting for him to draw another breath but he lay motionless on her lap, the dark patch spreading with each second. She rested her head on his, continuing to rock him, cocooning him in her arms.

"It's going to be okay, it's going to be okay. Just don't leave me, don't leave me." She stroked his face, murmuring, repeating the same phrase over and over, "It's going to be okay."

The bright light made her flinch; it aggravated the dull pain in her head. All she wanted to do was lie down. Her body felt so heavy, so numb. She swallowed several times, trying to suppress the bile rising up her throat again. The woman sitting on the chair beside her shot her a sympathetic smile.

"Have a drink; it may help," she encouraged, nodding towards the water bottle on the table in front of them. Mary did as she was told, grimacing as the cold liquid reached her raw throat. She remembered screaming; not so much the blood-curdling sound she emitted, more the feeling behind that scream. She hadn't wanted them to touch him, to prise him from her arms. She had begged, pleaded with them to leave her be. To let her hold him for a moment longer. She knew it would be the last time and she didn't want it to end. She had been clinging on to a tiny, false hope, that a miracle would happen. That the paramedics would spring into action and work wonders, bringing him back to life, instead of crouching beside him acknowledging their help was not needed. She had resisted as the policewomen – one of which was still by her side – had led her away, reeling off trite words of comfort and encouragement. But most of all, she had

191

regretted turning back for a final look and seeing the moment when they covered his body; like someone putting a towel over a spillage on the carpet. That was when the blood-curdling scream had reached its climax; she had screamed until her throat bled and vomit came out of her nose.

"Sorry to keep you waiting."

Mary looked up briefly at the man as he re-entered the room but didn't acknowledge his apology. He quietly put his notes on the table and sat down opposite her, eyeing her thoughtfully.

"We've picked Josh Higgins up. He's being brought in for questioning."

Mary nodded.

"And the little girl?" she whispered.

"Yes, my officers are there now."

She nodded again, clenching her teeth in a bid to stop the tears. As soon as she had been brought into the cold, starkly lit room, she had told them everything. Everything except the bit about her being pregnant; that was a secret she had kept with Richard and didn't want to share with anybody else. She had relayed the fight between Richard and Josh: Richard's beating from his grandfather, and her punishment from her father. She had stressed how Richard had only meant to scare Josh's family; how he had been pushed to the absolute limit by Josh, and how he was going to hand himself in after killing Jodie. She made it crystal clear that Josh had no idea his sister was dead when he had fatally stabbed Richard. She knew that people - both locals and the police - would make their own minds up about what had happened but she felt the need to defend him, to stand up for Richard and try to make them see what had driven him to such extreme lengths. She didn't want to think about Josh or how he had probably felt he had been driven to the same extreme lengths by Richard. She knew they were both in the wrong but she could forgive Richard, she could understand it. She could never forgive Josh.

"You're free to go for now, Mary. We'll take you home but we'll need to question you further at a later time." The inspector paused, casting an eye over his notes.

"Do you want to file a complaint before you go?" he asked.

"Complaint?"

"Against your father."

Surprised by his suggestion, she shook her head vehemently.

"No."

The policewoman sitting next to her leant forward.

"Mary, we can arrange for a support worker to ..."

"No!" she insisted. The inspector sighed inwardly. It troubled him how she had taken such pains to make them see Richard in a positive light despite his obvious crimes and yet, when she described the crime committed against her by her father, her choice of words had been very telling and her acceptance of it, very disturbing. He had heard of Donal O'Shea through the grapevine and she had just confirmed his suspicions of him.

Mary turned away from the inquisitive faces staring at the police car and following its progress as it approached the top of Main Street and drove through the archway by the café. Amanda, the policewoman who had been by her side for the past four hours, helped her out of the car. Bridget was at the back door, waiting for them. She tentatively held out her arms, her eyes filling up at the sight of Mary's drawn face. Mary accepted the hug, barely flinching at the pain it caused, her own body too drained to reciprocate.

"We'll be in touch tomorrow, Mary. If you need me for anything, you've got my number," Amanda nodded, getting back into the car. Bridget ushered Mary up the stairs and headed for the kitchen.

"I just need my bed, Mam."

Bridget gave her a strained smile.

"Of course. I'll bring you up some tea." She watched Mary climb the stairs to her room, then steeling herself, opened the kitchen door to face more of Donal's questions. By the time he had returned home from his afternoon of golf, word had quickly spread across the tight-knit community of the two murders and Josh's arrest, and Mary's name was on everybody's lips.

Mary lay on her side, staring at the window. She didn't register the bustle outside or the birdsong that pierced the early evening air. She hardly noticed Bridget placing a cup of tea on her bedside chest, or gently pulling her trainers from her feet. She didn't react when Bridget bent over to stroke her brow and softly whisper,

"Get some sleep. It will do you good."

She didn't want to sleep. She didn't want the day to ever end although she knew it must, but when it did, the last day that Richard spent on this earth would be over. A new day would dawn and he wouldn't be in the world. She wasn't ready to deal with that. She had to stay awake.

The footsteps she dreaded drew near and she closed her eyes, feigning sleep. Donal opened the door, stopping halfway across the room, hesitating. He called her name. It didn't jar like it usually did but she ignored him anyway. He quietly closed the door behind him as he left.

An hour passed before she was forced to move to go to the toilet. She refused to look at herself in the mirror as she cleaned her teeth; she didn't want to see the pain reflected in her face that she so desperately felt in her chest. She couldn't bring herself to change out of her blood-stained clothes even though the smell was making her feel sick. Sitting on the edge of her bed, she took the two books from her bag and hugged them, kissed them, then tucked them under the pillow on Richard's side of the bed. Brushing crumbs from the battered chocolate chip muffin, she placed it on the chest by his pillow.

"Your favourite," she whispered, burying her face in his pillow, breathing in his lingering smell of sandalwood. Unable to hold it in any more she howled his name and wept loudly, curling herself into a tight ball and cradling her small bump.

The bell chiming half past eleven stirred her from her trance, seated in her chair overlooking the street and church steps. Going through to the back room, she opened her window, pushing the warped, sash frames up high to stick her head out and stare across to Brow. Distant street lights flickered through the leafy trees and the bright moon threw eerie shadows across the alleyway below. She listened to the stillness of the night, waiting; straining her eyes to see through the darkness. Muffled sounds of laughter echoed from the other side of the street as the regulars drifted home but once they'd gone, stillness again. Sighing, she pulled the window down, leaving it open a little way, as she always did. She pressed her hand against the glass that had been his gateway to her.

"Come back to me. Please."

Chapter Thirteen

"Mary, can I come in?" Hannah's voice was a little too bright, too forced and Mary's first instinct was to ignore her but then she remembered Roddy. She opened the door. Hannah gave a concerned smile, trying not to look at the blood stains on the clothes she was still wearing from the previous day.

"I'm sorry to come round so early but I thought you'd need Roddy. And I wanted to see you." She glanced at her watch; she had seven minutes before her shift started downstairs. She had already loitered by the church steps for five minutes, waiting for Donal to leave for work. Mary took the basket from her and Roddy jumped out, complaining and purring all at once, weaving happily around her legs. She picked him up and buried her nose in his fur.

"I heard about what happened. How you saw your friend being stabbed," Hannah started. Mary nodded, sitting on the sofa, keeping her focus on Roddy. Hannah sat next to her. She was about to rub her back but hesitated, her hand hovering in the air before patting her knee instead. She sighed.

"I always had a soft spot for Richard. I know he had a terrible reputation in the village, especially when he was a bit younger but I thought he was a nice lad; troubled, but nice."

Mary closed her eyes. This was how it was always going to be; Richard had been right. He would never shake off his 'terrible reputation'. Not now.

"But to kill his own sister!" Hannah shook her head in disbelief.

"Who did?" Mary's eyes flew open, confused.

"Richard."

"You mean, he killed *Josh's* sister," Mary corrected. The look of pity on Hannah's face twisted her stomach.

"Jodie was *Richard's* sister. Didn't you know? That's what is so shocking. He must've been in a really dark place to do that."

"I don't understand," Mary breathed, letting Roddy drop to the floor. Hannah held her hand, patting it in a maternal gesture.

"She was Richard *and* Josh's sister. She's the reason Richard's dad left – because Josh's mum got pregnant. And she let everybody know! I think he just wanted a fling but ..." she tailed off, seeing the blood drain from Mary's face.

"Are you alright, love?"

Mary nodded, her head screaming in protest as doubt bombarded it.

"Did Richard know that Jodie was his sister?"

"Of course he did! Everybody knew. Jodie knew. It was a scandal at the time, especially when Gail came back to the village, parading about with Jodie. She made a few enemies, I can tell you! But this ... this is just awful. Jodie's dead, Richard's dead, and Josh'll go to prison for murder. This will completely destroy Gail." Hannah stood up, glancing at her watch again.

"I'm sorry, love, I have to go. Your mum's waiting for me." She sighed heavily, assessing Mary's pallor. "I'm really sorry about what you went through yesterday. I just wish Richard had known you better. I reckon he could've done with a friend like to you confide in. Such a waste of life." She put her arms round Mary and hugged her, gently rubbing her shoulder.

"If you need me to look after Roddy again, y'know, if your dad gets funny about him; just shout. I'm happy to help, love." With that, she left the room and hurried downstairs to the café.

Mary sat back down, stunned, reeling from what she had just learnt. Why had he never told her about Jodie? Right to the end, he had kept things from her, and Hannah's words stung, renewing the nagging doubt that Jodie's death had been an accident. After all, *she* was the reason his dad had left. *She* took his place in his dad's heart – and life. And now, the woman who had caused Richard's world to collapse, had just had her whole world destroyed too. By Richard.

"What did you do?" she screamed with frustration, running her hands through her hair and squeezing her scalp with her fingertips. A sudden wave of nausea hit her; no longer able to stand the smell from her clothes, she ripped them off and jumped in a scalding shower, scrubbing hard at her skin. She thumped the tiled wall repeatedly, grunting and wailing, completely helpless. Her mind kept turning over and over as the hurt and betrayal grew, and the frustration at not being able to do anything about it intensified.

Spent and with bruised hands, she stepped from the shower, wrapped herself in a towel and sat on the toilet seat, staring at the floor. A long list of 'what ifs' ran through her mind and as she let the scenarios play out in her mind, her anger with Richard subsided, and her hatred of Josh escalated. Jodie's death had been in the heat of the moment; she knew that, despite her earlier doubts. But Richard's death had been pre-meditated, plain and simple. Josh had even warned her of what he was going to do. And here she was, feeling remorse and sorrow for Gail Higgins when in fact, her own life had been destroyed too. Why did she always put everybody else first? Her life was in pieces, her heart ripped apart and yet, she worried about how others were coping.

"What is wrong with you, Mary!"

She knew the answer.

"Is Mary not eating again?" Donal asked, indicating to the empty place at the table.

"I took something up for her. She's not slept yet; I think she's best left alone to rest just now," Bridget replied, resisting looking at her husband when he drew in a disapproving breath.

"She needs to snap out of it. If you mollycoddle her, that will only make it worse."

"Donal, she saw a boy die!" she reproached.

"Yes," he nodded curtly. "We have all seen people die, Bridget. She will get over it; the sooner, the better. Tomorrow, she eats here, with us."

The phone rang in the lounge, interrupting their conversation. Bridget spoke for a while, then hurried upstairs with a message for Mary, leaving Donal to start his meal alone.

"You are not her secretary, Bridget!" he barked, his angry words hanging redundant in the air.

Bridget woke Mary the next morning, surprised to find her asleep in the chair by the window, but pleased that she had finally got some rest. She put the tea on the floor next to her and went over to the bed.

"I'll strip your bed now; get a wash on before I open up." Heeding Donal's words, she needed to get Mary motivated.

"No!" Mary launched herself, half asleep, from her chair to pull Bridget away, knocking the tea over in the process. Bridget stepped back, startled.

"But …"

"Please, Mam, just leave my bed be. Just leave it." She had a wild look in her eye, like a feral cat protecting its young. Bridget backed away, towards the bathroom.

"Okay. I'll just get something to mop that tea up with."

"It's fine, I'll do it. Please, Mam. Just … just leave me be."

Bridget nodded, seeing how close to the edge Mary was. She left quietly, putting a smile on her face as she went back in to the kitchen to prepare Donal's breakfast.

"She's much better today. She said she will join us this evening. I told you, she just needed time, that's all."

Donal's eyes narrowed but he didn't look up from his paper.

"Good. And remind me; what time is she meeting Mr Nelson today? And *why* is she meeting him?"

Bridget sighed quietly. They had already been over this the night before.

"He and his wife are taking her out for tea this afternoon. They just want to make sure she's okay, that's all."

"Why would she not be okay?"

"Because she was with that boy when he died." She closed her eyes, knowing she had missed the warning sign; that tone. He lowered his paper and fixed his granite eyes on her.

"Yes, she was. And where should she have been, Bridget? In her room! And where were you?"

She hung her head, knowing no answer was expected. She had none to give anyway.

"Make sure she is back on time and seated at this table for her evening meal," he commanded, folding his paper and standing up. "Can you manage that, Bridget?"

Mary pressed her hands heavily on the towel, soaking up the spilt tea. She looked at the wet patch; she knew it would stain but the carpet was so worn anyway, another one wouldn't make much difference. She straightened out her bedspread, picked up Richard's pillow and breathed in the smell, as she had done repeatedly for the past two days. She tucked the book she had been clutching all night – unread - back under the pillow and stared at the pink fabric, visualising his head resting on it. Although completely drained, tears still fell unchecked, trickling down her face. She knew she would never get over it and to be honest, she didn't even want to try.

Hannah knocked on her bedroom door promptly at four o'clock.

"You have visitors waiting downstairs for you," she smiled. She was relieved to see a little colour back in Mary's face. "That's a pretty top, love."

Mary nodded, mumbling her thanks. She found Nicola waiting for her in the café, talking quietly with Bridget. They both flashed bright smiles at her, Nicola quick to give her a comforting hug.

"Jim's outside in the car. I thought, somewhere quiet?" she suggested, glancing at the large group of weary backpackers that were dominating most of the room. Mary nodded. She followed Nicola outside, squinting in the bright sunlight.

"I know; lovely day, isn't it!" Nicola chirped, holding the car door open for her. Mary glanced down the street at the sea of heads turned to watch her. Somebody held up a hand in acknowledgment but the rest just stared. She ducked into the car, catching Mr Nelson's concerned face.

"Hello, Sir."

"Mary, call me Jim, please," he smiled. "Right, where to, ladies?"

It was only a ten minute drive to find a quiet tea shop away from Haworth. They took a table by the window overlooking the village green. Mary watched the passing traffic, listening to Nicola's light-hearted chat as they ordered tea and cakes.

She cast an eye around the room; it was quaint, prettily done up in a rustic style. There was a family on the other side of the room; two siblings squabbling over the coloured straws. A couple in the corner sat together, quietly planning the week ahead, their diaries in front of them. Their normality annoyed her. Her world had stopped and she expected everybody else's to have done the same. She wasn't even sure what day it was.

"How are you holding up?" Jim's question broke her thought process. She shrugged. He and Nicola exchanged glances.

"We had a special assembly yesterday," he started. "It's shaken the whole school. I can imagine Haworth is in shock too." He waited for her to respond. She stared at the table.

"I heard that Josh Higgins confessed straight away," he continued. "He's been charged with murder. So..." He widened his eyes helplessly at Nicola. She took over.

"Mary, I know it's probably none of our business but if you want to talk about what really happened, we're here to listen. To help in any way we can. I didn't really know Richard but Jim did," she said, shooting him a smile, "and he thought the world of him."

"So did I," Mary whispered. "But everybody else hated him."

"Not everybody. I know he was a troubled lad, and I know he spoke with his fists but he was calming down, growing up. And I think you helped him, I really do," Jim encouraged. "You changed him. I know you were worried about it at first but I'm glad you were friends."

"We were running away together, that day," she looked up at Jim. "He was helping me escape from my dad. I loved him so much! Josh should've killed me too!" her voice broke and she burst into tears. Nicola crouched by her chair, holding her. Jim couldn't mask his surprise.

"You mean, you two were …" he blurted. Nicola gave him a knowing look and he stopped himself, rummaging around in her bag for tissues to pass to Mary. The tears subsided eventually; she blew her nose and gave Jim a weak smile.

"He always said he wanted to thank you. It was instant, y'know. We both knew it."

"Oh, Mary, I am so sorry. This makes so much sense now but …" he gave her a searching look. "What can we do to help? We have a spare room if you need it." He looked to Nicola for approval. She nodded.

"Absolutely. How are things at home? Do your parents know about the two of you?"

Mary shook her head.

"No, but …" she hesitated.

"But?" Nicola prompted. Mary glanced at Jim. Reading her mind, Nicola patted his arm.

"Jim, give us a minute would you. Girls talk," she smiled. Nodding, still stunned by what he had missed picking up on, he went outside and wandered down the street. Nicola turned her attention to Mary. Mary took a deep breath.

"I'm pregnant. And so scared." She told her everything: how Richard had taken control, making plans and arrangements, finding them somewhere to live, and above all, always taking care of her. And without him, she felt completely lost and so helpless. Nicola listened intently, her heart aching for the frightened, bereft girl sitting next to her.

"You need to tell your parents."

"I can't!"

"Mary, you can't do this alone. What's the worst that could happen?" she reasoned.

"They'd throw me out."

"Then come to us. Like Jim said, we have a spare room." She smiled at the simplicity of her solution but could see Mary wasn't convinced.

"You'd be surprised how a baby changes things. The thought of a grandchild can soften even the hardest of men. You need their support, Mary."

"I'm not so sure that was the best advice, Nic. You don't know her father," Jim ventured as he and Nicola discussed Mary on their drive home to Keighley. "We should go back for her, before it's too late." He slowed the car down.

"It'll be fine, Jim. You worry far too much. You'll see." She patted his leg, touched by his concern for Mary. He always went above and beyond for his students, and he had taken the news of Richard very badly.

"So tragic though," she said softly. "Poor girl. Poor, poor girl."

Mary straightened her top, pulling it away from her stomach. It seemed that whatever she wore clung to her bump. She took a deep breath and opened the kitchen door. Bridget smiled with relief, noting how Donal eyed the clock on the wall. He didn't acknowledge Mary though, and that irked Bridget. It was the first time she had come down to the kitchen since Sunday and she deserved some kind of recognition for that.

"Hello, Mary. Did you have a good time? Sit down, I am just about to dish up." She made a big thing of gesturing her to her seat, as if she were in a restaurant. Mary hesitated.

"Actually, there's something I need to tell you, Mam." She swallowed, instinctively clutching her stomach. Bridget's eyes widened, staring at where her hands rested, then at her face. She saw the look in her eye.

"No!" she breathed. "Are you …"

Mary nodded. She glanced at her father. He slowly lifted his eyes to her, his body worryingly still.

"Who is … are you …" Bridget faltered, grappling with the bombshell. Mary waited for her to compose herself.

"Is the father going to marry you?" she finally piped up.

"He was, but he can't now," she replied, her voice threatening to break. Bridget licked her lips, shooting an anxious look at Donal. That wasn't the answer she needed.

"Why not?"

Mary dropped her head for a second, clasping her hands together.

"Because he's dead."

Donal slammed his hand down on the table, making them both jump, a vitriolic smile on his face.

"I knew it!" He got up from his seat, jabbing his finger in the air at her. "I knew it!"

It took a moment for Bridget to process, her face draining as she realised who they were talking about.

"Did he … did he force you?" she whispered, clutching at her chest.

"What? No! No, I loved him. He loved me," she stressed, horrified at the suggestion. Bridget's eyes filled up. "Mam, he *loved* me."

Donal snorted, leaning his clenched fists on the table.

"How would you know about love? You are just a child." His derisive look cut through her.

"Mam was eighteen when she had me. At least Richard was my age, not twelve years older!"

His eyes narrowed sharply.

"You hold your tongue!"

"No. He was my equal and we loved each other!"

"Your equal?" He moved towards her. "Your equal? He murdered a child. What does that make you?" he hissed. Incensed, she stood her ground.

"That was an accident! *You* drove him to it! If you hadn't beaten me, he wouldn't have been so angry. *You* did it; it's your fault she's dead!"

Crimson with rage, he lurched at her, grabbing a handful of long hair and dragging her out of the room. She stifled a scream, trying frantically to steady herself as her shoulder slammed against the doorframe. He didn't slow down, pulling harder when she stumbled on the stairs behind him. He kicked open her bedroom door and swinging her round, pushed her against the wall. Panting, trying to catch her breath, she stared defiantly at him. With one swift movement, she pulled her top off and threw it on the floor, turning to face the wall.

"Go on then; beat me some more. I don't care."

Donal growled, snatching up her top and throwing it at her back.

"Do you honestly think I would *touch you* … in your condition." His voice dripped with disgust. "Turn around."

She turned to him, holding her top against her, suddenly feeling vulnerable once the heat of the moment had subsided. He stared at her stomach, deliberating, fists still clenched. The silence seemed to stretch on for an eternity before he finally spoke.

"I need you to stay here, while I think this through." She thought she detected a note of compassion in his tone; sadness maybe, or regret. Either way, that unnerved her more than his blind rage did. He locked eyes with her and let out a heavy sigh.

"You are a disappointment, Mary. I hope you know that." He closed the door firmly behind him when he left, turning the key and pocketing it. She slumped onto her bed, completely drained once again.

Bridget bought her dinner up on a tray, placing it silently on the bedside chest, and again in the morning with a cup of tea. Mary made no attempt to leave her room although she planned to venture down once Donal had gone to work. The church bell chimed nine and he still hadn't left. It soon became apparent that he wasn't going to work that day. Bridget appeared shortly after midday with another plate of food and then again at six.

"Mam, what's going on?"

Bridget avoided looking at her.

"Your father will let you know soon enough," she said quietly and hurried back downstairs, once again pocketing the key. Mary ran through the possibilities in her head, round and round, all day. She concluded that the most likely scenario would be that she was sent back to Ireland, probably to Bridget's mother. She felt too empty to care. Anywhere away from her father would suit her.

Bridget woke her a little earlier the following morning, ahead of her alarm clock.

"You need to get dressed, Mary. We have an appointment at the hospital this morning."

Mary sat up, instantly wide awake.

"What for? Is it to check the baby?"

Bridget nodded.

"So, will it be a scan?" She knew she had already missed some important check-ups by keeping her pregnancy hidden.

"Yes. There will be a scan. Your father arranged it all yesterday." She looked sad, and it was clear to Mary that she was struggling to come to terms with everything. But for Mary, it lifted her spirits. Her heart beat a little faster, and the knowledge that she would be seeing her baby on the screen

207

filled her with such a bitter sweet mix of joy and grief. She ached for Richard; the only thing keeping her going was knowing that a part of him was still alive, growing inside her.

"Thank you," she murmured, sipping the hot tea, her mind racing ahead.

They pulled up outside the hospital and Donal got out of the car and slid into the back seat next to Mary. He hadn't spoken to her at all during the drive.

"You have an appointment here today."

She nodded, a tentative smile trembling on her lips.

"I know. Mam told me about the scan."

"It is a termination."

She gasped in horror, reaching for the door handle to bolt from the car but he grabbed her wrist, twisting it round until she sat still. She stared at the back of Bridget's head in horror.

"Mam?"

"Leave your mother out of this," he warned. He took hold of her other wrist, pinning them into her lap with a vice-like grip.

"Now, you listen to me. You have two options here. Option one: you go with your mother into that building and have the termination. We will help you heal, both mentally and physically. I will support you in your choice to go to university – I will even put money into your savings fund to help you. I understand," he dropped his voice, softening his words, "I acknowledge that you had feelings for that boy and I will help you move on. I have spoken personally to the staff here about your situation and they will do everything they can to help you through it."

Mary couldn't control the shaking in her body, and the compassion in his voice just amplified it. He released the grip on her wrists slightly.

"Option two: should you persist with this pregnancy, I will ensure that you are implemented in that young girl's death. I have enough … sway … to do that. Although you were not there, you knew of his need for revenge and you knew of his volatile nature, and yet you did nothing to stop him. You will get a police record. You will never be allowed near children, let alone teach them. I will make sure of that." He paused, letting her absorb what he was saying.

"I will also make it my priority to remind you, *every day*, of your sin. Of your deception. And I will punish you accordingly, for deceiving your mother, and fornicating under *my* roof." He moved his face closer to hers. "I warned you, Mary; nothing gets past me. I know what you did." He watched her eyes darting wildly, trying to avoid his malicious stare. He leant away again, drawing in a deep, deliberate breath.

"And finally, should you choose option two, I must advise you that the minute your baby is born, it will be taken from you. You are not a fit mother and its father was a child murderer. I will personally guarantee that you never see your baby. Ever." He released her wrists and climbed out of the car, holding the door open for her.

"Choose your option wisely."

Mary stumbled out, knocked sideways by what had just happened. Bridget stood beside her and watched the car pull out of the hospital. She took Mary's arm and guided her to a nearby bench. Mary turned to her, helpless.

"How could you, Mam?"

Bridget looked away.

"This is your father's decision. He knows what is best for us."

"So, you think he's right?"

Bridget deliberated her answer, watching the traffic build up around the car park.

"Mary, if you choose option two, it will never end well. You need to think about this carefully. You can go to university in a couple of months, away from ... your past. You will have freedom, be your own person. Your father will never allow that boy's baby to be a part of your life."

"His name was Richard, Mam. Please say his name!"

Bridget shook her head, infuriating Mary.

"I can't possibly do this! How could you even think I would? This is *my baby*, not just a problem that needs to be fixed. I thought you were going to help me!"

"Help you?" Bridget retorted evenly. "You got yourself pregnant. Why would you expect me to help you?"

"Because Richard is dead. He's dead, Mam!" her voice cracked.

"Yes. And you should never forget what he did before he died. He murdered a child. How can you allow a baby to be born with *that* stigma hanging over their head? That baby will pay for his father's sins forever. Your father will make sure of that. You know him. You know he means what he says." She turned to Mary, pleading. "Do the right thing."

She did know her father. She knew he could manipulate whoever he wanted to. She knew what he was capable of, and that knowledge meant he had a terrifying power over her. Without Richard, she couldn't fight him anymore. She had to be free of him; that left her with only one option.

"Stay with me, Mam," she pleaded.

It was after five by the time the taxi got them back to Haworth, and shops were starting to shut. Hannah was outside the café, wiping down the tables and sweeping the pavement. She looked up as the taxi turned in under the archway, widening her eyes at Mary, as if warning her of something. The pungent smell of bonfire hung heavy in the air. As Mary gingerly climbed out of the car, she saw her velvet chair, in bits, outside the back door. Flames billowed out from a galvanised incinerator, and a pile of ash smouldered on the path. Donal was standing by the fire, with a handful of books nestled in the crook of his arm. He watched Mary get out of the car and ceremoniously dropped the books into the fire.

"What are you doing?" she wailed. "They're *my* things! That's my chair!"

Behind the chair, she saw a pile of smashed records. Sacks of cooled ash were stacked up against the kitchen wall. It was evident that he had been busy burning things for the entire day. Mary ran to the back door but Donal darted in front of her and blocked her way.

"Do not take one more step," he warned. Mary's mouth dropped open, confused.

"What's happening? Why are you burning everything? My things!" She turned to Bridget for an answer but Bridget just hung her head.

"I don't understand. Dad! I did what you said. You promised to look after me, to help me!" she choked on her tears, panic ripping through her. Donal straightened up, folding his arms across his chest.

"It is a nasty feeling is it not, Mary? When somebody you trust turns out to be a liar! How could you possibly think I would allow you back in *my* home when you have been such a deceitful, dirty, little whore. You are the epitome of degradation and evil. You fornicated like an animal. Your boyfriend took a human life and you followed suit. You were right; you are his equal. You committed murder today, without much persuasion at all. What kind of a mother would do that?" he spat his words at her with a slow deliberation. "You disgust me!"

The ground swayed beneath her feet and her stomach dropped.

"You were testing me? All those things you said; was that a trick? You told me I had no choice!"

"I did not. I said, choose wisely. You chose the coward's way out. I expected nothing less from you." He placed a firm hand on her shoulder and pushed her backwards.

"There is nothing left for you here. If I see you anywhere near this building again, I *will* go to the police; I *will* carry out my threats. You have two minutes to get out of here." He lifted his wrist, gauging his watch. Mary stumbled through the archway onto the street. Hannah was watching from the corner of the café.

"Hannah! Can you find Roddy and keep him safe, please?" Mary sobbed. "He's thrown me out!"

"What's happened, love? I saw him burning your bed sheets and pillows; what is going on?"

"Just keep Roddy," she urged.

"Of course. You know where I am, just com …"

"Hannah, can I have a word?" Donal's voice resonated across the street. Mary took a last look at him and ran to the church steps, disappearing into the grave yard. She headed for the ancient tombstones towards the back, where she and Richard had been hiding only days before. Sinking into the long grass, she dissolved into tears, sobbing so hard it made her head pound.

Chapter Fourteen

The six o'clock evening chimes roused her from the exhausted sleep she had fallen into. As she gained consciousness she drew her knees up in a bid to ease the abdominal cramps and the feeling of being punched hard between her legs. Slowly sitting up, she stared unseeing at the weeds and ryegrass around her feet, going over the events of the past few hours. Her father had been right; she had taken the coward's option, but under such pressure from him. She hadn't been able to think clearly - if at all - since Richard's death, and the thought of trying to carry on without him was unbearable. Mentally she was a mess and physically, she felt like her body had been cemented to the ground. As the full impact of what she had done filtered through, her eyes focused on the grass by her feet and she suddenly remembered the makeshift engagement ring that she had wrapped up carefully in her jewellry box. A bereft wail escaped her lips. She knew it would be gone, along with her books with Richard's dedications in, her records that they loved to listen to, the beads from the bracelet he had bought her in York, and the pillow that smelt of him. There was nothing left. Everything he had given her, everything that reminded her of him, everything he had touched, had gone. She quickly got to her feet and headed for Hannah's house. She needed to find Roddy.

Avoiding the café, she had taken the back route to the bottom of Main Street and was just about to knock on Hannah's door when it opened and her husband politely ushered out their guest. He stopped short when his eyes fell on Mary, then darted a look at his guest. Donal straightened up, sneering at her.

"Have you not left yet, Mary? Did I not make it clear enough for you?" His loud, caustic tone echoed across the narrow street. "You are not welcome here – or anywhere, in fact. The whole village knows what you did and they are as sickened by it as I am. Now get out of here!" He ordered her away with a wave of his hand, his hateful eyes boring into hers. People had stopped further up the street, wondering what the commotion was, watching with baited breath. Mary turned and hurried towards the park. A bus was pulling up at the stop and she climbed on it, fumbling with shaky hands for her purse. Slumped in a seat with her head bent, she assessed the contents of her bag. A purse, a pack of tissues and a couple of Kirby grips were the sum total of her possessions. She didn't even carry any sanitary towels with her; she hadn't needed any for months.

She got off the bus on the outskirts of Keighley and hurried along the quiet pavement. Most people were indoors, winding down for the evening. She hadn't been to the Nelsons house before but she knew where it was. An end of terrace, it was part of a row of old weavers cottages that had been painstakingly renovated, and snapped up by prosperous young couples. Mary could see Nicola at the kitchen sink that overlooked the street, the window prettily framed by a rich crimson, climbing rose. She froze in her tracks. Jim came into the kitchen, kissed the back of Nicola's neck and cradled her slightly swollen stomach from behind. Mary recognised, all too painfully, that paternal smile on his face. It suddenly made sense; the 'hardest of men' that Nicola had referred to, hadn't been Mary's father at all. It had been Jim's. Ducking out of view, she ran back down the road towards the bus stop, completely out of places to turn. She was struggling to hold it all together and was aware of curious glances from other passengers as she rocked in her seat, trying to keep tears and the excruciating pain in her lower body at bay. Once back in Haworth, she headed for the allotments and let herself in to Mr Wood's shed. The familiar smell of trapped heat and fox pee hit her immediately but there was another smell she recognised. Scouring the dirty floor, she fell to her knees frantically gathering up crushed cigarette ends, and hugged them in her hand, tenderly stroking them with her finger. Looking around, she could see where Richard had slept; a pile of hessian sacks were bunched up in the corner as a make-shift bed. Spying a kitchen roll in amongst twine, pens and plastic plant labels on one of the crowded wall shelves, she tore off a piece and wrapped the cigarette ends up. Then she tore off a ream of sheets, folding them up into a thick wad. She was bleeding heavily and had nothing else to use. Disposing of the soaked, nappy-sized pad the hospital had supplied her with earlier into an old plastic bag she found on a higher shelf, she settled herself on the hessian pile. She hadn't eaten all day and her head thumped from lack of food and water. She looked around the shed from her spot in the corner, hoping to spy a packet of biscuits or a can of drink but to no avail. As the daylight faded, the heat drained from the wooden exterior and a chill settled in the air. Mary placed the parcel of cigarette ends next to where she rested her head. She gently put her hand on it.

"Goodnight, my love," she whispered, closing her eyes and willing sleep to claim her for an eternity. She didn't want to ever wake up.

She heard her name through the thick fog that clouded her brain. The soft Yorkshire tone sounded concerned, and called her again.

"Richard?" She forced her eyes open, pain gripping at her throat. Kelly's dad crouched beside her, gently shaking her shoulder. He smiled; the smile not quite reaching his eyes to mask the sadness there.

"Mary, you gave me quite a fright." He helped her to her feet, steadying her as she swayed. He frowned.

"How long have you been here?"

"Only last night. I'm sorry …"

"No, no," he stopped her. "Don't be sorry. I was worried you'd been here all week, only I haven't had a chance to get up here. My mate watered the veg but apart from that …" he tailed off. "Are you okay, love?"

She nodded. He offered the rickety chair to her and busied himself pouring a cup of tea from his flask, pressing it into her cold hands. She gave him a wane smile by way of thanks.

"It's none of my business but you've always been a good friend to Kelly and I feel a bit responsible for you," he ventured, waiting for her to explain. She sipped at the tea, sighing as the warmth hit her empty stomach.

"I'm sure Kelly told you," she offered as a reply. He snorted a laugh.

"Well, Kelly says a lot of things. I don't always listen – but you don't need to tell her that!" he winked, offering her a digestive biscuit from his bag. He watched her devour it and offered another one.

"Would you like to come home with me for breakfast? Pearl does a cracking fry-up and she cooks for the five thousand, y'know." His craggy face lit up when he spoke about his wife but his smile faded into concern again at Mary's reticence.

"I'm fine, thank you. I'll be on my way now." She stood up to leave but he held his hand out to stop her.

"No, no, you finish that tea first," he insisted, re-filling the cup. "I'll just be outside picking slugs. They're a mighty breed, resilient to every slug pellet going!" His laugh was a little too forced but his kind smile was a genuine one. Alone again, she gulped the scalding tea, pocketed the cigarette ends and stuffed the sealed plastic bag into her shoulder bag. She took another biscuit and stuck it in her pocket for later.

"Thanks, Mr Wood," she called as she headed for the allotment gate. He straightened up, a pot of slugs in his hand.

"Breakfast?" he offered but she shook her head, mumbling her thanks again. He watched her hurry up the incline and through the gate, his heart sinking. If the rumours were true, she must be traumatised. She looked broken.

Mary sat in the churchyard, waiting, watching the clock above her. Satisfied that the coast was clear, she went across to the café. Both Bridget and Hannah looked up in shocked surprise.

"You can't be here," Bridget hissed.

"Mam, please."

"Go away, Mary!" She turned her back; Mary caught a glimpse of a red welt snaking across her shoulder and collar bone.

"Mam, I just want to see you. Five minutes, please." Her voice trembled. "I'll be in the churchyard."

Bridget relented, giving her a curt nod. Mary hurried back and moments later, Bridget joined her on the bench, sitting some distance apart. Mary's eyes were drawn back to the angry lash mark, not fully covered by her cotton top.

"I'm sorry," Mary murmured.

"In general, or…?"

"I'm sorry you've been hurt. By him."

Bridget sighed indignantly.

"So, not sorry that you have shamed the family?"

"No. I loved him. I will always love him." She wanted her mother to understand that, more than anything.

"You fell for the wrong boy," she snapped.

217

"No! I fell for the *right* boy. He was my saviour." Mary willed her to look at her but she refused. They sat in silence.

"Come with me, Mam," she whispered. Bridget's head snapped round.

"What?"

"Leave Dad. Come with me."

Bridget stared at her aghast, mouth open.

"Are you out of your mind? Why would I leave your father? I vowed to honour and obey him, till death do us part. *In front of God.* Does that mean nothing to you?"

"But he hurts you. He punishes you," she tried to reason but Bridget was not listening.

"He corrects me when I make an error of judgment. He guides me and shows me my wrong doing. He is a good man."

Mary felt sick at the words coming out of her mother's mouth. She was horrified by the way Bridget excused his behaviour, his cruelty.

"Did you love Dad when you married him? Or did your dad just give you away to his protégé?"

"How dare you! You know nothing!"

Mary met Bridget's challenging stare, feeling more brave than she ever had.

"I know love, and I don't see it with you and Dad." She paused, knowing her words were hitting a nerve. "Richard was a good man. He loved me and he would never have raised a hand to me."

"He was a murderer, Mary!"

"It's Dad's fault; Dad did all of this," she reiterated her words of three days previously.

"That boy filled your head with poison!"

"No. Dad is poison. Dad is the bad man. Dad is the murderer," she said steadily. Bridget stared in horror, her eyes widening at Mary's insinuation.

"Don't think I don't know why we left Ireland, Mam. I know he murdered a man. I know what he did."

"Your father was an exemplary policeman," Bridget countered. Mary shook her head.

"He was a thug. He used his power to commit murder!"

"He was protecting his country!"

"Against what? The Irish? The other side that were also protecting their country? Terror fighting against terror; how is that ever going to resolve anything?"

She took a moment to calm down. She had surprised herself how incensed she had become, talking about her father.

"My Richard killed that girl by mistake…"

"She's still dead though," Bridget quickly interjected.

"Yes. But my father tortured that man for two days and then committed cold blooded murder! Oh, you think I don't have ears, Mam? You think I don't know what went on?"

Bridget, lost for words and caught unawares, just stared at Mary as she continued with her angry outburst.

"What makes me really sick though, is that Richard is dead and labelled a murderer, even though he was murdered himself! And yet, my father is alive, enjoying life and labelled 'a good man'. A good man! How is that fair?"

Having heard enough, Bridget stood up to leave but Mary pulled her back down.

"I'm sorry, I know I'm upsetting you but I need to know things, Mam."

"Like what?"

"After Granddaddy died …"

"Why are you bringing my father into this?" she snapped, bristling.

"After he died …"

"He was murdered! By - as you put it - the other side."

"I know," Mary acknowledged softly. "And you said that Dad changed after that. He became angry."

"He was very close to him. They were friends long before he became his son-in-law," she reasoned.

"I know. But … Dad didn't become angry *then,* not really. More angry, yes; but he has *always* been like that. He has always disapproved of me. He has always hurt me. And you. Long before Granddaddy died." She gave Bridget a searching look, pleading for an answer, wanting to understand. Bridget dropped her head.

"He was disappointed. He wanted a son."

There was a stunned silence.

"Then, why didn't you have more children? Is that really it?" Mary frowned, not ready to accept Bridget's explanation.

"Yours was a difficult birth. There were no more chances after that." Bridget looked away, not wanting to see the disbelief in Mary's face.

"So I've been punished? For not being a boy! And you have been punished for … for not providing him with a son. And you let him punish me because …? Why, Mam? Why did you never step in? I'll tell you why; because you think he's right to blame you. You think you did let him down!" She was spitting words angrily, furious at what she was hearing. "Well, you let me down too! The minute you looked away, the minute you condoned what he did to *both* of us, you let me down. I just accepted it because you did. I grew up thinking it was normal. I grew up thinking it was my fault!" She let out a furious growl. Bridget turned to her, eyeing her with contempt.

"Where did you learn such a temper, Mary? This isn't you talking; this is him. That boy. You would never have spoken to me like that before. How dare you judge me, after everything that you have done." She got to her feet, about to walk away.

"Your father has decided, we are leaving Haworth as soon as possible."

"Where are you going?"

Bridget shrugged, shaking her head.

"I don't know."

Mary could see she was lying.

"You're not going to tell me? Are you cutting me out completely? Am I being left behind? Mam?" She fired the questions at her, her voice rising in panic. She grabbed at Bridget's arm as she walked away.

"Mam, I'm your only child! You can't cut me out!"

Pulling herself free, Bridget turned on her heel.

"I have no child. Goodbye, Mary."

Knocked sideways, Mary stared after Bridget for several minutes after she had disappeared round the corner and back into the café. She kept hoping that she would come back, apologise, and talk over what had been said. But she didn't and it slowly dawned on Mary that Bridget had no intention of backing her up against Donal. She had been relying on Bridget to smooth the waters, as she always did. When Donal had sent her packing, she didn't for a minute think that it would be forever. However much she hated him, she hadn't ever contemplated the notion that she would be without her mother because of him. She had always assumed that Bridget would be there, on the side-line, in whatever capacity she could.

"Mary!" Hannah hurried towards her, arms folded across her apron, glancing behind her. She perched on the bench, a tentative smile on her lips.

"How are you, love?"

Mary shrugged, not meeting her inquisitive eyes.

221

"I'm sorry, love, but I couldn't find Roddy yesterday. By the time I managed to sneak upstairs, everything was gone from your room. I asked your mum but she just said he'd run away. He got out apparently." She saw the desolation in Mary's face. "Look, I get off at half three today. I've got the doctor's but I'll cancel it; your mum doesn't have to know. Come round then. I'll get us something nice for tea." She gently patted Mary's knee then hurried back across the churchyard.

Mary closed her eyes, drained. Eventually summoning up the strength, she walked up and down every lane in the perimeter of the café, calling for Roddy, peering over low walls and high fences for a glimpse of his glowing, ginger fur. She knew he would be scared and probably too cautious to come out of hiding, despite her calling. Extending her search radius, she headed down the road to the park; a gut twisting compulsion drawing her to the spot where her world had been destroyed. Remains of police tape lay in the gutter and remnants of sand were swept across the pavement; the dark stain it was meant to cover still plainly visible. Aside from that, there was nothing to mark the spot. No reminder that a life had been ended there. She knew for a fact that a bank of flowers had been placed outside Gary's house; juvenile writing and drawings dominating the scores of cards and messages left amongst the mass of teddies and heart shaped balloons that were secured by pink foil-covered weights. The village had ground to a halt to mourn Jodie's death. Nobody mourned for Richard, except her. She knew if she sat down on the kerb she would never want to leave so instead she went into the park and sat on the bench by the rhododendron, allowing herself time to reminisce. The last time she had sat on that bench, her body had been trembling with anticipation, excitement. Now it shook with unfathomable grief.

"Come in, love," Hannah smiled warmly, showing Mary into the front room. "Make yourself at home; I'll just fetch a couple of plates. Cup of tea, love?" she called from the kitchen. Mary sat down, instantly sinking into the soft seat. She could smell warm vinegar and batter, and her stomach growled with hunger.

"I got us a nice couple of bits of fish," Hannah gushed, putting two plates of steaming fish and chips on the coffee table in front of Mary. "Brown sauce? Ketchup?"

Mumbling her thanks, she ate quickly. She hadn't realised just how hungry she was. Hannah watched her wash the food down with gulps of tea.

"Mary, if I had known about … y'know … I would never have said what I did the other day."

Mary frowned, shaking her head.

"How do you mean?"

"Well, about him being your friend and that. I feel really bad now even feeling sorry for him. I couldn't believe it when your dad told me." She shook her head in disgust.

"I don't understand. What have you been told?"

Hannah hesitated. She didn't want to drag it up again but maybe Mary needed to talk and this would be the perfect cue.

"How he took advantage of you and got you pregnant. How he was forcing you to leave with him that day. And then you went against your parents' wishes and had an abortion as soon as you could but your father can't cope with it because it goes against his beliefs. They say he's heartbroken over it. I'm sorry love, but I never put your dad down as the heartbroken type. It just goes to show how little we know each other, doesn't it."

Mary let out a shrill scream of frustration.

"That's all lies! All of it! I *loved* him – he *loved* me. And we both wanted our baby more than anything in the world," she blurted, bursting into anguished tears. Mortified, Hannah passed her a box of tissues and held her hand while May told her everything.

"You have to leave, Mary. Get as far away from here as possible," Hannah determined. She had always felt there was more to Donal O'Shea behind that frosty, aloof façade, and it sickened her to think he had deceived everybody with his tale.

"I have nowhere to go."

"You're going to uni, aren't you? In York? I have a friend there. Let me give her a call. She runs a B&B and she said only the other week that she was looking for a chambermaid." She stood up, taking the plates and mugs with her. "More tea while I make that call?" she offered.

"Actually, would you mind if I used your shower, please?" Mary asked shyly. She was acutely aware of how badly she smelt.

"Of course you can, love. I'll find you some fresh clothes to put on. Come on, let me show you where everything is."

Mary gave her a searching look, something playing on her mind.

"Can you do me a favour," she gave a little laugh, " another one."

Hannah sat back down.

"Of course. Anything."

"Tell me about Richard; about his parents."

"Oh. Okay, what do you want to know?"

"Everything. We never talked about the past, we only focused on the future. The past just drags you down, y'know. Especially with a past like ours," she gave a derisive smile. Hannah nodded. She didn't know anything about Mary's childhood but she knew plenty about Richard's. And his parents. They had all known each other throughout school; Hannah, her husband Frank, Richard's parents Andrew White and Hayley Swales, and Josh's parents Tony Higgins and Gail Smedley.

"Hayley was the quiet one. She used to be friends with your Kelly's mum, Pearl. Gary Swales always had a black eye. On a Monday, he'd look like he'd been playing rugby, y'know, with cauliflower ears. Hayley sometimes had a black eye too, but everybody knew what her dad was doing to her." She could see by Mary's expression that she already knew that part of the story. She nodded.

" I was surprised when Andrew started dating Hayley. I always thought Gail was more his type but they seemed really suited somehow. He brought her out of herself, gave her a confidence she never had before. And then Richard was born; they absolutely doted on him. Then Gail married Tony. They were a right match for each other. He was a poser, she was a show-off, very shallow the pair of them. But happy enough."

"Then years later, Gail got bored and started flaunting it about, and Andrew got drawn in. I was disappointed in him, I thought him and Hayley were happy, but then Gail was the kind of woman that was hard to resist. Bubbly, vivacious and she *always* got her own way." She paused as a thought struck her. "I tell you who she reminds me of – your friend Kelly. That larger than life type. Anyway, they carried on for a bit, rumours started about them and then she announced to the world that she was pregnant. With Jodie. I don't think that's what Andrew wanted but he was in too deep. Then he died and she came back to Tony. I never did like Tony at school; a big show-off really, but as we got older I realised he's just a weak man hiding behind his trophy wife." She eyed Mary thoughtfully. "Does that help?"

225

Mary nodded.

"Yes, it does. I knew some of it but you've just made them real, thank you."

Hannah stood up, heading for the door.

"You know how Andrew died, don't you?"

"Yes, a heart attack," Mary nodded.

"No, love. He killed himself. He left a note saying he could never forgive himself for what he did to Hayley and Richard but he was trapped by what he'd done. He could only see one way out. Tragic really. Maybe Richard didn't tell you about Jodie because if he had, that would make it real. I think he just wanted to forget."

Mary went over and over what Hannah had told her as she stood under the warm water, her aching body eased by the powerful jets. She had thought talking would help but she felt even more bereft and deeply sad. She wished she had known; she wished she had been there to comfort Richard when it happened. He always seemed angry with his dad but it struck her now that the anger was more frustration and hurt, and the knowledge that there was no going back. He could never talk to his dad, argue it out, or vent his sense of betrayal. Death was so final.

Hannah tapped on the bathroom door.

"I nipped up the road, love, and got you a few bits from the shop. I'll leave them outside the door."

The 'few bits' were a pack of pants, two t-shirts, sanitary towels, a toothbrush and some deodorant. She stared at the pack of sanitary towels and the implications behind it. She couldn't allow herself to go there yet; that would undo her completely.

"Oh, you look much better, love; do you feel it?" Hannah greeted her when she ventured back downstairs and found her in the kitchen. Mary nodded, eyeing the bits of paper Hannah was clutching in her hand.

"Now, I've spoken to my friend, Eileen, and I was right; she is looking for a chambermaid. She can't put you up but her friend can for a month or so. And I want you to take this." She thrust a cheque in Mary's hand, shaking her head when Mary protested.

"Take it, Mary. It's not much but it'll help you." She glanced at the clock on the kitchen wall. Mary knew Frank would be home soon and she should leave before then.

"Do you know when Richard's funeral is?" She hated asking but she had to know. Hannah shook her head.

"He's not having one. His family have said it'll be a private cremation and no gravestone. Gary's left the village so it'll probably just be his mum."

"No grave? That's awful! It's like he never existed." Mary stifled a sob.

"I know love, but he killed a child. How do you ever get beyond that?"

"You don't," she mumbled. She hugged Hannah, whispering her thanks and pocketing the cheque and contact details. Once back on the street, she decided to do another scout around for Roddy. He had to be somewhere nearby.

Mindful of the time and watching out for Donal's car, she snuck through the archway and walked slowly down the alley at the back of the café. She just had a feeling that he would be there. Going in to the small cul-de-sac at the bottom of the hill, she called a little louder. A woman came out of her house.

"Alright, love? Have you lost something?" Shrewd blue eyes, partially masked by a greying mass of thin curls, assessed her.

"Yes, my cat. He's quite skinny, not very old."

"What colour?" Her weathered face showed a concern that Mary didn't like.

"Ginger."

The woman's face dropped and she took a step closer.

"I'm sorry, love. I found him yesterday. He'd been hit by a car."

"No! Oh, God, no! Where is he?" Her heart was pounding, pumping with adrenaline.

"Well, he was dead, love, so I put him in my bin."

Mary stared aghast, a rush of emotions hitting her at speed.

"He's dead? You ... you threw him away? You can't just throw my baby away! I want him back," she demanded loudly. The woman backed away, uncertain. Mary's eyes darted across at the neat row of bins by the curb side.

"Which one is your bin? Which one?" her voice continued to rise. The woman hurried over and opened the lid, pulling out a tied up bin liner. Mary snatched it from her hands, crouched on the pavement and ripped it open. Roddy's lifeless body rolled out. Whimpering, she picked him up. He was cold and stiff, his eyes glassy and black. There was a dark purple swelling visible just above his eyes. Mary parted the fur to get a clearer look. It was speckled with blood; definitely an impact trauma.

"Where did you find him?"

"Up there, on the path," the woman said, pointing towards the top of the alley.

"Not on the road?" Mary breathed.

"No, love. I thought that was strange but maybe he was hit and then ran away. I found him up by the back of the caff."

Suddenly drained, she sank onto her knees and carefully wrapped Roddy back up.

"Do you have a trowel or something that I could borrow, to bury him, please?" she asked quietly. The woman shook her head.

"Anything?" she asked again. The woman headed back to her front door.

"I recognise you now. You're that girl, aren't you. You were with that lad. Shame on you!" And with that, she slammed the door.

Mary hurried back up the alley, her anger mounting with every step. She knew Bridget would be closing up soon so she quickened her pace, clutching the bag with Roddy against her chest. Striding through the archway, she marched into the café. Bridget was there cashing up, and Marie and Gemma were giving the tables a final wipe. Donal was talking to Bridget by the till. They all turned when Mary pushed the door open.

"You bastard!" she screamed at Donal. "You killed my cat, didn't you!"

Donal didn't flinch, he just fixed her with a cold stare.

"Mary!" Bridget reproached.

"Shut up, Mam! Don't you dare stick up for him." She put Roddy on a table and rushed over to Donal, pushing him backwards. He steadied himself but didn't respond. Mary spun round when she heard Gemma gasp, appalled.

"He killed my cat! He beat Mam. He did this," she pulled off her t-shirt to reveal the welts across her back, still red and swollen. "Repeatedly. He is a bastard!" She swung back to face Donal. "You are a murdering bastard and I hope you rot in Hell. God has seen you." She marched back towards the door, putting her t-shirt back on. She grabbed a dessert spoon from the caddy and snatched up the bin liner with Roddy in.

"God has seen you too, Mary," Donal called after her in an infuriatingly level tone. She turned back to him.

229

"I don't care anymore. I wish I had stood up to you years ago. I wish I had seen what a weak, nasty bully you really are. Now everybody knows."

She hurried up the church steps, refusing to look back. She headed for Dimples Lane and the sanctuary of the moors. She needed to bury Roddy and there was only one obvious place.

Chapter Fifteen

Mary ducked her head as she passed by the allotments but Mr Wood spotted her nevertheless and called a greeting. She gave him a wave but didn't slow down. Her heart sank when she heard Kelly shout after her.

"Wait up!" She caught up with her and there was an awkward moment where they just looked at each other before Kelly put her arms round her and squeezed her. She swore softly at Mary.

"Where the hell have you been hiding?"

Mary shrugged, not wanting Kelly's kindness. She was too emotional and angry to have a heartfelt conversation. For once, Kelly seemed to sense it and tactfully avoided asking the questions she was desperate to.

"I'll never forgive him. He changed you and I lost my best friend," she chided lightly.

"He didn't change me; I was already changing. I loved him, Kelly."

Kelly nodded. She could see it.

"He wasn't good enough for you though."

"Yes, he was. He was the air that I breathe. He was the one who kept my heart beating," she said softly, repeating words once said to her.

"Are you quoting your bloody books again?" Kelly half-laughed.

"No. Why would I quote books when I had the real thing?" She forced a smile. "Kelly, I have to go. Thank you for not judging me." She surprised Kelly by being the one to offer a hug, and holding on for a little longer than she usually would. Kelly watched her walk away.

"I don't understand what you saw in him, Mary, but then, I thought Josh was alright. I was wrong there."

Mary turned and smiled.

"Nobody will ever know what I saw in him because he was so different with me. He was my world. And he loved me. Nobody can take that from me." Her voice cracked and she sniffed loudly, hurrying on up the path.

She sucked her fingertips, trying to dislodge the dirt from under her nails. They were raw from scrabbling at the soil and shallow roots that spread like spaghetti just inches under the surface. Digging a hole big enough to bury Roddy had proved much more difficult than she had envisaged. The spoon had quickly bent under the strain and she had resorted to using large fragments of rock and her bare hands. She laid him to rest in a shallow grave and covered him with bits of heather before scraping powdery earth over him. She made a cross with two branches of heather. It had taken all her resolve to put him in the hole, to finally let go. She had clung to his rigid body, stroking his bony head and ears of stiff velvet. She had wept into his fur, willing him to purr one more time as she whispered goodbye.

She sat next to the grave, hugging her knees, watching the water flow under the bridge below. Dusk was falling; she guessed it was near nine o'clock. It had been their favourite time of day. Nature's reminder that they would soon be together for the night. She hit the ground in torment.

"I want you back, Richard! I need you so much." She looked to the sky, listening for an answer amid the distant bleating and evening birdsong.

"I've got nothing left of you. Nothing! Not even a picture. The only pictures I have are in my head and all I can see is you dying, right in front of me. That's all I can see – the fear in your eyes." She choked as she sobbed. "I'm so scared that I'll forget you; forget your face, your eyes, that look you had. Your smell." She rocked back and forth, letting the tears flow. "All I can smell is your blood."

Pulling her bag onto her lap, she took out the small bottle of whiskey she had taken from the sideboard in Hannah's lounge, and the pots of pills she had taken from the bathroom cabinet. She had no idea that Hannah was on medication for depression but then, that must mean the pills were working. She did know that Hannah's husband, Frank, was on painkillers; Hannah talked about it often enough. All his aches and ailments were a frequent topic of conversation at the end of the day when she and Bridget were clearing away, and Mary invariably caught the tail end of it.

Straining to break the seal on the unopened whiskey bottle, she took a mouthful, grimacing at the burning sensation. The taste and smell reminded her of Adam's party. She took a deep glug. And another. She wanted to remember that giddy feeling of being drunk and infatuated. Of falling in love. She drank some more.

"I let them kill our baby. How could I do that? I'm so weak without you, I didn't have any fight left in me. And now I feel so angry! I want to hurt someone, smash something. I want to scream til I have no breath left. Til my throat bleeds." She let out a guttural scream, thumping the ground repeatedly. Finally spent, she tipped the tablets from each bottle into her lap and mixed them together with her finger, watching the colours merge in kaleidoscopic patterns. Scooping a handful, she dropped them into her mouth and washed them down with alcohol. It didn't burn anymore. She took another handful.

"How can I do anything without you? I need to be with you. I know you're missing me as much as I'm missing you, aren't you. I'm coming, my love. I'm coming to you." Swallowing the last of the pills and taking another drink, she lay down across Roddy's grave. She reached out and clumsily twiddled the cross between her fingers.

"I need to sleep. Stay with me, watch me sleep. Keep me safe, like you always do."

She heard a noise and tried to sit up. A voice in the distance, calling her name. The voice seemed to multiply, her name echoing across the moor, drawing closer.

"I can hear you, Richard! I can hear you calling me." She closed her eyes, the world spinning as she drifted into darkness.

She was running blindly, stumbling in her haste. A crowd surged forward, blocking her way. She pushed them aside, frantically searching the sea of faces staring at her but he wasn't there. She tried to call his name; her throat was raw, as if she'd swallowed barbed wire. Finally she reached the pool of light that had drawn her; a clearing in the crowd, so bright. So bright it hurt her eyes. She squeezed them shut then opened them, blinking. The brightness eased; she could see again. There was nothing to see. Turning, she realised she was alone. The crowd had vanished. She felt herself float upwards.

"Not again," she whimpered. She'd already battled with it earlier, fighting to stay on the ground. She needed to find him.

"Richard!" A pained, hoarse whisper escaped her lips, inaudible to even the sharpest ear. Staring, spinning on the spot, looking in every direction, there was nothing. Just bright light. She fell to the ground, banging her head against it in desperation. Where was he? She tried to call his name but again, a soundless croak was all she could emit. Taking a deep breath, she tried again. Her throat burst in agony and she started to choke, spluttering and gasping for air. Her head was swimming, the light was fading. And Richard wasn't there.

Mary woke with a start, a sharp pain tugging in her forearm when she moved it. Her other arm felt heavy and trapped, something squeezing it tightly. She tried to lick her cracked lips but her throat was even drier. Her stomach lurched and her head thumped. She was in a bed – not her own. The sheets were stiff with starch and the antiseptic smell in the air was what caused her stomach to lurch. Gingerly turning her head to the side, she became aware of Hannah and Kelly sitting next to her bed, watching her anxiously. She slowly closed her eyes and opened them again. They were still there. She glanced down at her arms. A monitor cuff was strapped round one; the long lead attached to a nearby trolley. The pain in her other arm, she realised, was from a canula, secured in place with a mass of tape. A bag of fluid was hanging above her head; Kelly had been watching it rhythmically drip along the clear tubing into Mary's arm. Their eyes met. Kelly welled up, reaching for her hand and giving her an encouraging smile. Hannah hurried into the corridor and returned moments later with a nurse who gave Mary a bright smile.

"Hello, Mary. My name's Helen, I'm your nurse for tonight." She checked Mary's pulse, tapping the drip tube and adjusting the pressure, all the while watching Mary.

"Good," she smiled, nodding. "I'll just let the doctor know you're awake. You can have a sip of water to wet your mouth but no more for now."

"Why?" Mary croaked, swallowing at the intense pain in her throat. "My throat hurts."

"It will for a while. You had a stomach pump, and sometimes the tube catches when it's pulled out again. Your throat did bleed for a bit but you'll be fine." She patted her shoulder, made some notes on the clipboard at the bottom of the bed, and left the room. Mary searched Hannah's face.

"Who found me?"

"Kevin," Kelly replied. "And our dad." Her lips trembled, struggling not to give in to tears.

"As soon as I realised what you'd taken from my bathroom , I got a search party together," Hannah chipped in. "Frank went to Kelly's and she'd seen you go up the moor, so we all went there."

"I guessed you'd be where Richard used to go," Kelly added. Mary closed her eyes again. It was an effort to breathe.

"Mary, if I'd known what you were planning yesterday, I would never have let you go off on your own. I'm sorry," Kelly whispered. Mary opened her eyes again.

"Yesterday?"

"Yeah, you've been unconscious for nearly twenty-four hours. I didn't think you were …" she stopped short, turning away as emotions got the better of her. Hannah rubbed her arm, comforting her.

"Does Mam know?"

Hannah nodded, looking awkward.

"Yes, the police told them."

Mary swallowed, flinching at the pain.

"Did they … did she come here?"

Hannah shook her head.

"Sorry, love. I offered to bring her but …" she shrugged. Mary nodded. They lapsed into silence, so many questions hanging in the air. Kelly was the one to eventually voice her thoughts.

"Richard would've hated what you tried to do. I know he was a dope-head but he hated anything like that; drink, drugs. Suicide." She swore under her breath, apologising quickly to Hannah, who smiled and shook her head. Mary tried to sit up. Pain ripped across her midriff and her stomach lurched again.

"I'm sorry. If I had known what my dad did, I would never have done that! He's going to be so angry with me," she half-smiled, not really convinced his anger would last long.

"Your dad is?"

"No. Richard," she stressed. Hannah and Kelly shot each other a look. Hannah put a maternal hand over Mary's.

"Richard's dead, love," she explained softly. Mary shook her head.

"No, that's just it – he's not dead. How can he be? If he was, he would've been there to meet me. I tried to find him but he wasn't there." She gave a little laugh of relief, nodding at them both.

"Mary, you need to rest, love," Hannah soothed.

"No, don't you see? My dad did this, I know it!"

"How?" Kelly asked bemused. Hannah shot her a warning look.

"He *is* dead, Mary," she stressed again. Mary grew impatient.

"Did you see him? I was dragged away from him by the police. Police who know my dad. I begged to see him at the morgue but they wouldn't let me. Why?"

"Because you're not family," Hannah ventured.

"No. Because he wasn't at the morgue. He didn't have a funeral. Why?"

"I told you why."

"No! Because he's not dead. It makes so much sense now. My dad made them trick me. That's what he does. He lies, he

237

tricks, he plots. Not this time," she rasped. Kelly straightened up in her seat, trying to change the subject.

"When you're allowed to leave, you're coming home with me. Mum's going to look after you," she smiled, nodding encouragement, her smile fading when Mary shook her head again. She gave Kelly a sympathetic look.

"Kelly, you have to understand: my home is with Richard. He's waiting for me, somewhere. York, probably. I just need to find him and we'll be together again, you'll see. You'll see."

Kelly stared at her, hardly breathing.

"But …"

May turned away to look out of the window, a wistful smile spreading slowly across her face.

"I'll find you again, Richard, I promise." Her tone was hushed and intimate, momentarily oblivious to anybody else in the room. "They don't understand. They don't know you like I do. You would never leave me. Never. I know you're waiting for me somewhere."

"Mary?" Kelly prompted quietly. Turning back from the window, Mary reached for her hand; Kelly took it with both of hers.

"Mary, you're scaring me," she started to cry. She could feel how Mary's hand trembled as she joined in with silent tears. The two friends locked eyes, silently pleading with the other for understanding.

"Please, Kelly. Just … just let me keep him alive," Mary whispered. "I wanted to die but I couldn't. I can't cope without him. I *need* to keep him alive."

Kelly leant across the bed, hugging Mary tightly, shaking as she sobbed.

"Okay," she agreed. "We'll both keep him alive. I loved him too, y'know. Not like you, you jammy cow," she joked, laughing through tears, "But I did love him once. He was my mate, my Prince Charming when I was five, and I let him down. I won't let *you* down now. I owe him that much."

She gently eased Mary to one side of the bed and lay down next to her, cradling her and stroking her hair.

"So, we've got six months of catching up to do then. First kiss – when was that?" she asked brightly.

"Adams' party." She laughed at Kelly's shocked face, then turned to the window again, whispering, "I'll never let you go, my love. We'll be together again. Soon."

Kelly swallowed the lump in her throat, deep concern clouding her face as she watched her. She tried to keep her voice light.

"Adam's party? You mean after I worked my magic on you, made you all beautiful and everything." She squeezed Mary. "You can thank me later. A bottle of Malibu will do," she joked. She smiled but inside she was shaking, aching to scream with relief and delayed shock. The two murders and Josh's arrest had rocked the village; Mary's attempted suicide on top of that had turned Kelly's world upside down. She would never forget the look on Kevin's face or the vision of her dad running with Mary's limp body to where the Land Rover was waiting. She would never forgive herself for not seeing the signs that day; for letting Mary walk alone into a pit of despair. She squeezed her again.

"We'll get through this, Mary. Together. That's what besties do."

✳ ✳ ✳

THE END

Coming soon

Brianna has the perfect life; happily married with a job she loves, beautiful home in the country and three successful children away at university. She's embracing hitting fifty – after all, everybody knows that's when life really begins. Then fate deals her a blow that unravels her perfect world so fast and leaves her fighting for her life. The one person that comes to her aid is the same person she's trying to avoid, but quickly realises she can't live without.

Anam Cara is a tale of love, loss, strength and endurance against all odds.

Also coming soon

When the tanks start to arrive in the New Forest, the residents of Brockenhurst just know their village is once again going to play a part in the war. Life had barely got back to normal since the end of the last one. For three local brothers, Reg, Fred and Bert Greene, the second world war was about to change their lives forever and tear their world apart.

Whispering Trees, book three of the *Cobbled Streets* saga, follows the brothers fate as they enlist to fight in the campaign in Europe, leaving loved ones and childhood behind.

Acknowledgements

As ever, a huge thanks to my family, Team Griffiths: Simon, Carina, Dino, Anton, Lou, Damon & Heidi. Not forgetting my feline trio, of course. I couldn't do any of this without you.

Thanks to the residents of Haworth, the lovely Brontë Parsonage staff and friendly shop keepers. You've all made my stays in Haworth so special. Thanks also to the fabulous staff at the York Minster. Love that place so much!

To my family & friends, my Facebook family and my readers, a massive thanks for keeping me going, for reading my stuff and saying lovely things to me. I really appreciate it.

Finally, thanks to Paolo Nutini and Stereophonics who kept me company throughout – the perfect writing buddies.

20242390R00149

Printed in Great Britain
by Amazon